"Seth offered to take us fishing. Is that okay?"

Victoria took a second to let this all sink in, wrapping her mind, and her heart, too, around the fact that he'd offered to take her two favorite kids fishing. Why would he do this? There was absolutely nothing in it for him, other than perpetrating an act of kindness. Well, except for some incredibly fun fishing. That thought left her with a grin, and the absolute confirmation that Seth James was good people.

The hopefulness on her daughter's precious face nearly brought tears to her eyes. The handsome, funny sweetness that was Seth James smiling eagerly in her direction had her stomach flipping in a very nice way. Probably a way that she should ignore but really didn't want to.

"Who am I to resist this kind of united front?" she answered. "On one condition."

"What?" Scarlett said, barely hanging on to her patience.

"That I can go with you?"

Dear Reader,

I have a confession. Seth James was never supposed to get his own book. But when he strolled onto the page in *In the Doctor's Arms*, all cocky and funny and adorable, and taught his sister, Iris, how to fish, I fell in love. His heart, his humor, even his mega-confidence as the self-described "best fisherman in the world" was endearing. I couldn't stop thinking about him and the type of heroine who might capture his heart.

She had to be a woman who could match his skills and challenge his ego and show him that there's more to life than catching the biggest fish or the first fish or the most fish. There's also the art of fishing. You know, she had to leave him reeling! Meet Victoria Thibodeaux. Competing for every angler's dream job as a professional angler and spokesperson puts them at odds in such a fun way. With a love of fishing in common, falling in love proves to be the easy part because only one of them can be crowned the best.

Enjoy Seth and Victoria's story. Thanks for reading!

Carol

HEARTWARMING

Catching Mr. Right

———

Carol Ross

HARLEQUIN
HEARTWARMING

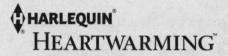

HARLEQUIN®
HEARTWARMING™

ISBN-13: 978-1-335-17974-6

Recycling programs for this product may not exist in your area.

Catching Mr. Right

Copyright © 2021 by Carol Ross

This edition published by arrangement with Harlequin Books S.A.

For questions and comments about the quality of this book, please contact us at CustomerService@Harlequin.com.

Harlequin Enterprises ULC
22 Adelaide St. West, 40th Floor
Toronto, Ontario M5H 4E3, Canada
www.Harlequin.com

Printed in U.S.A.

Carol Ross lives in the Pacific Northwest with her husband and two dogs. She is a graduate of Washington State University. When not writing, or thinking about writing, she enjoys reading, running, hiking, skiing, traveling and making plans for the next adventure to subject her sometimes reluctant but always fun-loving family to. Carol can be contacted at carolrossauthor.com and via Facebook at Facebook.com/carolrossauthor, Twitter, @_carolross, and Instagram, @carolross__.

For Dad and Uncle Boyd.

I would give anything for just one more day of fishing on the river with the two of you.

CHAPTER ONE

THE KID COULDN'T be more than ten or eleven years old, Seth James decided. He watched the kid's skillful maneuvering of the well-used bass boat toward the shady cypress cove. Seth had a pretty good view from his seat on the opposite bank of the channel just up from where it spilled into the flat water of Louisiana's picturesque Lake Belle Rose.

Skinny and long-limbed, the kid wore faded coveralls, and a bucket hat shielded his face from the rays of the afternoon sun. Standing on the bow with the easy confidence of a practiced angler, he simultaneously worked the electric motor's foot controls and readied the fishing rod he held in his hands.

Open-faced reel, Seth noted, as the boat slowed. That alone suggested a measure of skill. A notion the kid proceeded to prove with a smooth flick of the wrist, casting in among the trees. The lure sailed smoothly through the air, sliding perfectly into place under a thatch of low hanging branches with a quiet plop. Tipping the rod up and to the left, he reeled in and cast again and again in rapid succession, each time placing the lure a little to the right of the previous attempt. And then, on maybe the fifth cast…

Bam!

The line went taut, the rod bowing as a fish hit the lure and bolted. He reeled, steady and smooth, keeping the line nice and tight. The fish fought, jumping and showing itself to be a good-sized catch. Calmly, like he'd done it a million times, he smoothly landed the largemouth bass. Seth felt himself grinning with equal parts of admiration and envy. A distinctive feeling, which his own lifetime of angling experience had convinced him only this sport generated.

Working quickly and efficiently, the kid slid a thumb inside the fish's mouth to grip its bottom lip, and then removed the hook. Holding the fish vertically to prevent any harm, he lowered to his knees and produced a portable scale, clipped it in place, took the weight, and then snapped a photo with a cell phone. Then he leaned over and, with gentle hands, released the fish back into the water.

When Seth had pulled into Bayou Doré RV & Campground Resort, he'd immediately spotted the sign reading Lake Belle Rose 32nd

Annual Junior Fishing Derby. The number of parked vehicles with empty boat trailers suggested it was a popular event. The registration office was unlocked, but no one was inside. A note on the counter instructed visitors to head toward the dock, "where someone will be with you shortly." He'd found the dock easily enough, but it, too, was devoid of people. Spotting a pair of empty Adirondack chairs several yards away and shaded by a patch of trees, he'd wandered over and taken a seat.

Minutes later, boy and boat had motored around the corner, and up the mouth of the channel where he'd proceeded with his unintentional bass master tutorial. Seeing how Seth had arrived in the state only hours before, it felt like the perfect introduction. Especially since he knew he was early and had some time to kill. He was glad for the opportunity to get his bearings and soak in the beauty of the lush surroundings.

The warm air felt pleasantly heavy. Tiny insects flitted and buzzed around him. To his left, trees and thick vegetation provided shade from the heat of the waning sun's late spring rays. Some of the trees he could identify like tupelo, willow and, of course, the giant cypress with its scarf-like strands of Spanish moss swaying gently in the breeze. Bushes, flowers, vines, he wasn't as confident about, but they all mingled together in an extremely pleasing way. The landscape couldn't get much different than his home on the southern Alaska coast.

And that was okay with him. He'd traveled to plenty of other states and countries, and so long as fishing was the common language, he got along just fine. He had no doubt that the reps from Romeo Reels would see that about him, too, once they arrived. Upon being notified about their flight delay, Seth had decided to rent a vehicle and find his own way to this idyllic Louisiana outpost.

As one of three finalists shortlisted for a spot on Romeo Reels' pro staff, this was the next step. A very big step. Not only did the contract guarantee a position as a sponsored angler, but it also included the coveted title as the fishing gear and tackle company's spokesperson, their "star ambassador." Seth had every intention of being the new face of Romeo Reels.

Even though this junket felt like a bit of a respite, these last few weeks would be intense. Romeo wanted to see each of the final competitors out in the field, interacting with other anglers and the public in a setting different than they were used to. For the next few days, he and two representatives from Romeo Reels would be fishing with fellow finalist Vic Thibodeaux.

Next, Vic would head to Minnesota to fish with the other finalist Henry Foster. Seth would then host Henry in Alaska. When the individual trips were completed, the three finalists would be flown to Maritown, Florida, for the Pro Plus Fishing & Outdoor Expo, one of the largest fishing shows in the world. There, they'd present workshops, participate in demos, interviews, events, and meet with Romeo Reels executives and members of the spokesperson selection committee.

Seth, focus still on the water, watched as the kid suddenly turned and squinted toward the shoreline. Two things occurred then; he realized that the boy was actually a girl, and said girl went wide-eyed as her gaze latched onto his. Grimacing, she set the pole to one side and removed something from her pocket. A pair of clippers he realized when she snipped the lure from the end of the line and tucked it into her pocket. The move made Seth smile again because he knew she was stowing it out of sight of fellow derby contestants. He would have done the same thing. Settling at the helm once more, she nudged the throttle and motored straight toward the dock where she hopped off the boat and hastily secured it to the dock with an expert cleat hitch.

"Hello, there," she called with a wave, every

trace of the grimace now buried beneath her pleasing accent and friendly smile. Slender with long legs, she strode across the wooden planks in a deliberate, graceful manner that reminded him of his sister and fellow triplet Iris.

When she reached the end of the dock, she jogged over to stand before him. "Can I help you, sir?"

Both taken with and taken aback by her professional demeanor, Seth muttered, "Oh, uh, I don't...know. Maybe. Do you work here?"

"Yes, sir, I sure do. My family owns this place. Are you here for the derby? Or checking in as a guest?" She removed the sun-faded cap from her head, and now he could see her hair twisted into a bun low on the back of her head. Pausing to take this all in, Seth noticed that her sense of style was more reminiscent of himself and his sister Hazel, who comprised the final third of his sibling trio. The coveralls she wore were faded and knee worn, and her dingy tennis shoes sported mismatched laces. One had a hole in the toe. Slung from one shoulder was a tattered and stained fishing vest, the pockets bulging with bait and tackle. He owned a nearly identical vest, albeit in a much larger size, currently packed in his suitcase.

"No. And yes. But aren't you competing in the derby? I don't want to keep you." Seth gestured at the water, recalling how competitive he'd been at her age. Who was he kidding? He was still *that* competitive when it came to fishing.

Valiantly fighting a scowl, she answered, "No, sir, I am not."

"But I just saw you land that monster bass. Well done, by the way. I know people who've fished their whole lives who couldn't make those casts."

"Thank you." She didn't even try to stop the grin that erupted across her face. "Biggest one of the derby, by far."

"I thought you just said you weren't competing?" How else would she know that if she wasn't? Offshore, Seth noticed an airboat cruising in their direction.

The sound must have reached her, too, because she glanced over her shoulder. When she faced him again, a staid expression was back in place, and she answered with a cagey, "Yeah, I'm not."

"Can I ask why?"

Nostrils flaring slightly, her mouth formed a tight, flat line. The topic obviously irritated her, but she was trying to suppress it. Sighing, she looked down and nudged the ground with her toe. From the worn hole in her sneaker, it looked like a habit she might often employ in times of stressful interrogation. Yet her answer was spoken with straight-up diplomacy that Seth could only admire. "My mama says I have an unfair advantage."

"I see." Seth knew the feeling. Knew it well. And disagreed on principle. It reminded him of the time he'd covertly entered a local junior fishing derby after his dad told him he shouldn't. Ultimately, the win had been worth the admonishment he'd received after his dad found out. "Because you're so much better than other kids your age?"

"Yes." Nibbling on her lip, she seemed to be struggling not to say more.

"How is it your fault that other kids choose to spend their time engaged in any activity that isn't fishing? You're not complaining because they're better at some video game or have a longer *snapstreak* than you do, am I right?"

"Exactly!" She cried, throwing up her hands. "Put down your stupid phone and go get your fishing pole for crying out loud! I'm not stopping you."

They laughed together.

"Spinnerbait?" he asked, tipping his chin toward the lake.

Grinning slyly, she nodded and threw a sidelong glance at the water. "Mmm-hmm. Need something flashy today. Water's still a little murky on account of the rain we had last week." Not, Seth noted, offering up the brand, type, size or color of the lure. A true angler and a kindred spirit.

They were chatting about all things bass related—lures, water conditions, weather, the spring spawn—when the airboat pulled up to the dock. Peripherally, Seth saw a brown-haired tallish woman exit the vessel and tie up next to the bass boat.

He was too intent on the mini-Seth standing before him to observe anything further. Not only was the girl entertaining, she was also a wealth of angling information. Information that could prove vital to him in the following days. The woman headed their way, and, sensing she was about to interrupt the conversation, he realized he hadn't introduced himself.

Reaching out a hand, he said, "By the way, my name is Seth, Seth James."

Still smiling, she said, "It's real nice to meet you, Mr. James. I'm Scarlett."

"Please, call me Seth."

"I'm not sure if Mama or my grandmas will like that, but I'll give it a try."

As he'd suspected, the woman approached and asked, "What won't we like, Scarlett?"

"If she calls me by my first name," Seth answered for her, finally looking at the woman.

And for the first time since he'd stepped foot in Louisiana, he was admiring something more beautiful than the scenery. Like her daughter, the woman was slender with long limbs and narrow shoulders. An effect that made her seem taller than she was, he realized, as she stood next to Scarlett. Her brown hair was a shade or two lighter than her daughter's and tinged with more red. Although, that could have been because more of hers was glistening in the sunlight, piled as it was up on top of her head. They had matching green eyes, too, and hers were sparkling with affection when they settled on Scarlett.

He wondered if she liked to fish as much as her daughter. What would that be like, he wondered, to be with a woman who liked to fish as much as he did? Or was there a husband in the picture? Scarlett had said her family owned the place, so maybe this woman's husband was Vic Thibodeaux? Probably not a good idea to admire the wife of the man with whom he'd soon be fishing with—and competing against.

"That does feel a bit familiar," the woman said good-naturedly.

Tilting her head, Scarlett nudged her eyebrows upward in a lighthearted I-told-you-so expression.

"You can ask Mémé what she thinks if you

don't like my answer?" Scarlett's mom suggested.

Scarlett groaned. "Very funny. I already know what she'll say. She won't even let me call Mr. Landry by his first name, and I've known him since birth."

"Hey, I call him Mr. Landry, too, and I've known him since my own birth." Her arm went around Scarlett's shoulder and gave it a gentle squeeze.

The woman turned a polite smile on him. "What can I do for you? Is Scarlett taking care of you? Are you checking in? Doing some fishing?"

"Yes, Scarlett has been extremely gracious and helpful. And I will be checking in *and* doing some fishing. I'm supposed to ask for Vic Thibodeaux?"

"Oh." Surprise had her eyebrows drifting up onto her brow. "You're early, I think. Aren't you?"

"I am a bit. I hope that's not an inconvenience?"

"Not at all," she assured him.

"Is he here?" Seth asked and then found himself blurting what he really wanted to know, "Is Vic your husband?" *Nice, Seth,* he chastised himself as heat crept up his neck, *very subtle*.

The woman's expression had twisted with

uncertainty while he was busy embarrassing himself with tactless curiosity.

"No, I'm—"

"She doesn't have a husband," Scarlett interrupted brightly.

"Vic," the woman finished at the same time, reaching out a hand. "I'm Vic, Victoria Thibodeaux, your fellow finalist. I'll be your fishing guide while you're here in Louisiana."

"Seth James," the man introduced himself, clearing up any lingering uncertainty Victoria had about his identity.

Seth James, her competition. He enfolded her hand in his, agitating the awareness already coursing through her. What was up with that?

She'd been helping her grandmother and her mother run Bayou Doré her entire life. It wasn't like she was a stranger to handsome men. In fact, that's how she'd met Scarlett's daddy. A relationship that, aside from Scarlett, had caused her nothing but misery and regret. Victoria hadn't invited another man into her life since. And she had no plans to do so, especially with the Romeo Reels spokesperson contract within her grasp. Which, now that she thought about it, was undoubtedly the reason behind the tummy spin. Nerves. This guy was her rival for a job that would change her life, a job she'd do anything to earn.

Short of winning the lottery, she couldn't imagine anything else that could compare. Except, where the lottery was all luck, she'd worked her tail off for this opportunity.

"Nice to meet you, Mr. James, and welcome. Have Mr. Drewson and Ms. Rivas arrived then, too?"

"Please, call me Seth. No, they haven't. Did you not get the email saying their plane was delayed?"

"Thank you for letting me know. I'm sure I probably did get it, but I've been out on the lake and haven't checked my email."

The derby had taken all her time and energy today. And yesterday, too, for that matter. As fun as it was, the annual event tended to wear her out. Tired and nervous was probably not the best way to begin this endeavor. The Romeo Reels reps would be watching her every move, assessing, evaluating, judging. Even though this was her home turf, she needed to be on her game.

At least, the delay gave her some extra time to get her wits about her. And, she realized, it also lent her the perfect opportunity to assess her competition.

"Scarlett, will you head on up to the house

and let your gram know that Mr. James is here? He's going to be staying in Cabin 3, and I'm not sure if the bed has been made yet. Grab the key, and we'll meet you there in about fifteen minutes, okay?"

"Yes, Mama," Scarlett answered and jogged away toward the office.

Vic turned on her most gracious smile, honed from a lifetime of working with the public, and faced her rival. "All right then, Mr. James, if you'd like to walk with me, I'll give you a quick overview of our facilities here at Bayou Doré."

While I take a quick overview of you.

CHAPTER TWO

SETH KEPT PACE beside Victoria as they strolled along a footpath running roughly parallel to the lake.

"I'm afraid that in this day and age, the word *resort* has come to mean something different than what we offer here at Bayou Doré," she told him. "You won't find any towel-art animals in your bathroom or chocolates on your pillow. We don't have a spa or room service or any of those fancy amenities. We're basically a campground with a handful of rustic cabins. What we do have is—"

They were past the dock when a voice interrupted from off the trail. "Hey, Ms. T."

Seth saw a boy stand from where he'd been crouched under a nearby tree amid some brush and tall grass.

Victoria stopped, prompting Seth to do the same. Lifting a hand in greeting, she called, "Hey, Quinn, what's up?"

The kid wore a pair of camo-green cargo shorts and a Louisiana Gators T-shirt. Shaggy blond hair curled up from beneath his base-ball cap. He had that too-skinny, rangy-limbed look that middle school boys often have when they're in the midst of a massive growth spurt. Seth estimated him to be around twelve years old.

"You wanna see what I found?"

"You know I do." Victoria was already veering in his direction like she'd anticipated the detour. Seth followed, and as they approached, he noticed the kid held a wad of thick, twisted rope in his hands. He couldn't help but think that it wasn't much of a discovery.

Until it moved. Seth froze while his brain attempted to process what he was seeing. Not rope. *Snake.* Fear bolted up his spine, across his scalp and out through his arms, leaving a tingling trail. His sister Iris's warnings about the vast array of dangerous snakes inhabiting Louisiana flashed through his mind. Why hadn't he paid closer attention to those photos she'd shown him? Thinking fast, he realized he'd retained only enough to process that it wasn't a copperhead. Yep, that was the extent of what he'd learned. He and Hazel had opted to tease Iris about her wildlife paranoia instead. Alligators had seemed a bigger concern.

"My goodness, Quinn, that is a beauty. Look at those markings."

Seth relaxed slightly at Victoria's praise. Probably not dangerous if she was passing out serpent-ish compliments.

"Isn't it? Young one, too. You wanna take a guess what kind it is?"

"Mémé calls them chicken snakes, but I believe the proper term is Texas rat snake?"

"Excellent. That's right!" Quinn said, deep dimples framing an approving smile.

"Thank you. I've learned from an expert. Very cool, Quinn."

"I knew I'd convert you eventually."

Victoria chuckled. "Now, I wouldn't go that far. But I do appreciate knowing what I'm looking at." She glanced at Seth, holding his gaze for a beat, and he wondered if she could see his fear. At least it wasn't panic-inducing like his dislike of heights.

"Quinn, this is Seth James, a first-time guest, here to do some fishing. Seth, Quinn Duquette. Quinn is our neighbor, a close friend and resident herpetologist."

"Aspiring," Quinn corrected. "I don't have my degree—yet. Hi there, Seth."

"Nice to meet you, Quinn. I'd shake your hand, but I really do *not* want to."

Quinn chuckled, the sound low and soft, and Seth presumed he was taking care not to startle his slithering companion. To Victoria, he said,

"Another of the uneducated masses here, I see. Would you mind taking a pic for me?"

"Sure thing." Victoria removed a cell phone from her pocket and snapped some photos.

Seth asked, "I take it that thing isn't poisonous?"

"No," Quinn said, wearing a smirk that suggested he found Seth's remark amusing.

"Is that a stupid question?"

"No, sir," Quinn said. "Like my daddy says, the only stupid question is the one you don't ask. Especially when it comes to snakes. He's a wildlife biologist. But rat snakes are constrictors and are neither poisonous nor venomous."

"Uh… There's a difference between those last two?"

"Yes. You'd have to eat the snake in order for it to be poisonous."

"Seriously?"

"Yes. But don't worry, it's a common misconception. Venom is injected. You know, like through a bite. Poison is ingested."

"Huh. Makes sense. I guess I've never thought about the distinction. But to be fair, I'm from Alaska, where the most dangerous critters all have fur."

"Yeah." Quinn nodded knowingly. "That explains a lot. Alaska only has one snake species, which is nonvenomous. Must be kind of boring walking through *your* woods, huh? Not having to worry about where you step and all."

Seth chuckled. "That's one way of looking at it, I suppose. Another would be that the danger in our woods is large and formidable, which can be plenty exciting. We've got wolves and cats and bears—grizzly bears. That's kind of scary, right? In its own way." Seth wondered if he'd ever before defended his home state in terms of its danger factor.

Quinn went thoughtful for a second before agreeing. "Fair point. And Scarlett wants to go to Alaska, so I'll give it to you. Speaking of." He shifted his focus back to Victoria, "Is Scarlett around? I want to show her this guy."

"She is," Victoria assured him. "I'll text her and tell her to get on out here. She'll definitely want to see this."

Seth took the opportunity to ask Quinn, "How many types of snakes are there in Louisiana?"

"Forty-eight, seven are venomous. But you won't find every variety here in the southern part of the state."

"Only seven?" Seth repeated in a wry tone. "And to think I was worried about alligators."

Quinn flashed him a knowing grin. "That's what everyone says. But our gators are like your grizzlies. Attacks are rare. And you should know that here in Louisiana, the worst danger is always the one that sneaks up on you."

SCARLETT ARRIVED TO check out the snake, handed a key to Victoria along with a nod, and promptly joined Quinn in admiring his discovery.

"To continue," Victoria said, once they were back on the path. "We have full hook-ups, tent spaces and cabins."

Seth relaxed and enjoyed the tour—asking questions, listening attentively, and generally dragging it out as much as possible. He knew that once the Romeo Reels people arrived, everything would change, and he figured this might be his best opportunity to get to know his intriguing challenger one-on-one.

While she talked, he took a moment to study her easy, quiet beauty; the attractive shape of her jaw and cheekbone, soft green eyes outlined with spiky lashes and dark brown eyebrows that sloped gently across her brow line. And she seriously had the cutest nose; turned up just slightly at the end and delicately dusted with freckles.

Only when she met his gaze did he realize that she'd stopped talking, and the not-so-subtle hoist of one eyebrow told him he'd been caught staring.

He smiled.

She frowned.

Hmm. Glancing away, he scratched his cheek just for something to do, to hide the sudden uncertainty coming over him. Something vaguely intimidating about her, he realized. Surely that would pass once he got to know her better.

He decided to concentrate on doing that. "So, Scarlett said her family owns this place. Did she mean you?"

"She means my grandmother, Effie Thibodeaux. I help run it along with my mother, Corinne. And now, Scarlett."

No mention of the husband that, thanks to his not-so-subtle inquiry, he knew she did not have. Or a dad or grandfather either, for that matter. He couldn't help but wonder what had happened to the men in her life. Definitely too personal of an inquiry at this stage in their relationship.

"So, you grew up in Louisiana?"

"I did."

"Have you lived here in Perche your whole life?"

"I have," she answered simply.

"Did you go to college here, too?"

"No."

Seth waited for her to expound. No, she didn't go to college in Louisiana or no, she didn't go to college at all? A few seconds passed before he realized that she had no intention of enlightening him.

Stepping ahead, she pointed to a narrow rectangular clapboard building situated perpendicular to the lake. "Those are the restrooms for campers and day-use customers." It was painted in the same attractive scheme as the other structures, deep forest green with white trim and a red door. "All the cabins have their own bathroom with shower, though, so you won't have to worry about that."

Lifting her other hand, she explained, "Laundry facilities are at that end of the building. I'm guessing you won't be utilizing those either, so I don't need to advise you to get there early. There's only one washer and dryer. Behind the building are a gazebo and picnic area. There's a horseshoe pit, beanbag toss, badminton net and a playground. It's a very popular area with our campers." A loud cheer and accompanying stint of laughter rang out from the general vicinity, an almost comical underscore to her assertion.

Stopping near the water's edge, she nodded toward the dock. "And of course, the boat launch, which is popular with the locals. There's a faucet, sink and outdoor shower on the far end of the building."

"And you rent boats as well?"

"We do. We have a few boats, some canoes, and kayaks. We also rent fishing gear. Our little store, which you undoubtedly saw when you arrived, sells basic groceries and supplies, bait and tackle, sunscreen, insect repellent, snacks and other essentials." He had seen the store, attached as it was to the registration office where he'd first gone when he'd arrived.

"Sounds good." Seth spun a slow circle, memorizing the details, admiring the scenery and all the while wondering about the woman standing beside him. He couldn't help but speculate about how many times she'd given this spiel in her life? Not because she wasn't great at it. Because she was. Professional, articulate, word perfect. And yet, he felt a vibe radiating from her that he couldn't quite decipher. Tense, but trying not to be. Polite, but not quite friendly. Definitely not inclined to talk about herself, and possibly growing bored with talking to him.

"I think that's about it. We try to keep things simple and let nature speak for itself. Maintain as much unaltered beauty as we can. Any questions, feel free to ask. In the meantime, welcome to Bayou Doré."

"Thank you. I'm thrilled to be here. This place is extraordinary."

"We think so." Thumb up and out, she gestured toward the office. "I'm sure you're ready to see your cabin and relax a bit. Should we go get you checked in?"

"Uh, yeah…" he said but didn't budge. A gray-and-white bird appeared overhead before dipping low above the lake and then landing gracefully on the water. Seconds later, another one joined it. Seth pretended to be distracted by the action as he pondered her blatant attempt to wrap up his tour and send him on his way. So much for his plan to get to know her. Victoria Thibodeaux was giving nothing away.

Maybe if he opened the door a little about himself, they could get a dialogue started. "For me, an Alaskan boy, this feels a bit like traveling to another country."

Gaze pinned on his, her brows inched up onto her forehead. Her tone seemed to hold more censure than surprise when she asked, "I take it that means you've never fished the South?"

"I've been to the Florida Keys a couple of times and—"

"Pfft," she interrupted with a rather ungraceful snort. Surprising, after the complete and total professionalism she'd displayed until now. He liked it; hoped it was a genuine glimpse of the woman beneath the slick facade.

Seth chuckled. "What was that for?"

"Florida Keys is not the South."

"Uh, have you looked at a map lately?" he joked.

"It's not about geography."

"Okay," he agreed because he knew what she meant. "So, I'm guessing bonefishing in Belize, and offshore fishing in the Cayman Islands and the Bahamas don't count as South either?"

Her head started shaking long before he'd finished the statement. "No, sir. Not even close."

"Hmm," he answered because he wasn't sure what to say to that.

A little huff escaped her, almost like she couldn't help herself, and Seth had to ask, "What?"

"You've been to Florida and the Bahamas and the Caymans." Raising one hand, she pushed it up and through the air in a long slow arc. Mimicking the path of an airplane, he realized as she added, "Which means you flew right on over some of the best angling in the entire world…" Dropping her hand, she trailed off with a shake of her head. "You people. Why do y'all do that?"

He hesitated to answer, letting her words settle into him. He really liked her voice, he realized. And not just her accent, although he enjoyed that, too. It was the rich, buttery tone that held him spellbound. She had the kind of voice that would be suited to broadcasting or acting. He wondered if she could sing, too.

She frowned, and he realized his hesitation had dragged on a bit too long. Again. He must be making quite an impression. Quickly, before she could retreat again, he asked, "We people? What type of people do you think I am?"

Too late, he realized, when she cleared her throat and said, "I meant people in general."

No, you didn't, he wanted to say because it was obvious she was hedging. Something about him bothered her, and that bothered him. What that was and why he had no idea. Of course, there was the simple fact that they were competitors. But could it really be *that* simple? It was easy for him to put their rivalry aside as he gawked around this exotic paradise. But maybe not for her. But still, just because they were competing didn't mean they couldn't be friends, right? Or friendly at least.

With a sheepish shrug, he grinned and said, "Well, I'm here now, and I plan to savor every second."

Nodding, she nibbled on her bottom lip, and Seth got the sense she was contemplating a response. He waited, hoping she would say something to give him a hint about what she was thinking. Another long moment stretched between them, heavy and awkward. He didn't think he'd ever had so much trouble conversing with a fellow human in his life.

When she gazed longingly toward the office, he knew the moment had passed. Sensing that she was about to start moving again, he scrambled for a topic not quite as personal that might keep her talking.

"Doré, I assume that's French. What does it mean?"

Victoria looked in his direction again. Reluctantly. "It means golden."

"Golden," Seth repeated, shifting his body so that it faced the lake. "Golden Bayou."

"That's right," she said and then angled her body, too, as if to admire the scenery right along with him. A soft sigh escaped her lips, but Seth couldn't tell what it meant. Was it a happy sigh or a sigh of discontent? Or was she annoyed with him? He had no idea.

"Do you know why? Other than it sounds pretty?"

"I do." She produced a half smile and kept her focus on the lake. "Mémé, that's my grandmother Effie who you'll meet here soon, is Cajun. Acadian specifically. She inherited the property from her parents and then started this resort with my granddaddy. Mama tells this story of when she was a little girl, maybe four or five years old, and she used to play over there near where the dock is now. One evening, she stayed too late, and her grandma, Mémé's mother, came down to the lake just before sunset to fetch her.

"She claims they stood right there by that tree looking out at the setting sun glowing on the water. Then Great-Grandma put an arm around her shoulders, and, with tears in her eyes, she whispered, *Regarde, mon cher, le bayou et plein d'or*. Look, my love, the bayou is full of gold. Since that day, this place has been called Bayou Doré."

Two years of high school French meant Seth was far from an expert, but her accent sounded so lovely he wanted to ask her to repeat the phrase. Which would probably be weird and not help his cause. So instead, he asked, "Why do you say claims?"

Brow scrunching, her mouth settled into a frown. "What?"

"You said your mom claims that's the story. Is there another version?"

"No." Something like frustration flickered across her face but was there and gone so quickly Seth was left wondering if he imagined it. "I mean, no, I didn't say that…" Features twisting with uncertainty, she said, "Did I?"

"You did."

"Oh, uhm…" She chuckled, but it sounded forced. "Huh." Gaze shifting along with her feet, she said, "Well, I didn't mean to. I just meant that's the family lore. My family has been here forever, I'm sure you can imagine we have a whole lot of lore."

"I can imagine," he said. "We have a bit of that in my family, too."

"Tons of stories," she reiterated. "Some of which you'll undoubtedly be hearing tonight." Glancing at the watch on her wrist, she did start walking this time as if she couldn't spare another second. She confirmed that with, "I need to get back to the derby." Seth fell into step beside her. "Your cabin is ready. After check-in, I'll show you where it is, and you can get settled and relax a bit. And then I'll see you at the house later for dinner."

HE'D LOST HER at Belize.

Although, Victoria knew that if she were completely honest with herself, she'd begun retreating long before that. It was the question about college. Not that she was proud of the lukewarm reception she'd given the guy, but she couldn't help it. It was that topic. It stung. Every time. And sometimes it filled her with an anger so intense she couldn't think straight. Why that had happened today, she wasn't one hundred percent certain.

True, there was a lot at stake here with this job. She finally had a second chance, an opportunity to, if not rectify the mistakes of her past, then at least overshadow them with something bigger. So much bigger. And, quite frankly, she was tired of competing with people who had all the advantages in life. Like Austin, her ex-husband, and his father, Linus, the men responsible for derailing her life and destroying her dreams in the first place.

Maybe there was a bit of that with Mr. Alaska here, too, she decided, almost excusing her behavior. Because, like Austin, Seth James did not strike her as a person who'd faced much in the way of adversity. Objectively, she knew she was reaching. Nothing that had gone wrong in her life was this guy's fault.

But come on! Bonefishing in Belize! He'd just had to weave that into the conversation, didn't he? No doubt in an attempt to intimidate her. And the worst part was that it worked.

Victoria had barely been to Biloxi. She highly doubted he'd be impressed with her stories about catfishing in Carlotta, Mississippi. That thought made her snicker as she crossed the wide expanse of green grass toward the dock.

No, she didn't have a college degree, she hadn't traveled the world knocking angling hot spots off some inauthentic, social-media-induced, corny hash-tagged bucket list, but she had spent countless hours on the water right here in the South. Fishing, observing, intuiting and flat-out practicing. Casting until her shoulders ached and her fingers were so stiff she couldn't keep hold of her pole. And loving every moment, especially when that time was spent with Mémé.

Plus, a lifetime of working at the resort meant she knew how to connect with people. Real people. People like her. The type who purchased Romeo Reels products. There wasn't any aspect of angling she couldn't handle, any technique she could not learn, or any person with whom she could not find common ground. All of which she believed would be important in securing this job. And, if parenting had added anything to the mix, it was patience. Another trait that was beneficial to a true angler.

Already feeling better, she crossed the dock to her airboat, untied the line, and climbed on board. The engine started smoothly, and she motored away from the dock and into the derby's fray, where she intended to busy herself until dinnertime.

She could do this. No way would she let some pretty-boy Alaskan who'd likely had everything handed to him in life mess with her head. All she needed to do was stay focused on her strengths.

CHAPTER THREE

"*MAAACK-SHAW, IS THAT RIGHT?*" Seth tried again, massacring the pronunciation of the spicy corn and pepper dish and making Scarlett howl with laughter.

"*Nooo*," Scarlett drawled and then slowly enunciated the name, "*macque choux*. It's more like mock-shoe than mack-shaw."

Mémé was sitting across the table watching the interplay with a tight-lipped, narrow-eyed expression that could only be described as suspicious. Victoria could relate. She was also relieved. She should have known that her cautious grandmother would share her wariness where the too-charming Alaskan was concerned.

While Mémé had been working at the resort and Victoria had been off weighing bass and chatting with derby participants, Mama and Scarlett had, evidently, been here entertaining their guest. Instead of his enjoying a little R & R in his cabin, in the isolation where she'd left him, she'd returned to find him, her mama and her daughter engaged in a raucous game of cards on the front porch. Scarlett had also gleefully reported that while Mama had been working in the kitchen preparing this feast of Cajun delights she, Quinn and Seth had "obliterated" the campers in space C-4 at a game of horseshoes.

Taken aback, Victoria had slipped inside the house, apologized to Mémé for running late and urged her not to wait dinner. Heading upstairs to shower, she couldn't help wondering if she'd been the topic of any card playing conversations. Had befriending her mother and daughter been his way of trying to get information about her? She'd been extremely careful not to divulge any personal details about herself. What had Mama told him? What had Scarlett said? What could her daughter have inadvertently disclosed about their situation, about Austin, the man who was her father?

Panic had sent her heart racing. Breathing deeply, she reminded herself that Scarlett didn't know most of the dark details about her past. Not even Mémé or Mama knew everything. Austin, or his father, were the only ones who could ruin this for her, and they had no reason to do that. Even if Austin was tempted, he would never risk the reputation he'd cultivated for himself by attempting to destroy Victoria's. Political aspirations kept his behavior in check.

The meal was on the table by the time she returned. As she'd settled in, Seth had smiled a greeting, but she'd pretended not to notice. Now, laughter and conversation and a Cajun language lesson flowed around her while she fixed her plate.

He tried the word again with equally disastrous results. Same reaction from Scarlett. Standing near the stove where she'd gone to check on a batch of corn bread, her mama chuckled. Mémé, bless her, remained stone-faced. Vic felt herself frowning and made a concerted effort to stop. Rudeness did not have a place at the dinner table, no matter how disconcerted she felt.

"I give up. Even if I could get the pronunciation right, it wouldn't sound nearly as cool as the way you guys say it." Seth winked at Scarlett and scooped up another serving. His second helping, Victoria noted, of both the *macque choux* and the *choupique*. "No matter how you pronounce it, I've never eaten such a delicious meal, Ms. Thibodeaux, Ms. Effie." By Ms. Thibodeaux, he referred to her mother, whose name was Corinne. Almost everyone called her grandmother Ms. Effie, except for her and Scarlett, who called her Mémé.

"My pleasure," Mémé said politely.

Corinne said, "Why, thank you, Seth. What a sweet compliment."

"I am not exaggerating in the slightest. Please do not tell my mother or my Aunt Claire that I said that."

Ever since Victoria had learned she'd made the final round of this competition and would be hosting a fellow finalist along with two representatives from Romeo Reels, Mémé and her mama had started in with the meal planning. She'd told them it was unnecessary, that they were judging her and not the resort, but they insisted on "doing their part." The absence of the Romeo Reels people at tonight's feast hadn't deterred them in the slightest. They'd gone ahead with the traditional Cajun fare as planned. An even grander menu was in the works for tomorrow's meals.

"My lips are sealed," Corinne said, "as long as you start calling me Corinne." Mama, it seemed, was already taken in by his charms.

"Mine, too," Scarlett agreed. "'Course I'd have to know her to tell her, wouldn't I? Where does your mama live?"

"Rankins, Alaska," Seth answered Scarlett. "Most of my family lives in Alaska."

"Alaska!" Scarlett cried.

Oh dear, Vic thought and braced herself, surprised the topic hadn't already come up amidst their earlier antics. In addition to fishing, Scarlett shared her desire to travel the world, preferably with fishing gear in tow.

"Mama and I want to go to Alaska so bad. We are for sure going fishing there someday."

"Do you now?" Grinning, he slid a glance at Victoria as if he'd just learned some big secret. "Your mom did not mention that."

The familiarity made her bristle, and it took effort not to roll her eyes. Every angler dreams of fishing in Alaska, she wanted to say. Instead, she offered a small, polite smile. "That is our plan."

"I highly recommend it. What kind of fishing are you interested in, Scarlett?"

"I've never been fishing in the Pacific Ocean, so I'd like to catch a salmon. A big ol' king salmon or steelhead. Mama *really* wants to catch a steelhead. I think that'd be epic, too. I've heard they fight like mad."

"Excellent choices. Steelhead is probably my very favorite fish to catch. It's one of my specialties." Again, with the sliding glance. Victoria pointedly ignored him, spearing corn kernels with her fork, while he went on, "You guys should come up and visit us in Rankins. I could *hook* you up."

Scarlett and Mama laughed at the silly pun. As he continued to ramble, Vic silently, grudgingly admitted that the guy had a very appealing manner about him, unassuming with an edge of self-deprecating humor. Confident yet down-to-earth.

"I happen to have my own boat," he was saying. "Two of them actually, and my dad is a commercial fisherman. I could take you out myself. My cousin also owns a very nice guide service if you'd rather have a more structured schedule. We know all the best places. The James family and fishing—it's kind of our thing."

"Really?" Scarlett asked.

It was only one word, but the yearning in her daughter's tone, the unabashed admiration in her eyes, made Vic's heart hurt. Next summer, she promised herself, she would find the money to take her daughter to Alaska. Unless she were to land this job with Romeo Reels. Then she might not have to try so hard to find the funds. But she knew that for now, she needed to tamp down on longing and dreams and concentrate on her performance. Job first. Dream granting second.

"You're officially invited. You could come this summer."

"No. Way! Mama, did you hear that?"

Unless someone decided to lay those dreams at her daughter's feet, where she was forced to deal with them in the here and now. "I did. That is a very generous offer." She managed to smile in Seth's general direction but didn't meet his gaze for fear he'd see the fire of irritation flickering there. Not everyone had the money to fly to Alaska, stay in hotels, purchase out-of-state licenses, and take expensive guided excursions. Vic wanted to strangle him for planting this seed of hope in her child's head. It was difficult enough to watch her daughter not having the luxuries that other kids did.

Scarlett, on the other hand, was already boarding the plane. "I cannot wait! That would be so cool. What's your family like? Do you have any brothers and sisters?"

"My family is awesome. I have five siblings and a bunch of cousins."

"Five! That is so great. I wish I had five brothers and sisters. I'm an only child. The only child of an only child, like my mama and Gram. Are you the oldest or the youngest or somewhere in the middle?"

"Technically, I share the title of youngest with two of my siblings."

He was a triplet? And his cousin owned an Alaskan guide service. Annoying how the guy seemed to get more interesting every time he opened his mouth. Scarlett was going to love this, and any second now… Sure enough, she was only about a beat behind Vic in figuring it out.

"Are you even kidding me right now!" she cried. "You're a triplet?"

"Scarlett," Vic admonished. "Please stop screeching. It's impolite."

"Sorry, Mama. But that's supercool, huh?"

Seth grinned, clearly enjoying her excitement. Which might be endearing under different circumstances. "I think so."

"Are you guys close?"

"We are."

"Where are they right now, your... What do you even call a triplet? Twins just say 'twin,' so is a triplet a 'triple'?" Scarlett asked. "Are you all boys? Are you identical? What are their names?"

Scarlett's barrage didn't faze him. He smiled and began ticking off answers, "Well, in my case, they are my sisters, Iris and Hazel. So, no, not identical. And they don't look all that much alike either. I think Hazel and I are the most similar. And we *think* an awful lot alike. They call me their trip, and I call them my trip-pas, but those might be more like nicknames? I don't know. I think most of us three-borns just say triplet or sister or brother.

"And to answer your first question, Iris is a

doctor, and she currently lives in Alaska. Most of the time."

"What about your other *trippa*?" Scarlett asked. "Is she in Alaska, too?"

"Hazel sort of lives all over the world. She's currently hiking and adventuring in New Zealand. She's a travel writer and blogger."

"Wait!" Victoria interjected a bit sharper than she intended. Heads turned her way. Dialing it back, she asked, "Your sister is Hazel James? Of *Hazel Blazes Trails*?"

"You've heard of her?"

"I have," she answered, trying to quell her envy. A wildlife guide for a cousin, one sister a doctor, and the other one Victoria's favorite travel blogger. Hazel's adventures had provided her inspiration to apply for this spokesperson job.

What other highly educated and skilled professionals were lurking in this close-knit family of doctors and high achievers, she wondered?

"What does the rest of your family do?" Scarlett asked, unintentionally chaffing at Vic's insecurity with the question.

"Mom is a school principal. My brother, Tag, is a pilot, my sister Shay runs a hotel, and my sister Hannah is a state senator."

Vic tried to prevent her spirits from plummeting any further. But seriously, what was next? With her luck, she'd soon discover that the third applicant vying for the Romeo Reels job was a Hollywood movie star or a member of the royal family. Good thing Romeo Reels wasn't basing their decision on pedigree. The problem was, though, in her experience anyway, the wealthy and connected often had an advantage.

"More tea, Seth?" Her mom asked, hovering at his shoulder, pitcher of sweet tea in hand.

"That would be great, Corinne, thank you." She topped off his drink.

Victoria frowned at her empty glass, waiting for her refill offer. Instead, her mother asked Seth another question and sank back down into her seat. *Nice*, she thought wryly, completely ignored in her own home for the novelty at their table. You would think this family had never had a guest for dinner before. Admittedly, they'd never had one quite this engaging but still. "Um, will you please pass—"

But her mom was already up and moving toward the kitchen again to fetch who knew what.

"I've got it." Seth picked up the pitcher of tea and poured her a glass.

His gaze collided with hers, and he smiled in that same too-familiar way as if he knew what she was thinking. A mix of humor and apology danced in his brown eyes. Victoria felt her cheeks go hot. So, only ignored by her *family*, she thought with a forced smile.

"Thank you," she told him quietly.

He acknowledged her with a tip of his head.

"Mémé and Gram grew all these vegetables in our garden, too," Scarlett carried on. "They know everything about gardening."

"No wonder the corn tastes so sweet," Seth said.

Mémé executed a single courteous nod at the compliment. Ha. It would take more than corn praise, Alaska invitations, triplet status, doctors, pilots, or semifamous travel blogging awesome sisters to sway her grandmother. Effie Louise Thibodeaux, bless her, was not easily impressed.

Hefting his glass, Seth asked, "What is the secret to *this*, by the way? I've never tasted anything quite like it. It's like drinking sweet liquid velvet."

Nooo. Victoria barely managed to suppress a groan.

"Tea leaves," Mémé answered flatly.

"No, no way," he argued lightheartedly. "This is not your average run-of-the-mill sweet iced tea. Something is different."

"Well, it's made with loose tea," her grandmother conceded. "Tea leaves, not those powdery leftovers they scrape together and stuff inside those smelly bags."

Ever since Victoria could remember, her grandmother had harbored an innate distrust of tea bags, insisting that some vague entity she called "they" were trying to unload this inferior "smelly" product on unsuspecting consumers. It was unclear to Victoria exactly why this conspiracy existed or what the offending odor could possibly be. She'd spent an embarrassing amount of time sniffing tea bags as a child. They smelled fine to her. But Mémé's beliefs were as convincing as concrete in their firmness.

"I see," Seth chuckled. "There's a method, too, though, right? I bet if I dumped tea leaves in a pot of water and added some sugar, it still wouldn't taste like this."

"There might be a little something to it," Mémé admitted reluctantly.

"Is it a difficult technique to master? Is it a secret family recipe or one that you could share? I'd love to learn how to make it and teach my mom. She loves sweet tea, but she always says it only tastes right in the South. She spent a semester at Louisiana State University when she was in college. Now I believe her."

And here we go... Vic watched the tight lines on Mémé's face begin to soften ever-so-slightly.

Mémé firmly believed it took both a discerning palate and superior intellect to recognize superior tea brewing. Not easily impressed, Vic silently amended, except by gratuitous tea flattery.

"I suppose I could give you a crash course."

Victoria exhaled a soft sigh. Had someone taken Mr. Alaska aside and clued him in on how to win the hearts of her family? Good thing they weren't the ones judging this competition either. But that just strengthened the question: Why was he going to so much trouble to charm her family?

THREE GAMES OF horseshoes with Quinn and Scarlett followed by card playing with Scarlett and Corinne, and then dinner with the entire family had yielded Seth precious little in the way of details about Victoria. Aside from more evidence of her carefully concealed dislike for him, that was.

Granted, he hadn't asked her family anything personal about her. He hadn't wanted to come across as overly interested, even though his curiosity had officially moved beyond the professional. It bothered him that she didn't like him; he wasn't used to people not liking him. That little hiccup notwithstanding, he was having a blast.

After dessert, the women adamantly refused his offer of help with the dishes, so Seth thanked them all and stood to leave.

Corinne, stacking dessert plates, asked Scarlett, "Scarlett, honey, would you go get the basket we put together for Seth?"

"Sure thing," Scarlett said and scurried toward the kitchen. Returning quickly, she handed him the bundle. "There's muffins, bread, jam, fruit, milk, hardboiled eggs, cheese and ham. Gram made the muffins and bread."

"Wow. Thank you so much," he said. "I'm getting spoiled." The cabin's tiny kitchen was stocked with a percolator and coffee, so he assured them he was all set for the morning.

"And once again, thank you, ladies, for everything. I hope I get a chance to repay your hospitality. Maybe that will be soon when you come up to Alaska."

Scarlett's face lit with a smile. "Did I remember to put the butter in here?" Stepping closer, she pretended to peek inside the basket and whispered, "There's something else in there for you, too."

Seth started to ask what it was, but she shushed him with a wide-eyed look followed by a loud, "Yep, there it is." Retreating a few steps, she added an enthusiastic, "Good luck tomorrow, Seth."

"Thank you."

Still facing him, she added a wink. "But you understand that I can't wish you more luck than Mama, right?"

"Of course," he said, and grinned.

Everyone laughed. Even Victoria, who then said, "I'll walk you out and give you the details about tomorrow morning real quick."

Outside on the porch, she walked to the stairs before turning and facing him. "So, we'll meet tomorrow morning around six thirty near the dock. The cooler will be stocked with water and snacks. We'll come back here for lunch, so don't worry about packing any of those provisions." She tipped her head toward his basket.

"I'll be there. Thanks again for everything. Dinner was out of this world. You have an incredible family. Your daughter is terrific. And Quinn is, too."

"Thank you," she said. "Yes, she is. We adore Quinn. He's a great friend to Scarlett."

The tight smile was back. The one that precluded him from asking questions. Among the most burning were, *How long have you been divorced? Is Scarlett's father a part of her life? Who taught you to fish? Where is your dad? And your grandfather? How did we get off on the wrong foot? What can I do to change your mind about me?*

"Listen, Seth, I, um, I appreciate your kindness toward Scarlett."

"Well, I appreciate her kindness toward me. I enjoy throwing horseshoes and playing cards. I had a blast. She's a sweet kid."

"I understand that. Scarlett *is* a sweet kid, but she's also just that, a kid. And that means she doesn't understand the abstract nature of an invitation like the one you extended."

"Abstract nature of my invitation?" he repeated carefully.

"Yes—you know, it's one of those invitations you extend to people that you don't truly mean. Like when you tell the mean girl who you went to high school with who turned into the mean wife of the mayor 'Let's get together real soon' when you don't have any intention on following through. You just say it because it sounds nice and pretty."

"I see," he returned carefully. "But that's not what—"

"What my Alaska-obsessed eleven-year-old heard is 'Alaska' and 'fishing' and 'I'll hook you up' and all of a sudden the vacation of her dreams seems like a real possibility."

"But it is," he answered, talking fast, trying to undo this well-intentioned faux pas. "I mean, it could be a real possibility. I can make it happen if you want. This summer even. I would be happy to make arrangements, host you guys myself, show you around, take you fishing. Steelhead guaranteed. Bring Quinn, too, if you want. If you're not comfortable with that, with me, I mean, then check out my cousin's website. His name is Bering James. There are some incredible photos on there. I can get you the friends and family discount."

"Why would you…? You don't even know us."

"I know enough." He circled a hand around, encompassing her and the house. "Kindred spirits here. Real people like me, like my family, who love to fish. Besides, I have a feeling by the end of this thing we'll know each other a lot better. Maybe we'll even be friends." There, he put it out there. Because why wouldn't she want to be friends with him?

"Okay," her tone was flat. Her gaze went squinty, skeptical. "I'm not sure what your strategy is here. Brewing tea and befriending my family isn't going to help you get the job, you know that, right?"

"Are you being serious right now?" Up until now, Seth had been patient. But now she was just being difficult. "You think I'm being nice to your family, to your grandmother, to your *child* because it could somehow help me get this job?"

Her shrug suggested she couldn't imagine any other reason.

"The Romeo Reels people aren't even here yet." He gestured helplessly around at nothing. "That doesn't even make sense."

"Maybe not," she conceded insincerely. "But I don't understand—" She clipped off the rest of the sentence, her expression suggesting it pained her even to be standing here with him much less having this conversation.

"Victoria, I'm not sure what you're afraid of exactly, but I don't have any ulterior motive here."

"I am not afraid," she said, but with an edge, and Seth knew he'd nailed it. *What* was she afraid of, though? He couldn't begin to imagine.

She sighed. "Look, maybe you are truly just a nice guy." Her tone told him she believed that couldn't possibly be true. She was good at that, making a statement while implying the opposite. "If that's the case, I'll be straight with you about a few things. Number one, if I could afford to take Scarlett to Alaska, I would."

It was her turn to gesture around. "As I mentioned earlier, and by now I'm sure you've confirmed for yourself, Bayou Doré, while a wonderful and special locale and an angling paradise, is essentially a small rustic campground. A five-star resort it is not.

"Bringing me to my next point, I am a single mom who lives with her mother and grandmother. The why in that should be obvious considering what I just revealed." She inserted a deliberate pause as if to give him time to catch up. "I'm telling you this so that you understand that I am not in this competition to make friends."

He knew he needed to be careful about how he responded to that. Part of him wanted to give her a shrug and a "Fine, whatever" and walk away, but he sensed that's what she wanted. Another part—the bigger part, evidently—wanted to win her over. There was so much about her that intrigued and interested him, including this fiery, determined-not-to-like-him side.

Patiently, he crossed his arms over his chest. "I'm not in this to make friends either, but why can't that be something that happens?"

Ignoring the question, she stated, "I plan to win."

"So do I."

"I am deadly serious. I am going to do whatever it takes to get this job."

"Me too."

"Fine. Good. Then we're on the same page. The way I see it, even if we were already friends, at the end of this thing, we couldn't possibly *still* be friends, so why start now?"

CHAPTER FOUR

SETH OPENED THE door of his cabin where he was greeted by a waft of balmy morning air already thick with humidity. The choir of chirps and tweets and buzzes from the myriad of unidentifiable insects and birds was almost shockingly loud. And so very different from what he was used to. Slipping off the top layer of fleece he'd impractically donned, he tossed it back into his room, and then took a moment to get his bearings.

This was it. The first day of competition was about to begin. A coil of nervous energy gathered inside of him, surprising in its intensity. He tried to pinpoint the source.

The fact that he'd never fished for largemouth bass didn't bother him. He'd done his homework, and he'd gone after plenty of other unfamiliar species to know that he'd adjust. Objectively, he was the most skilled angler he knew. In this case, he planned to use a lack of experience to his advantage; impress the Romeo Reels reps with how quickly he picked up the skill. So, yeah, the fishing he could handle. Then why did he feel…off?

Maybe it was the conversation with Victoria the evening before. He'd stewed about it for too long into the night and then hadn't slept well. Suggesting that he was being kind to her family to somehow get a leg up in this competition was insulting. And, ridiculous.

And he didn't agree that because they were competing for the same job, they couldn't also be friends. People did it all the time; coworkers vying for a promotion, salespeople competing for accounts, professional athletes for a starting position on the team, students for the top grade. The list was endless. Now, here he was, starting off the most important day of his life all tired and irritable.

Walking the path toward the dock, he couldn't help but think about snakes—thank you very much, Quinn. Head down, he trod carefully even though the area was illuminated from the glow of mercury vapor lights strategically hung from nearby trees and posts. Nearing the dock, he discovered that Victoria was already there and conversing with two people who he assumed were the Romeo Reels representatives.

"Hey, Seth," she called with a jovial tone and a wave.

Hmm. Apparently, they could be *friendly* but not friends? *Whatever*, he thought grumpily, but cheerfully returned the greeting.

Tipping her head back, she laughed at a remark he wasn't close enough to hear, and he couldn't help but note how the sound of her laughter was as pleasing as her voice. Her reddish-brown hair was pulled back into another messy bun with loose strands framing her face. Like him, she was wearing shorts, and he admired her long, shapely legs. She might not want to be his friend, but she couldn't stop him from appreciating her beauty, now could she?

Probably, he should let this go. Certainly, he needed to focus on the day before him. She might be in this competition to win, but so was he. And there hadn't been many times in Seth's life where he'd set his mind on winning or being the best that he hadn't succeeded.

A woman stepped forward as he closed the distance. "Good morning," she called cheerfully. Medium height, she looked fit with sculpted shoulders that were nicely defined in a snug, long-sleeved T-shirt. She'd paired the top with lightweight cargo pants, and her feet were encased in sporty water shoes. A long black braid fell over one shoulder. She reached out a hand to shake. "You must be Seth. I'm Marissa Rivas."

"Nice to meet you, Marissa," Seth said. "Sorry about your flight issues yesterday."

She flipped a breezy hand through the air. "Yeah, well, it was a bummer, but not much we can do about bad weather except complain, right? I'm glad you decided to head here instead of waiting around the airport for us."

"Me too," Seth confirmed. "It's been fun. This place is incredible. Victoria and her family are excellent hosts."

Glancing at Victoria, he found the warm smile still in place. Evidently, she was performing for a new audience now.

"Gerard Drewson," the man introduced himself with a firm handshake. Gerard was a few inches shorter than Seth's six-foot-two with a stocky build and the thickly muscled neck of a wrestler. He wore a pair of long shorts, T-shirt, mesh sneakers and a baseball cap emblazoned with the Romeo Reels logo. He sported a thick, neatly trimmed beard of red that was a few shades lighter than the hair showing beneath the cap.

They chatted for a few minutes before Gerard said, "I think we're about ready to get going here. We just have a few things to tell you guys before we head out on the water."

"Okay," Seth replied. Victoria nodded.

"So, you might be surprised to hear what we

have in store for this phase of the selection process. We're not interested in straight-up tournament competition like you may have been anticipating. We're not going to keep track of who catches the biggest fish or who lands the most fish or hooks which types of species. This isn't a fishing derby. This is about technique, adaptability, finesse and how you handle certain situations."

Pausing to look pointedly from Victoria to Seth, he continued, "Our next Romeo Reels spokesperson will go on to experience a variety of angling conditions, both unfamiliar and familiar. Like you will be doing today, Seth. While Vic, you'll be in your comfort zone. We want you both to know that we are aware of this. And we are also very aware that this makes the experience different for each of you. *That's* what we're interested in—how each of you handles this unique experience. The conditions will change again next week when Victoria travels to Minnesota and joins Henry on his turf, and then when Seth hosts Henry in Alaska. Marissa, you want to add anything?"

"I do," Marissa said, inhaling deeply and then addressing them both. "I'd like to expound a bit on Gerard's point about how you guys perform in these situations. At this stage in the process, you've already proven your angling skills. We know that all three of you can catch fish. We know that you're all used to winning and being the best. Don't get me wrong—knowledge and skills are important, and showing us that aspect is a factor, too. But this job is going to entail more than just knowing how to use our gear. Our next spokesperson is going to be the face of Romeo Reels for at least the next three years. Sure, it's about promoting our brand. But you are also selling yourself. So essentially, what we're looking for is an element beyond skill." She paused for a moment to let that sink in.

"Who loves fishing the most? We can't truly judge that, can we? But what we can judge is who conveys that passion in the most appealing way. In a way that others will want to share. With all that being said, you might be reeling right now, forgive my pun, because this might not be exactly what you were expecting. My advice is to just be yourselves. Let your personality shine through. We want to see the person fishing at this stage, as much as we want to see that person catching fish. Maybe more."

Reeling was putting it mildly, Seth thought, as the morning's twinge of uncertainty erupted into a full-blown bout of anxiety. How was he supposed to compete for something so…intangible? He'd been fully prepared to prove that he was the best angler. But he had no idea how to gauge his success within these subjective parameters.

Victoria, on the other hand, appeared not only unfazed by the news, she looked elated.

"All right then," she said with a bright smile. "If y'all want to climb on board, I'm going to take you fishing."

"RIGHT OVER THERE," Victoria said once they were on the lake and slowly puttering along. One hand remained on the wheel while the other drifted off to the right. "Is where I lost the big one."

"Ouch," Gerard said sympathetically. "Why do we always remember the one that got away?"

"Well, in this case, it was a very expensive loss."

"Bass?" Gerard asked while Seth wondered the same thing, thinking maybe she lost a tournament here.

"Camera," she returned dryly.

"A what? A camera?" Marissa repeated the words slowly, her expression turning thoughtful. "Is that a type of fish I haven't heard of?"

"Nope," Victoria answered on a chuckle. "It's exactly what you're thinking. I was ten years old, and my mama told me under no uncertain terms was I to take her brand-new digital camera near the lake. I realize I'm dating myself here, but that was almost two decades ago, and digital cameras were fairly new and very expensive—at least here in our little enclave. So, obviously, that was a perfectly reasonable request for a mother to make. It's one I'd make myself as a mom.

"And I probably would have complied, except for the fact that my nemesis, Billie Drake, used to live right over there." Victoria pointed back behind them to the southwestern shore, where a white-painted tidy-looking house was perched near the water. "One day, he challenged me to a bass catching contest."

"Uh-oh," Marissa said.

"It gets worse," Victoria said. "He proposed that the loser would have to buy the winner a milkshake from Dairy Daisy every Sunday after church for the entire summer. Now, I need to interject here and add that I've been working at my family's resort for as long as I can remember. I mean, since I was a teeny-tiny thing." With one hand, she indicated a height a few feet from the ground.

"Before I worked for a paycheck, I received an allowance. My mama and grandma believed that was the way to teach me the value of money. It worked. And at that age, much like today, there was nothing more valuable to me than fishing gear and my weekly postchurch milkshake from Dairy Daisy.

"That being said, I knew Billie's throw down was nothing more than an elaborate ruse designed to steal my secrets. I'd placed first in the junior bass tournament the year before and was always outfishing him. So, I agreed to the competition on the condition that we follow derby rules and not fish together. This created a problem of how we were going to keep track of our catches. In a stroke of self-perceived genius, I suggested we take photos of every fish we caught alongside a measuring stick. Which, I have to say, worked like a charm right up until I landed the moneymaker, or in this case, the milkshake maker. Six pounds, two ounces— I could not believe how big it was. I knew it would seal the win for me. I could literally taste my milkshake-flavored victory as I grabbed Mama's camera and started snapping photos. I was going for one final shot when… *Thud*. Boat drifts into a stump. And then *splat*."

Marissa cringed. "Is that the sound the camera made when it dropped into the lake?"

"Yes, ma'am, it is. Slipped right out of my hands," Victoria said, and then sighed dramatically. "In my defense, my judgment was unduly impaired."

"Unduly impaired?" Gerard repeated, shaking his head in amusement.

"Absolutely," Victoria returned dryly. "My fixation on Dairy Daisy's banana caramel shakes was akin to a mind-altering state. To the point where it could be argued that it unduly impaired my judgment."

Gerard laughed. "We may have to find a way to use this story for promotion."

Marissa was smiling and nodding. "I get it. My mom used to bribe me to get good grades in school. Straight As and I could order whatever I wanted from this restaurant where we were regulars. To this day, my mother credits my graduating with honors to a dessert called the brownie cookie collision."

"Thank you!" Victoria said, "You do understand. Unfortunately, my mama did not." She paused to chuckle. "I spent the rest of my summer working to pay off that camera. No money left over for my own milkshakes or fishing tackle. On the positive side, that is the summer I got serious about making my own lures."

It was all Seth could do not to snort his disbelief. Who was this woman? This chatty, engaging, funny woman was not the same Victoria Thibodeaux he'd met the day before. The one who'd given him the rote tour of the resort and then curtly dropped him off at his cabin like a tired pair of shoes. Nor was it the pensive, serious woman he'd sat across from at the dinner table the night before. And definitely not the surly one who'd chastised him for being kind to her daughter before informing him in no uncertain terms that they were not going to be friends.

Not only was this Victoria charming and entertaining, she seemed completely comfortable that the fishing job they were vying for had suddenly turned into a personality contest. Like she'd known all along and had been practicing and saving all her content for this very moment. And suddenly Seth was wondering how in the world he was going to compete with that, with her? His confidence took a hit while his already-rattled mental state deteriorated further.

"What about you, Seth?" Marissa asked. "Have you done much bass fishing?"

"Uh, no, I have not," he answered, trying to get his head in the game. "I've never fished for largemouth bass if you can believe that."

"In that case, I think you should have only one goal in mind today, Seth," Victoria said brightly, and Seth knew—he *knew*—he was walking into a trap. But for the life of him, he couldn't see a way out.

"Oh, what's that?" he asked, helplessly playing along.

"To beat the Alaska state largemouth bass record."

"We don't have largemouth bass in Alaska," he returned, trying not to sound overly smug about this piece of misinformation she'd just surprisingly imparted.

"Well, actually, you do. Or you did have, anyway." Her smile was pure mischief, and her voice was full of teasing good humor, and he knew she had him right where she wanted him. "In 2018, a seven-and-a-half-inch largemouth was legally caught in Sand Lake near Anchorage."

"Seriously?" Marissa asked.

"Seriously," Victoria confirmed. "Wildlife officials don't know how it got there. Planted most likely. Seth is right that they're not native, but a record is a record nonetheless."

Gerard laughed.

Seth felt his neck heat with embarrassment. How did he not know this? He prided himself on his expertise regarding every aspect of Alaska's fisheries. He recited fishing facts the way other people did baseball stats. He knew how many sockeye salmon were harvested in the Copper River every year. He could list the weights of the top ten largest halibut ever taken in the state's waters. His fingers itched to grab his phone and fact-check her, but he knew better. The confirmation he'd undoubtedly find would make him look worse.

"Don't you worry, Seth," Victoria said. "I'm going to make sure you beat that record today."

Frustration rippled through him. He wanted to tell her that he didn't need her help, that there wasn't a fishing record he couldn't break and he certainly didn't need her assistance in doing so. All of which would make him sound crabby and childish. Not to mention that Gerard and Marissa would be observing it all.

So instead, he forced a smile and played along, "I hope you're right about that."

"Oh, I am," she said, steering the boat toward the right.

Then Gerard asked her to "Tell us a little about the most important aspects of bass fishing in southern Louisiana."

"I think knowing their behaviors and needs and learning the water are key to bass fishing success," she explained in the rich-as-cream voice he'd once found so pleasing but now felt contrived. Even though he knew it was silly to think she would alter the tone of her voice. "I'm so glad y'all are here during the spawn because it increases the opportunity to hook a true monster. These largemouth are the most aggressive when defending their nests.

"As far as *where* we're going to fish, an important aspect to keep in mind is that the bass spawn is all about water temperature. Of course, that differs from pond to swamp to river to lake, but it can also vary a lot within a body of water, especially in larger lakes. Lake Belle Rose has a lot of depth variation. So once those temps edge up into the high fifties or sixty-degree range, the fish will move into shallower water to lay their eggs. Bass like a hard, flat surface for their nests, so all you need to do is find the nooks and coves…"

She went on, and Seth listened, spellbound, while she expounded on the intricacies of bass behavior in conjunction with water depth, temperature, clarity and even the effect of moonlight.

Still talking, she maneuvered the boat through a short channel that widened into a large cove. "This here is one of my favorite spots around this time of year. As you can see, there's tons of cover." Willows and thick patches of tall grass surrounded the perimeter. At the far end, there was a small grove of cypress trees that reminded Seth of the area at the resort where he'd watched Scarlett land the bass.

"We've got nice, flat light this morning and the water temperature has been steadily warming the last few days. They should be moving right on in here to spawn. We'll work our way around from this end." She shut off the motor and picked up a rod outfitted with a bright chartreuse-and-yellow jig.

"Seth, why don't you start by pitching this one toward that tangle of branches jutting out there." Handing it over to him, she then motioned toward the bank.

Seth wanted to disagree. If it were up to him, he'd head straight to the far end of the inlet near the cypress patch for a full-frontal assault, so to speak. Again, the presence of Marissa and Gerard kept him subdued.

Dutifully, he took the pole and did as she instructed. Then reeled in the line.

"A little to the right," she advised. "And closer in if you can. Don't be afraid to get right on up in that cover. And don't worry about getting caught up. Nothing there we can't get out of."

"Okay," he muttered and cast again. Nailed the placement, thank you very much.

"Perfect," she acknowledged. "But, I'd slow down the retrieval a bit."

"Don't I want a quicker presentation, though?" Seth countered because, on this point, he felt strongly. He'd read about how aggressive bass were during the spawn and how you could spark a response with a quick approach. Which made so much sense. As he prepared to try again, it occurred to him that she might be setting him up. Uncertainty prickled his scalp. Should he protest and follow his instincts? How many unsuccessful casts would she allow him to make with this bogus rigging before *she* cast the lure she knew would work?

"Okay, for this one, try dropping it a little to the left…"

Not sure how to politely decline, he did as she instructed, and this time when it hit the water, she reached over and placed her hand on the pole. "Wait… Feel the bottom? There. And go." She lifted her hand, and, like a conductor, directed him to raise the line.

"There it is!" she said at the exact second he felt the line go taut.

She was right, he thought as the fish struck hard and fast in that way a truly big one will. You feel it, and you just *know*. He tugged on the line, setting the hook, while a burst of adrenaline surged through him, followed immediately by an awareness of the fish's strength and weight. He tried to play it cool, but this was his first bass, and he could tell it was a dandy!

"This is a nice one," he said, unable to

squelch his enthusiasm. Sneaking a glance at Victoria, he kept a steady pressure on the fish. The last thing he wanted to do was slack the line or jerk the hook out.

"I can see that." The smile she gave him felt electric. He let his gaze connect and mingle with hers and he could feel her sharing his excitement. For the life of him, he could not figure this woman out. Moments like these were what fishing was all about. He wanted to tease her and ask if this meant they were friends now. But having an audience was different than he'd imagined, inducing a constant awareness and a check of his behavior he hadn't anticipated.

"Looks like a nice chunky female, too. Better than five pounds, I'm guessing. Certainly, bigger than seven and a half inches," she joked.

"Five pounds, are you kidding me?" Seth repeated, not even trying to stifle the thrill coursing through him now. Worried about losing it, he concentrated on the task and soon landed the bass without a problem. Working quickly, he unhooked the fish while Marissa produced a scale.

"Five pounds four ounces," she declared. "You know your bass, Victoria."

"Hot dog!" Gerard said video camera in hand. "That's the way to start us off."

Seth was ecstatic. "My first bass," he said. "Thank you, Vic."

"My pleasure, Seth." Beaming now, she executed a little bow. "I am absolutely honored to be the one to introduce an angler of your stature to the delights of Louisiana largemouth bass fishing."

Only then did it dawn on him; his smile froze in place as he recalled the advice and guidelines Gerard and Marissa had established this morning. Like a fish on her line, he'd played right into her hands. This might be his catch, but it was Victoria's win. And she'd executed it all so brilliantly.

His admiration didn't last long as fear welled up and squeezed it out. Victoria was everything they were looking for. Doubt hardened into a cold stone in the pit of his stomach. This was going to be so much more difficult than he'd anticipated. Had he overestimated himself? Was he out of his league?

He wasn't ready to accept that possibility. He'd worked so hard to get here. Fishing was his life. This job was his dream. But if he was going to have any chance of competing with her, he would have to drastically up his game.

CHAPTER FIVE

VICTORIA COULDN'T QUITE believe what was happening. She was on fire. Seth, on the other hand, was barely smoldering. That might be a bit of an exaggeration as he was still affable and witty, but to her, he seemed like a different person. She'd seen him at his best, agonized over the fact that he was going to be stiff competition. Where was that confident, world traveling, smooth talker who'd won over her whole family in less than a day? Not that she didn't appreciate him taking a back seat and making her look good. But surely, he could do better than this.

The rest of the morning proceeded in much the same fashion, with Victoria driving the boat to a location of her choosing where they'd discuss the conditions, talk strategy, confer about lures, and then catch some bass. Victoria dispensed advice but was careful not to dominate either the conversation or the fishing successes. By noon, she couldn't see where she'd made even one misstep while Seth, on the other hand, still seemed content to let her take the lead. Definitely not a strategy she'd employ either on her home turf or when visiting another's.

They headed back to the resort for lunch after they'd landed nine bass among them. Seth had caught three, Victoria five, and Marissa one. For the most part, Marissa and Gerard were observing, filming, taking photos and making notes. But at Victoria's urging, Marissa had tried her hand with one of Romeo's newest level wind reels and caught the second-largest bass so far.

At the resort, they agreed on a two-hour lunch break. Mama, with assistance from Mémé and Scarlett had prepared gumbo, shrimp po' boys on homemade crusty bread and fruit salad with plenty of sweet tea to wash it all down. A platter of molasses cookies and pecan balls were laid out for dessert.

In the kitchen, Seth helped her mom dish out the gumbo while Mémé and Scarlett assembled the sandwiches. Vic couldn't hear what they were saying as she set the table, but chatting and laughing like they were, she couldn't help but note how he already seemed like an old friend. Especially when she watched Scarlett approach him.

Vic could tell her daughter had something important to say, and she could see that Seth picked up on this, too. Hands stilling, he tipped his head to listen, giving her his full attention. After a moment, he set down the bowl and ladle he'd been holding, replacing them with an invisible fishing rod. Scarlett giggled as he then proceeded to fight an invisible fish. They continued like this, laughing and chatting and acting out some silly fishing scenario. Completely different than what Scarlett was used to with Austin and his perpetual busyness and impatience where his daughter was concerned. Vic felt a stab of gratitude and an accompanying rush of affection that shocked her with its intensity. He could be chatting up Marissa and Gerard and working on making a good impression, but instead, here he was clowning around with her daughter.

Corinne filled the remaining bowls, and Seth and Scarlett placed them around the table along with the other dishes. Everyone found a seat and, at Mama's urging, dug in with unabashed enthusiasm. As usual, the food was perfection. Victoria silently conceded that Mama was right; this was just one more good impression for her to leave on the Romeo Reels team. There might not be a place for hospitality on the score sheet, but it certainly couldn't hurt her chances.

"Corinne, have you ever considered opening

a restaurant here at the resort?" Gerard asked between appreciative mouthfuls.

"I have tossed that idea around," Corinne answered. "I bake cakes and desserts on special order and for the bakery in town. But I always feared cooking would lose its flavor if I made it my job."

"I get that," Gerard said, nodding enthusiastically. "It's interesting, isn't it? How sometimes the things we want, and work so hard for, don't turn out like we anticipate?"

"That is a fact," Mémé replied. "Being careful what you wish for is one of life's most interesting challenges."

Victoria couldn't help but think of the life she'd wished for with Austin. Wealthy, educated, from a family who had been here for a million years, she'd thought he was the answer to her desire for something different, something of her own.

Mémé had warned her that he was not what he appeared. She hadn't listened. Her dream of a different life had been too tempting. Even after she'd confessed to a crime she didn't commit and sacrificed her own future for his, she'd held on to hope that he'd deliver on his promise. How could she have been so naive? Not only had he not delivered, he'd nearly destroyed her in the process.

With everyone still happily nibbling cookies and discussing Cajun cuisine, Victoria slipped out and headed back to the dock. It was time to strategize for the afternoon.

The sun was bright, the day had heated up considerably and the water was beginning to clear, conditions that would be challenging from an angling perspective. They all knew this, which presented the perfect opportunity to showcase her knowledge and experience where bass were concerned. If she could get the combination right.

There were a variety of lures in the tackle boxes Marissa and Gerard had brought along. Now she took a few minutes to study and mentally catalog them; many were of the tried-and-true variety, some she'd never seen before but looked promising, and a few she knew would be useless under the current conditions.

Movement caught her eye, and she looked up to find Seth approaching. Alone. Her stomach took a nervous plunge. This would be their first private conversation since they'd spoken the night before and she'd set him straight. Possibly with a bit more force than had been necessary.

Setting aside her wariness, she had to admit he was a very nice-looking guy. Well-muscled with broad shoulders, he was bigger than he appeared at first glance. It was the way he moved, she decided, watching him navigate across the dock's planking. Unlike the lumbering gait displayed by most big guys she knew, he was light on his feet, graceful, even. Athletic.

"Hey, there," he said, stopping when he got close. The corners of his mouth were curling up like he was trying not to smile, making Vic wonder if he'd somehow heard her thoughts. Just the idea of that sent a warm flush creeping up her neck. "Need some help?" he asked looking directly at the open tackle box.

"Not really. Just familiarizing myself with our options for this afternoon," she explained. "How was your lunch?"

"Amazing. Do you guys eat like that all the time?"

"Pretty much. There's usually less variety at a meal, but yeah."

"Scarlett said she made the gumbo."

"That's right. Mama taught her."

"How old is she again?"

"Eleven."

"That is impressive. Can you all cook like that, too?"

"Not quite as well as Mama. She really should be working as a chef or a baker somewhere. I'll have to show you a photo of the bass cake she made for Scarlett's birthday. Seriously, it was so lifelike, it was almost weird to eat it."

Seth chuckled. "I would like to see that."

"Scarlett loved it. But to answer your question, I can put a decent meal together. Mémé is an excellent cook, too. She taught Mama, or at least initially. And they insisted I learn."

"Did you not want to learn?"

"Mmm." Tipping her head, she took a few seconds to think about the question. "I wouldn't say that exactly. It's more that I didn't have a choice, or it certainly didn't occur to me that I had a choice—if that makes sense? It's that way with a lot of things around here."

"Everyone has to pull their weight type of thing?" he asked, and Vic felt unsettled by the intensity of his gaze.

"There's that, for sure. Mémé's adamant that we all contribute equally, and that means knowing how to do every job around here and performing that job up to her standards. Which are high. But it's more that my family is all about passing on knowledge and skills. Another of Mémé's maxims is 'Learn by doing.' Most things I've been doing so long, I can't even remember learning them exactly. And I was made to feel like it was an honor to learn them." Victoria paused to smile. "The woman has an endless amount of patience, too. Something I only realized after I had Scarlett and started teaching her the same way."

"I see. So, in addition to running this resort and cooking and gardening, your grandmother keeps bees, brews beer, sews, hunts, fishes, makes her own lures for fishing and, Scarlett told me, builds things out of wood, including canoes, in her spare time?"

"That is all true," Victoria answered, somehow not surprised that he'd learned so much about her family in such a short time. Honestly, what surprised her more was his seemingly genuine interest in what Austin condescendingly referred to as their "simple existence."

"What else?"

"What else can she do?" At his nod, she said, "Uh, let's see… Pretty much anything she sets her mind to. She can build or fix just about anything. She and my granddaddy built the house we live in and the dining room table. She plays the piano, she's fluent in French and she's the best at horseshoes I've ever seen."

"Wow. That's…phenomenal. I'm suddenly wondering what I've been doing with all of my time. Is she single?"

Vic laughed. "Mémé does not tolerate much in the way of sitting still. I'm sure you can imagine her opinion about kids and screen time. That's why I'm so terrible about my phone. I didn't have one until I was sixteen. I wasn't allowed on social media, and now I don't want to be there. We have one small television in the family room that we got when Scarlett was six years old. I kid you not, I have *never* seen her watch it. Although, truthfully, none of us watch it much."

"So, does that mean you can do all of that stuff, too?"

Still smiling, she said, "To varying degrees. All except for the piano and the canoe making. Woodworking is Mémé's hobby, although Scarlett has taken an interest."

"Did you ever play the piano?"

"Nope. I took violin lessons for about ten years. I wasn't bad, but practicing always felt like a chore. She let me quit when I joined the church choir."

"You sing?" His face erupted with a wide smile, an inordinately cheerful-looking one, in her opinion.

"Uh, yeah. Do you sing, too?"

"No. Not a bit." Head shaking, exuberant grin still intact, he kept his eyes pinned on hers. What was he thinking? Something just occurred to him, so he asked, "Were you home-schooled?"

"I was through the eighth grade."

"And Scarlett?"

"Yes. She'll have the option of going to high school in town like I did, even though she says she doesn't want to. Although, that might change as she transitions into those dreaded teenaged years."

Victoria had wanted to go to school, but if Scarlett didn't, that was fine. Especially if she continued to participate in sports and extracurricular activities where she had a nice network of friends and plenty of socializing. And either way, Scarlett had Quinn.

"That's cool. No wonder you're all so intelligent and accomplished. You have a very interesting life here."

"Thank you. It's nice that you see it that way." And it was. Vic appreciated the fact that he didn't judge her for being homeschooled and isolated. She'd encountered a lot of reactions on that front over the years.

"That's because that's the way it is. Lots of people homeschool where I'm from."

"It's funny because on paper Mémé has an eighth-grade education, and yet she's the wisest, most intelligent, skilled and capable person I've ever met. People in this town seek her advice and counsel. My respect for her only grows the older I get, and the more I learn about the world. There are a lot of paths you can take to acquire an education."

Marissa and Gerard came into view, heading toward the dock.

Seth nodded. "I get that. Some of the smartest people I know have the least amount of formal education."

"Oh yeah?" That interested her, too. She enjoyed researching successful, self-educated people. "Like who?"

"Well, me for example. My grades were lousy in high school. I spent too much time goofing off and getting into trouble, the harmless kind. Or I was skipping to go fishing. I knew I wanted to fish so, for me, college didn't feel like the best use of my time. And, when it comes to fishing, I've met very few people I couldn't out-clever, or at least hold my own against."

Taken aback by the knowledge that he hadn't gone to college either, Vic was left speechless. She wondered why she had assumed that he had? Momentarily distracted, the rest of his statement was slow to sink in…

With Marissa and Gerard rapidly closing in on them, she hastened to ask, "What is that supposed to mean?" Even though she knew, didn't she?

Mouth twitching, eyebrows drifting up, he gave her an easy shrug. Taken together, the casual gesture had the opposite effect. No doubt, exactly what he intended. A rush of nerves flooded through her and sent her pulse racing. Victorian knew a challenge when she heard one.

THEY'D BEEN BACK on the water for nearly two hours with very little action and only one small bass. And as Victoria grew increasingly edgy, Seth came to life. Joking around with Marissa and Gerard like they were best pals. Telling stories. All laid-back and nonchalant like he didn't have a care in the world.

But Victoria could feel it, the intensity radiating from him. The confidence was back, along with something else she couldn't identify. It was like a spark had been lit inside of him. So much for that lack of competitive fire. He was up to something.

Pressure building, she steered the boat into a shaded cove ringed by tall cypress trees.

"There are some nice flat-bottomed areas for nesting here," she explained as she attached yet another lure to the end of her line. "Like my grandmother says, 'There's no such thing as a fish that won't bite, just a fisherman who doesn't know what to feed it.' My mama, the master chef, would say it's all about the presentation. But either way, it's merely a matter of figuring out the right lure for the conditions."

"I agree," Seth piped up. "In fact… Now, you all know I'm no expert on largemouth bass or

Louisiana water. But what I am is pretty good at is scoping out new territory and conditions. When I first arrive in an unfamiliar locale, I like to take some time to absorb it all and then figure out my plan of attack."

"That's an effective tactic, for sure," Gerard said. "I like to do that, too. I'll even talk to the locals. See if I can get any information out of them. Or even better, watch them fish if I can."

"Exactly, Gerard. Me too," Seth said, removing a small object from his shirt pocket. It looked like a wad of paper. "I did both when I got here yesterday afternoon." He squinted skyward. "In fact, time of day and conditions were about the same as they are today. Water's maybe a little clearer now. Anyway, I got to talking with a local angler and learned that it's been a bit cloudy from all that rain last week." Unhurriedly, deliberately he began to unwrap the scrunched paper.

Gerard and Marissa looked on with interest. But Victoria already knew it was a lure. The only questions she had were, what was it, and where had he gotten it? What *local angler* could he have spoken with? Likely, he was making it all up. But she had to give him credit; it made for a good show.

"Now, I should probably qualify this by telling you it isn't a Romeo Reels product."

"That's okay!" Marissa said. "Whatever works!"

"Definitely," Gerard agreed. "Not to mention, that's how we come up with new products."

"That's what I was hoping you'd say." Keeping his back to Victoria as he attached lure to line, he added, "Because I also watched this same local angler land a dandy of a fish with this little guy."

What a load of nonsense. Every local angler she knew had been out on the lake for the derby. Well, except for…

"She was generous enough to loan it to me, and I'm curious what might happen if I give it a try."

She. Scarlett!

Seth was already pitching the lure between two stumps. Beautiful placement. He reeled it in. Tried again. Victoria found herself holding a breath…

Bam!

"Woohoo!" Seth yelped. "Fish on! Feels like a nice one."

Victoria could tell it was. Even without the scale that Marissa was scrambling to retrieve, she knew it would be the biggest catch of the day.

"Six pounds, twelve ounces," Marissa announced proudly, confirming Vic's assumption.

"Way to go, Seth!" Victoria cheered with feigned enthusiasm that she hoped was convincingly portrayed.

"Well done, my friend." Gerard clapped him on the shoulder. "That's exactly the type of resourcefulness we like to see. That is what makes a successful angler right there."

"Indeed," Vic agreed, still wrapping her brain around the fact that she'd been unintentionally sabotaged by her own daughter. A testament, she knew, to how far Seth had already ingratiated himself into her family. Scarlett guarded her fishing secrets like the priceless treasure trove they were. Aside from herself, she'd known Scarlett to share them only with Quinn. And then only under certain conditions.

"Thank you, guys," Seth replied humbly. "I'm thrilled it paid off." His gaze slid to Victoria, where it lingered long enough for her to see both amusement and triumph. Holding up the spinnerbait for her to see confirmed that it was indeed Scarlett's, not that she'd had any doubt. In the other hand, he hefted the fish and a big cheesy grin so Marissa could snap some photos.

Then, locking eyes with Victoria again, he said, "It really pays off when you make friends with the locals, doesn't it?"

Victoria felt her confidence slipping away.

Clever didn't even begin to describe this little performance. But beyond that, she could see a much bigger problem; Seth acted, and sounded, exactly like a professional spokesperson should.

CHAPTER SIX

WITH THEIR SECOND day of fishing complete, Seth was on the way back to his cabin after fetching some ice from the cooler outside the office. Mémé had generously given him his sweet tea tutorial and he'd successfully produced his first batch. According to both her and Corinne, he needed a tall glass of ice in order to enjoy it properly. Who was he to argue with the experts?

Passing by the house, he spotted Scarlett and Quinn on the porch. They were chatting quietly, Scarlett perched on the table's attached bench, head bowed over her hands. Quinn lounged on the top of the table, feet on the bench, elbows resting on his thighs.

"Howdy, Seth" Quinn called with a friendly wave.

Scarlett looked up and smiled. "Hey, Mr. James."

He veered toward them, and as he got close, he could see that Scarlett was busy tying a lure of some sort.

"Hey, what are you up to there?" he asked, peering closely at her project. "That's not for bass, is it?"

"Sac-a-lait," Quinn said.

"Umm…" Seth reached up and scratched his cheek with one thumb. "Sack of what?"

Quinn and Scarlett busted out laughing, exchanging amused glances. Quinn sighed and shook his head slowly with exaggerated pity at Seth's ignorance. "Y'all don't have sac-a-lait in Alaska either, do you?"

"Not that I'm aware of…"

"Sac-a-lait is a fish," Scarlett informed him. "Also known as white perch. Or crappie. They are tons of fun to catch, and you've never tasted a fish fry more delicious. This," she declared, holding up the finished project, "is a jig of my own design."

"Interesting. Perch I've heard of. You guys going fishing?"

"Hoping to," Scarlett said, frowning just a little, and Seth knew her well enough by now to know she was fighting not to elaborate.

Quinn explained, "They're spawning right now over in the Tchelaya Swamp. Ms. Thibodeaux won't let Scarlett go without an adult."

"We never miss the spawn, but she's been real busy," Scarlett added, and Seth could see she was putting on a brave face. "She said maybe tomorrow."

"Ah." Seth nodded, thinking about how true that busy part was.

This morning, he, Victoria, Marissa and Gerard had risen before dawn and driven south to the gulf where Romeo Reels had secured a charter boat for their exclusive use. They'd traveled offshore where they'd spent a few hours fishing for yellowfin tuna and wahoo. The trip had been absorbing, successful and, much to his relief, genuinely fun.

He knew this was partially because he'd felt far less of a disadvantage. Redeeming himself yesterday had certainly helped. And with his background as a commercial fisherman and charter boat captain in Alaska, he had more overall experience in deep water than Victoria. As a result, he'd felt more like himself. Relaxed yet focused. And confident.

Victoria had been more chill, too. Less wired, he imagined, from the responsibility of being the one in the know. And she wasn't unfamiliar with the gulf, having fished there a fair amount growing up. By silent mutual consent, they'd both seemed intent on enjoying the experience. Victoria landed the largest yellowfin of the day, but Seth had caught the most fish. (Just because Marissa and Gerard weren't keeping track of their catches didn't mean he couldn't.)

All in all, Seth wanted to believe the day had ended in a draw as far as Romeo Reels' mysterious and subjective standards went. But truthfully, he had no idea. What he did know was that he was absolutely wiped out. He couldn't imagine how Victoria felt.

In addition to the long hours of fishing they'd put in, she'd kept up with her work around the resort. Even this afternoon, immediately after Marissa and Gerard had departed for the airport, she'd gone straight into the office. He'd just seen her there when he'd passed by, seated inside at a desk studying a monitor screen. She touted her grandma and mom's accomplishments, but she had plenty of her own.

"How far away?" he asked the kids.

"Maybe twenty minutes."

"By boat?"

"Yep. We go through a channel out by the island. Tchelaya is just a swampy part of Lake Belle Rose."

"Sold! Let's go."

Quinn's face erupted with a huge grin while Scarlett went wide-eyed and hopeful. "What? Seriously?"

"Yeah. Pretty sure I qualify as an adult, and I'd love to…sack some lays. As long as it's okay with your mom. I'll go put this ice in my cabin and meet you guys at the dock. I'm leaving tomorrow, so I was planning to head out on the lake anyway."

"Let's do it!" Quinn slapped his palms on his kneecaps.

An exuberant Scarlett was already on her feet and moving. "I'll go ask Mama."

VICTORIA CLICKED THE mouse to place an order for the store. The derby had nearly cleaned them out of chips, soda and ice cream bars. Sitting back in her chair she let out a sigh, finally allowing the relief to settle into her.

Marissa and Gerard had departed. Seth was leaving the next day. Vic was thankful to have these two days complete. Not that she hadn't enjoyed them. She had, and much more than she'd expected. Especially today. Marissa and Gerard were easygoing and fun. Funny how she now thought of them as Marissa and Gerard instead of as the "Romeo reps." Like they were friends.

Then there was Seth. She'd never met anyone quite like him. He was so…attractive. Like, as a person, not as a man. Well, of course, there was that part, too, but what really drew her in was how easy he was to be with. How comfortable he always seemed to be. Just completely pleased with who he was. And yet, he was pleased with others, too. Accepting and curious and genuinely interested.

At first, she'd been suspicious of his motives. Admittedly, that was changing. Because he was friendly with other resort guests, too. And today, everyone he met from the charter boat captain to the bait boy to the waitress at the café where they'd gotten take-out coffee and donuts, was treated with the same degree of kindness and respect. Including her. Even more so with her. Despite her initial treatment of him, he liked her. She could tell.

And she liked him. A niggle of regret churned inside of her thinking about the conversation they'd had that first night, the lecture she'd given him and how emphatic she'd been that they couldn't be friends. Because the truth was, if the circumstances were different, she could see them as friends.

A new email landed in her inbox. A reservation request, which prompted her to check the bookings for the approaching weekend. Also, she needed to call Austin. Her ex had left several messages in the last few days asking her to get back to him.

"Mama!" Scarlett busted into the office while she was still scanning the reservation list.

"One second, Scarlett," she replied holding

up a finger. They were going to be busy. Busy was good. And lots of out-of-towners, which was even better because that meant most of them wouldn't be showing up before noon the next day. Sac-a-lait were spawning, and she'd been promising Scarlett they could go fishing. If they headed out first thing in the morning, she could be back in time to check in the bulk of the campers. Mémé had a meeting in town, but Mama could handle any early birds.

"Hey!" she said, smiling at her daughter's eager face. "What's up?"

"Can I please go sac-a-lait fishing?"

"Yes, we sure can. How's tomorrow morning sound?"

"No, I mean right now. Quinn and I will—"

"Scarlett, honey, I—"

"Mama," Hands up, palms down, she interrupted. "It's okay. I know you're probably tired and busy catching up and all. Mr. James offered to take us."

"Excuse me? Young lady, did you—"

"No! Mama, I did not ask him to take us, I swear." She inhaled deeply and then delivered her pitch in one long, sprawling and enthusiastic breath, "Me and Quinn were talking on the porch while I was tying jigs, and Mr. James came up and asked what I was doing, and I told him they were for sac-a-lait, and he didn't even know what a sac-a-lait was—he said 'sack of what?'" Scarlett paused to laugh, and Vic chuckled because she could see him saying that. "And then we told him, and they don't even have them in Alaska, and he said he'd like to learn how to fish for them, and then he offered to take us. Is that okay?"

Victoria took a second to let this all sink in, wrapping her mind, and her heart, too, around the fact that he'd offered to take her two favorite kids fishing. Why would he do this? Marissa and Gerard were long gone. Closing in on exhaustion herself, she knew how tired he had to be. There was absolutely nothing in it for him, other than perpetrating an act of unselfish generosity. Well, except for some incredible fishing. That thought left her with a grin, and the absolute confirmation that Seth James was good people.

She was opening her mouth to reply when a soft rapping sounded on the doorframe an instant before he appeared.

"*Heyyy,* Victoria," he called in a sing-song voice. "How are you?" Then he looked eagerly at Scarlett and switched to a comically loud stage whisper, "What'd your mom say?" The whole thing was such a perfect dramatization of kids secretly conspiring that she had to laugh.

"Just a sec," a grinning Scarlett loud-whispered

her answer. "I don't know yet." Scarlett turned toward her again, eyes silently pleading, and she could feel Seth's gaze on her, too. "Mama?"

Their enthusiasm was contagious and reminded Vic of everything she loved about fishing: the anticipation, the thrill of the catch and especially the camaraderie. The hopefulness on her daughter's precious face nearly brought tears to her eyes. The handsome, funny sweetness that was Seth James smiling eagerly at her had her stomach flipping in a very nice way. Probably a way that she should ignore but really didn't want to; she was having a blast.

"Who am I to resist this kind of united front?" Shaking her head, she answered, "Her mom says yes, on one condition."

"What?" Scarlett said, barely hanging on to her patience. "I already finished all my homework and I even started on my book report. What's the condition?"

"That I can go with you?"

VICTORIA FINISHED UP, closed the office, and then hurried into the house to let her mom know they were leaving. After stuffing a few things in her daypack, she was on her way back out the back door when she heard the front doorbell chime.

Not an unusual occurrence. The office and

store were closed, but guests knew they lived onsite. Mostly, people were extremely considerate and didn't bother them at home unless it was important. Unfortunately, they had the occasional entitled guest used to five-star treatment who assumed the "staff" would be available to fetch their emergency marshmallows or ketchup or beer 24/7.

"I'll get it!" Victoria called into the kitchen where Corinne was busy baking something undoubtedly amazing that had the whole house smelling like vanilla. Mémé was out in her woodshop.

Cheerfully, she opened the door. Not a guest. Austin. Resentment flooded through her at the sight of her ex. A sensation even more unpleasant than usual since she'd been buzzing with the anticipation of a fun-filled evening. One that included Seth. *Seth.*

She did not want Austin anywhere near him. She could not bear the thought of Seth getting even a glimpse of the woman she'd once been. The idea of him learning her history made her blood go cold. Would she ever accept that her past was well and truly buried?

Quickly, she stepped out onto the porch and shut the door behind her. "What are you doing here, Austin?"

"I've left you four messages in the last week,

and you have not returned my calls. I'm here to see my daughter." He looked pointedly around her toward the house, asking without words if he could come inside.

Victoria ignored it. "Avery isn't here." Avery was the daughter he had with Amber, the woman he'd left her for. Austin, Amber, Avery; Team Triple A, as she secretly referred to them. With poor Scarlett serving as some sort of second-string player.

"You know very well that I am referring to Scarlett."

"But…it's Friday."

"I am very well aware of what day it is, and the parenting plan states that I get her every other Friday at 4:00 p.m."

"Seriously?" she shook her head as irritation and anxiety gave way to confusion. "Since when are you abiding by the parenting plan?"

"I always *try* to abide by the parenting plan, Victoria."

"Do you know how many Fridays you've actually had her in the past year?"

"I know I've missed a few but most of them for sure."

Victoria felt her blood begin to boil with anger and a host of other negative emotions. She reined in everything except for the amused contempt which seemed to annoy him the most.

"If you mean you've missed all *except* for a few, then yes, you're right. You've picked her up on exactly three Fridays in the last year."

Vic could even tell him which weekends they were; Avery's birthday, Amber's birthday and Austin's birthday. Each of those events had called for a "special getaway" trip; one to Florida's grandest amusement park for Avery's birthday, another to New Orleans for Amber's, and then to the Gulf Coast for Austin's. Scarlett had patiently waited for the phone call that would reveal where they'd all be going for her own special birthday trip.

That call never came. When the Friday before her birthday rolled around, Austin texted to say he couldn't fit her in that weekend because he was going to Baton Rouge. Victoria had been livid while a devastated Scarlett cried in her arms. He'd dropped a gift off on his way out of town and promised to take her out for ice cream later. For about the ten-millionth time she wondered how such selfish, self-centered genes could have contributed to her child. It also served as continual validation for not giving Scarlett his name.

"You keep track?" he snapped, irritation flashing across his face.

Interesting, she thought, he was usually much better about keeping his emotions in check. A deliberately casual shrug of one shoulder conveyed her answer. He'd also missed more than half of his Wednesday visits.

His look felt probing. "Is that how far your records go back, a year?"

"No." They went back much further than that. All the way to the beginning, in fact. She'd been keeping records of his visitation, and everything else, since the day he'd left. Initially, Mémé had insisted that she do it. She'd acquiesced. Later, it had become a source of justification for her animosity. An animosity she was careful not to let Scarlett see. Thankfully, those feelings had dissipated. Somewhat. Now, not only was it a habit, but it also felt prudent. Protection, if they ever ended up in court again, a real possibility if he kept neglecting his daughter. And yet another reason she loved her grandmother.

"Well, that's something anyway. At least, you're not keeping track of every misstep I make."

No way was she going to fall for that trap. She let the seconds tick by waiting for him to get to the point.

Austin had this annoying, theatrical way of sighing where he opened his mouth, inhaled deeply, and then huffed out the breath through his nose. Which he did now, before haughtily inquiring, "When are you going to get over this, Victoria?"

Never, she replied silently. *I will never get over your making me promises that you did not keep, including your and your father's promise that if I took the blame for you so you could finish law school then I'd get my turn at college. Or the promise you made to forsake all others while you cheated with another woman and then tossed me and my daughter aside.*

"Don't flatter yourself, Austin. This isn't about me. It's about Scarlett. She has plans tonight. If you want to start adhering to the parenting plan, you're going to have to provide me with some notice."

"I tried to, Victoria. That's what the phone calls were for."

"Well, I'm sorry, Austin. You should have left a message. It's not going to happen tonight. We're in the middle of a special evening. You can have her tomorrow."

"That's not going to work."

"Why? No one is having a birthday."

"What?" he said with a flash of irritation.

"Never mind. Why can't you just get her tomorrow like you usually do? When you *do* get her, I mean."

Another dramatic Austin huff, and then he

confessed, "We have a family portrait scheduled for tomorrow morning."

"How sweet," she gushed sarcastically.

"Can you just go get her? Please?"

Wow. A please from Austin Galbraith. The truth was that Scarlett would probably be thrilled to be included in their family portrait. She adored her little sister, Avery. And Scarlett hadn't quite reached the point where she was ready to give up on her dad. That was a conclusion that Vic knew she couldn't force; Scarlett had to make that decision on her own. Putting Scarlett first was always the right thing. Guilt immediately flooded in to temper her anger.

"What time is the photo shoot?"

"Ten."

"I'll drop her off in the morning."

"Really?"

"When have you ever known *me* to say I'd do something and then not follow through?"

"Vic, I—"

"Do not call me that. You are not allowed."

"I…know." Raking a hand through his hair, he turned and squinted off into the distance as if gathering for a speech. That's when Victoria noticed the lines of tension on his face. What was going on with him? After a second, he gave her a tight smile and said, "That would be great. Thank you. I truly appreciate it."

"What is she supposed to wear? Are you doing like a color scheme? How does Amber want her hair done?"

"Uh…" He shrugged helplessly.

"Have Amber text me."

"Thank you."

"Yep." Two thank-yous in less than a minute. Definitely something strange going on with him. Not her business, and definitely not her concern. Hefting one thumb, Victoria pointed over her shoulder. "I need to go." Stepping backward with a final wave, she turned around and was almost to the door.

"Victoria?"

"Yeah?" she said, spinning to face him again.

"I, uh…" He slid a hand across his cheek to grip the back of his neck.

Victoria recognized the gesture. Stress. Regardless of their history, she felt this…something for him. Concern, she supposed, if she was being honest. After all, he was Scarlett's father.

"Hey, are you okay?"

His eyes widened like he was surprised by the question. With good reason, she supposed, as she wasn't prone to inquiring after his health.

"Oh, yeah, absolutely. Just tired." He waved a breezy hand. "You know what, never mind. I can see you need to get going. We'll talk about it later. Have a good evening, Victoria. Thank you again." And with that, he descended the stairs of the porch and walked away.

Hmm. Very strange, indeed.

CHAPTER SEVEN

"So, what's it going to be, Scarlett?" an animated Victoria asked as she guided the boat across the lake. "Loser has to... Let me think. Clean the restrooms for a week?"

"Gross!" Scarlett shot back. "No one should have to do that all by themselves."

"True enough," Vic agreed. "Especially when it's my sweet little daughter who will surely be the lone toilet cleaner."

"Yeah, you wish. Everyone knows I'm just being kind to my feeble old mama."

"Wow." Quinn laughed. "There is some serious trash talking taking going down in this boat right now."

"I'd say so." Seth agreed. "A fishing wager?"

"Oh, yeah," a chuckling Victoria answered. "You'll have to forgive us, Seth. Sac-a-lait tends to bring out our competitive natures. And not always in the most attractive way. We always have a friendly bet. Most fish or biggest fish or both."

She gifted him a warm smile, and Seth was

struck by how genuinely relaxed and carefree she seemed. He liked this Victoria even better than the one he'd fished with this morning.

"Loser has to eat one of Gram's hot peppers?" Scarlett suggested.

Victoria winced. "Please, don't make me."

Scarlett giggled. "I won't. Okay, how about loser has to do all the garden chores next week?"

"Wait a second here." Seth held out a hand. "I want in on this. So, it has to be something I can enjoy watching you guys do before I leave."

Scarlett sputtered out a laugh and shook her head. "I don't think you want to do that, Mr. James. You're never going to—" She bit off the rest of the sentence as if suddenly realizing how that sounded. Bug-eyed, she attempted to change course, "I meant, I mean, uh…"

Trying not to laugh, Seth leveled her with a playful scowl. "Never going to do what, Scarlett? Catch as many sacks of lays as you? I do possess some general knowledge of fishing, you know?"

Quinn howled with laughter. To Scarlett, he joked, "You talked yourself into a tight little corner right there, didn't you?"

"No, wait, I," a red-cheeked Scarlett stammered, embarrassed by the idea that she may have offended him. "I just meant because you've never fished sac-a-lait."

"She sure did," Seth agreed with Quinn, pinching the pad of one finger against his thumb and holding it aloft. "Tiny little corner she can't get out of without letting me in on this."

"Fine," Scarlett said, fighting her grin in a way that reminded him of her mother. "But don't say I didn't warn you."

"It is on! I'm going to win, and then you ladies are going to…" He looked at Quinn. "What can I bet?"

"How about we team up?" Victoria suggested. "And the losing team fries up this mess when we get back? And does the dishes."

"That works," Seth agreed.

Scarlett nodded. "Sounds good. Me and Quinn versus you and Mr. James?"

Vic grinned conspiratorially at Scarlett; two ladies sharing a secret. "Nothing else would be fair. If we were on the same team, it wouldn't even be a contest."

"Wow," Seth said dryly and then gaped exaggeratedly at Quinn. "I wonder where Scarlett gets it from?"

"You know it," Quinn replied in a similarly dry tone. "They are both insufferable. I don't see how we can accept this insult and still hold on to our collective manhood."

"I agree. That settles it," Seth said.

"Ladies versus gentlemen!" Quinn declared.

"Quinn," Scarlett returned flatly. "Have you lost your ever-loving mind? We will smoke you, and you know it."

"Now, Scarlett," Vic said in an overtly conciliatory tone. "Be nice. There is no doubt in my mind that these boys are a force to be reckoned with." Countering the statement with a sad shake of her head, she made a show of cupping her hand to her mouth and whispering loudly, "This is going to be pathetic." Clearing her throat, she then announced, "It is on! But please remember that Scarlett and I do not care for our sac-a-lait either overbattered or overcooked."

VICTORIA TOOK A seat on the cooler to change jigs and accepted the reality that it had been way too long since she'd had this much fun. Doing anything. She'd spent months planning and fretting about making the final round. Then, when she'd learned she had, she hadn't even celebrated. Instead, she'd jumped right into preparing, practicing, creating a workshop to present, developing her strategy. All while trying to keep up with her normal life of helping run the resort, teaching Scarlett, parenting Scarlett and spending time with her family.

The sweet sound of her daughter's belly laugh drew her attention. Seth was telling a story about his sister Iris casting her pole into the ocean.

"The only reason she was even on the boat in the first place was because Hazel bribed her. She promised to do Iris's chores for a week. Our dad tried so hard not to be upset. Iris had never been halibut fishing before, and he was thrilled that she'd agreed to come along, so he gave her this brand-new, expensive rod and reel to use. And then she just..." Swinging both hands, he simulated an exaggerated cast. "Heaved the whole thing up toward the sky. It was like a cartoon. Dead silence on the boat while we all watched it fly out of her hands. Up, up and away... And then *splash!* When I think about it now, I still, I just..." he trailed off with another bout of laughter. "Lose it."

Scarlett and Quinn joined in, and Vic couldn't help but admire how he treated the kids. She already knew he had a way with Scarlett, but he was every bit as good with Quinn. They all spent nearly as much time laughing as they did fishing. A world of difference from Austin who... Enough thinking about her ex and whatever affliction had taken hold of him.

Why in the world would she be comparing the two men anyway? She and Seth might be closing in on a friendship, but they couldn't be more than that, could they?

"I want to meet them," Scarlett said. "Iris and Hazel. And your other sisters—Shay and Hannah, right? And your big brother, Tag."

"I would love for you to meet them, and my cousins, too, and my parents. You can meet everybody when you guys come up to Alaska."

What would he do if she took him up on this trip that he kept offering? Although she knew what he would do, didn't she? Just like his generous spirit, his invitation—the one she'd initially taken with suspicion and skepticism—was completely sincere. Longing hit her fast and hard, and for a moment, she indulged in a good old-fashioned daydream of what that trip might look like. Seth showing them around, taking them fishing, introducing them to his family.

He spun around then as if he could feel her eyes boring into him. The smile he turned on her felt different. It held the same bold self-assurance and lighthearted humor she'd become familiar with, but there was also affection there and what might be…heat? As if to confirm the suspicion, his gaze dipped to her mouth and back up again to her eyes.

Then something happened that Victoria hadn't experienced in years. In fact, she'd done her level best to avoid anything even remotely like it. Her heart leaped. Like an actual, literal shock zapping the inside of her ribcage. The sensation prompted her to raise one hand and lightly rub her breastbone as if she could calm the agitation now raging there. Except, it wasn't only agitation, and there was a part of her that didn't want it to stop. Another vision materialized: her and Seth standing toe-to-toe, his arms coming up to embrace her, dancing brown eyes staring into hers, him leaning close to press his lips to hers…

"Vic?" he said, in a low voice tinged with concern and curiosity, and she wondered, despaired, about how many of those thoughts had shown on her face. "You okay?"

Inhaling deeply, she became aware of the rapid pace of her pulse and how her skin felt funny. Tingly. And overheated. Bringing her chin up, she stared back at him, right into his eyes, desperately searching for… There was no need. She could see he felt it, too. This charge between them, electric and heavy and alive, like the way the air feels during a thunderstorm. If she reached out a hand and touched him, she knew, irrational as it might be, that she'd get a jolt.

At that moment, she realized that she no longer wanted just his friendship. What she wanted would be so much better. And the revelation made the wanting so much worse.

Somehow, she managed a weak smile. "Yep. Yeah, absolutely. I'm, uh, I'm fine." Pivoting around, she flipped her line toward the bank. "Just a little heart…burn or something."

"What a coincidence," he said, and then added so softly she could barely hear him, "Something fishy going on with mine, too."

"WINNER, WINNER, SAC-A-LAIT DINNER!" Seth made a fist and punched the air as Quinn's line stretched tight.

"Pass the tartar sauce!" Quinn confirmed, smoothly reeling in the final fish of the evening. Under the rules they had agreed upon, whoever had the most sac-a-lait in two hours would be victorious. Collectively, they'd already caught and kept enough for dinner, so Quinn quickly released his prize.

"Well, Quinn, looks like we managed to make it a *contest* after all."

Quinn nodded solemnly. "Not much of one. I almost feel bad about it, but, you know, what did they expect when they allowed the two best fishermen to be on the same team?"

"Truth."

Scarlett sighed and lowered her pole. She looked at Victoria, a helpless expression stamped across her face. "I want to say something about what bad sports they're being, but I know that if we would have won—"

"We'd be even worse?" Victoria finished while Scarlett nodded. "I know it, Scarlett. I was thinking the same thing. Well, at least we don't have to worry about them destroying our dinner."

Seth scoffed and looked at Quinn. "Did I hear that correctly? Are they now trash-talking our *cooking* skills? After we annihilated them in this fishing competition?"

"That is what I'm hearing, Seth."

"Can you think of anything worse than a sore loser?"

Quinn slowly tipped his head one way and then the other as if considering the question. "An obnoxious winner, maybe?"

"Yeah. Good thing we're not that."

"Gracious is what we are," Quinn agreed with mock seriousness. "I didn't even point out how we won by four fish. Four, Seth. Four is a lot. But I would never mention that and make them feel worse."

"Restraint is another sign of good sportsmanship, Quinn. You are an inspiration to would-be gloaters everywhere."

Seth made a dramatic show of turning toward Victoria and Scarlett. "Do you ladies have any idea what day it is today?"

Victoria, trying not to laugh, shook her head in the negative.

"What day is it, Mr. James?" Scarlett replied, drawing out the words like someone who knew she was about to be on the receiving end of a bad joke. Victoria could not have been prouder.

"I do believe it is, wait for it… Fish-fry-day!"

"And, ladies," Quinn added, only containing his laughter enough to throw Victoria's earlier taunt back at them, "Please remember that Seth and I do not care for our sac-a-lait either over-battered or overcooked."

Seth and Quinn bumped fists and then howled with laughter.

Victoria and Scarlett exchanged gloomy, amused headshakes and began storing the gear. Then, with the boat full of laughter and happy chatter, Victoria set a course for home.

WHEN THEY RETURNED to Bayou Doré, Victoria said, "Scarlett, why don't you and Quinn go on ahead and get these fish to Gram and Mémé and help them start frying. Gram texted and said they've got everything else about ready. Seth can help me clean up here."

Seth agreed, thrilled to have a few minutes

alone with Victoria. To explore this…whatever was happening between them. He didn't know exactly, but he wasn't ready for it to end.

"Sounds good," Scarlett answered. "I'm starving."

"Me too," Quinn replied, hoisting the cooler up and securing the strap over his shoulder. With his other hand, he grabbed a tackle box. "I hope your gram made corn bread."

"Oh, I can guarantee you she did," Scarlett said, gathering up another tackle box and two fishing poles. Seth liked how the kids did their part without having to be asked. It reminded him of his own family. "No fish fry would be complete without it…" Scarlett and Quinn continued the conversation as they headed for the house, speculating about what other culinary delights might be in store for them. Seth couldn't help but share their enthusiasm. Corinne had mentioned something about bread pudding for dessert. Made with real vanilla bean.

Working in tandem, like they'd been performing the chore forever, he and Victoria set about unloading and tidying the boat.

A few minutes of companionable silence passed before Seth asked, "I have to know. Did you and Scarlett let us win?"

"What? Absolutely not!" Victoria whipped around to face him. "Let's get something straight here, Alaska, I do not *let* anyone win. Especially when it comes to fishing. You can ask Scarlett for confirmation on that one. I fall into the 'kids need to learn to lose gracefully' camp. I stopped letting her win every game we played when she was about five years old." Stepping toward the boat, she checked the lines a final time.

"That's probably wise seeing as how she doesn't have a bunch of siblings to lose to. In our house, we also learned to lose at a very early age." Seth walked across the dock and deposited the remaining items on the pile of provisions to pack into the storage room, which he knew was located in the small supply building next to the restrooms.

Victoria joined him. "Exactly. I remember losing to Mémé at checkers when I was so tiny that I still had to sit on the big dictionary at the dining room table to see the checkerboard."

"Oh, we lost a lot at checkers—and other games, too. Our sister, Hannah, is next above us in age, and she's good at everything. Like freakishly good. She beat our older siblings, too. Even when we teamed up, we were rarely a match for her. And she showed us no mercy."

Mouth curling at the corners, she crossed her arms and looked him over.

Good naturedly, he threw his hands up.

"What? Are you wondering how big of a loser I am right now?"

Grinning outright now, she shook her head. "No, that's not it. I just… I like how you talk about your family. You almost always say 'us' when you mention your childhood, are you aware of that?"

"What do you mean?"

"Other people usually say when *I* was a kid, or when *I* was younger, but you say *us* and *we*. When *we* were younger, Hazel and I did this, or the three of *us* played that. It's really sweet. And it tells me that you're very connected to your sisters."

"Yeah, well, I like to joke that when you spend eight months in a tiny cramped womb space together, your perspective is forever altered. It's like they're a part of me."

"That makes sense. I sound like Scarlett now, but I'd love to meet them. I bet I could learn everything I want to know about you."

Surprised by her assertion, Seth didn't move. Warmth unfurled right in the center of his chest. She wanted to know stuff about him? Did that mean she wanted to get to know him, too? He wanted to encourage her to ask anything she wanted. But he didn't want to lose this connection they'd forged. It felt wispy and fragile as if one wrong move could cause her to bolt.

So, he kept it light. "Ha. Good luck with that. We are very loyal to each other. They would never tell my secrets."

"Maybe not—" Victoria drawled, pulling one shoulder up into a little shrug "— on purpose."

"Unfortunately," he rushed forward with the lie, "I already asked them. And neither of them wants to meet you. Ever. So, too bad for you because they are pretty cool."

That made her laugh hard. "We'll see about that. I think they'll want to meet the woman who aces their brother out of *the* job as Romeo Reels spokesperson."

Seth followed Vic to the outdoor sink, where they washed their hands before walking back to the pile of gear.

Before she could begin to collect it, before he could talk himself out of it, he said, "Can I ask you another question?"

"Sure," she said.

"What changed?"

"What do you mean?"

"I think you know what I mean, but I'll go ahead and say it. Why are you being nice to me now? Genuinely nice. Not for the sake of this job nice. Don't get me wrong—I'm enjoying it. I just… You're hard to read, and I want to know that this change is for real."

CHAPTER EIGHT

VICTORIA'S FACE SETTLED into a frown as she looked away. Seth almost regretted the question and pondered how to take it back or soften it somehow.

But then she caught his gaze again and held it. "I do know what you mean, Seth, and I owe you an apology. I'm sorry about what I said that first night. It was just that you seemed too..." She exhaled on the word as if thinking. "Nice. You were so nice. And I didn't trust you."

"That part I picked up on. What I don't understand is why. What did I do?"

"Nothing. It wasn't you. You were perfect. Believe it or not, that was the problem. I've had trouble where men are concerned. Nice guys who...aren't. Specifically, a bad marriage that turned..." Trailing off, she searched for a word. "*Ugly* might work."

"I'm sorry," he said, even as he pondered all the implications of the word *ugly*. The thought of someone mistreating her made him angrier than he probably had a right to be, and brought up questions he knew he didn't have a right to ask.

"Me too. My ex-husband, Scarlett's dad, he broke…" Trailing off she shook her head.

"It's okay." He took a step closer. "You don't need to talk about it now. I've had one of those myself."

"You've been divorced?"

"No, sorry, I meant heartbreak. I thought you were going to say he broke your heart."

"Oh…"

"Victoria." Tentatively, he reached out a hand and tangled his fingers lightly with hers. She curled her hand into his, and he relished the sensation. Like he'd captured a moonbeam or calmed a skittish butterfly. "I know it's not the same. Divorce is painful in ways I could never understand. And I know the fact that you have a daughter changes everything."

"My ex, he… I actually wasn't going to say that he broke my heart. What he did was way worse. I was going to say that he broke his promises. So many promises. I married him for the wrong reasons. I was pregnant, and there were false pretenses…

"But I was committed. We were just married. I hadn't even had Scarlett yet when I found out he was cheating, had been cheating the entire time we'd dated. With the exception of Scarlett, our relationship was a disaster. And all these years later, I still can't understand how he could be so different than what I thought. He shattered my trust. I resent him for so many things, but the biggest one is how he changed me. I'm leery of people, of relationships. I can't help it. Normally, I'm good at hiding it. But you were so… You seemed too good to be true. I think I wanted to believe you had some hidden motive. You know, to protect myself."

What was she saying here? Because it sounded like she was afraid of liking him too much. "Well, if there's one thing I can assure you of where I am concerned, what you see is what you get. Always. I will never pretend to be something I'm not." He thought about his own heartbreak, about Ashley, and how she'd made him feel bad about who he was, tempted him to try and be someone different. Eventually, painfully, he'd realized that he could never be what she wanted.

"I believe that," she whispered. "I can be distrustful and suspicious." She tried to smile, but he could see it hurt her to say the words. "Just know that I don't want to be like this. I wasn't until him. I was…"

"I think you're pretty amazing just the way you are." Stepping closer, he lowered his chin to brush the top of her head. "And under the circumstances, being cautious is completely understandable."

She nodded.

Slowly, he brought his arms up, wrapping one around her waist and pressing the other lightly to her upper back. He half expected her to push him away, so he was surprised and so very pleased when her hands came up and gently gripped his shoulders instead. Emboldened, he tightened his hold and pressed a gentle kiss to her temple.

She stretched her arms around him, hugged him. Nice and tight, and for a moment, Seth couldn't move. He was…dazed. Overwhelmed. Her warmth, the smell of her hair, the feel of her hands lightly gripping his back. How could anything be better? Thoughts and emotions collided inside of him, unprecedented ones that he couldn't quite get a grip on.

His heart felt full and exposed at the same time, which was both exhilarating and terrifying. He wanted to kiss her. Too soon for that, he decided, because he needed her to trust him. He wanted to be the one she trusted.

Was that even possible when they were competing for the same job? And not just any job, but a career-making opportunity of a lifetime that only one of them would be granted. Could they reconcile that? He needed to consider all of this. But it was too late for that, wasn't it? He couldn't unfeel any of this. And he knew she felt something, too. Otherwise, she wouldn't be here in his arms.

With a soft shake of her head, she pulled back slightly like she might be dazed, too, which was oddly reassuring. Reaching out, he took one of her hands and turned it palm up, and rested it in his other hand. Using one finger, he lightly traced a twisted pattern on her palm.

"Do you know what this is?" he asked.

"No," she whispered, and he liked that she trembled a bit from his touch.

"It's a Celtic knot that symbolizes loyalty and trust." And love, but he didn't mention that part. "I'm not sure what is happening between us here, and I know you're not ready to trust me. But I'm making you a promise. I will earn your trust, Victoria. If you'll let me."

For a few long seconds, her gaze searched his. "I want to," she said, her voice cracking around the edges. Nodding, she stepped forward and rested her cheek against his muscled chest, and he held her again.

"Wow," she breathed softly. "I wish you weren't leaving tomorrow. I wish this didn't have to end."

Seth brought one hand up to curl around the back of her neck. "Me too," he whispered, even though he knew in the deepest part of his soul that this was only the beginning.

TWO DAYS OF travel had Hazel back from New Zealand, home in Alaska for a week of "vacation" from her life as a travel blogger. A few days behind Seth's own return from Louisiana.

"Why do you keep checking your phone?" Hazel asked, handing him a steaming mug of coffee and then sauntering into the kitchen of their parents' home.

Iris had been in Washington, DC, for work and timed her return trip to coincide with Hazel's. Last night, Tag had met them both in Anchorage and flown them to their tiny town of Rankins on Alaska's southeastern coast.

Hazel always stayed with their parents when she came home.

Their large, two-story arts-and-crafts style house had five bedrooms and plenty of space to raise six kids. After they'd all left the nest, he'd wondered if his parents would downsize. But with the number of grandchildren increasing at a rapid pace, and his mom's penchant for family gatherings, he doubted it. There might be less people living there now, but it was full of memories and still felt cozy, warm, lived-in. The perfect place to fill his sisters in on all the details he knew they'd want to hear.

Even though they checked in with each other almost daily, he'd been vague about certain aspects of his experience, namely the ones related to Victoria, which undoubtedly would interest his sisters the most.

"Uh…" Seth stared at the still blank screen, willing a message from Victoria to appear. Or Scarlett. Something to let him know they'd received the packages.

He'd worked quickly to set this whole thing up, planning it before he ever left Louisiana, wanting it to happen before she departed for Minnesota. Crazy how nervous he felt now that the delivery day was here.

He and Vic had been chatting daily via text and exchanging nightly phone calls, getting to know each other better. Mostly, he kept things lighthearted, funny, friendly. No mention of where they might be heading or what the future might hold. Until now. This gesture could definitely be construed as an effort to take things up a notch. Which is exactly what he wanted. But now that it was happening, what if it was too much?

"I told you that you'd love Louisiana, didn't I? Was it superhot?" Returning with two more mugs, Hazel passed one to Iris, who was seated near Seth on the large sectional sofa in the great room.

"You did," Seth agreed, glancing again at

the lifeless display. "And no, not miserably so. It was nice."

"Are you expecting an important text?" She took a seat on the adjacent cushions and swung her feet up onto the ottoman.

"Uh, yeah, sort of." He scrolled through to reread Quinn's message: The eagles have landed.

Initially, the words had made him chuckle. But he should have heard something from Victoria by now. Or Scarlett at the very least. Louisiana was three hours ahead. He'd enlisted Quinn's help to ensure the safe and coordinated delivery of the packages, and his abstract reference had reassured him. Quinn had loved the fishing vest he'd sent him, too.

Seth looked up to find both his triplet sisters staring expectantly.

"Who is she?" Hazel asked.

"Ashley?" Iris queried at the same time.

"Ashley!" Scowling, Hazel whipped her head around to look at Iris before then turning again to half shout in his general direction, "Why would Ashley be texting?"

"Not Ashley," Seth said and felt a tiny flicker of guilt. Ashley had been texting, and he'd finally agreed to her lunch invitation. There was nothing to feel guilty about, he reassured himself, he and Ashley were just friends. Granted, she'd been a little friendlier than usual lately, but he'd written that off to her satisfaction with her new job working for their brother Tag's air transport company. Getting back on her feet after her divorce and all that. He wasn't interested, hadn't been in a long time. And he intended to reiterate that at lunch, which was the reason he'd accepted the invite.

"Please tell me you're not seeing her again."

"No, Hazel, I'm not."

"Then why would Iris ask if you were expecting a text from her?"

"Did she ask that?" he asked absentmindedly.

"Yes, she did," Hazel returned sharply. The only reason Ashley is interested in you again is because she thinks you're going to be famous."

"Hazel, I love you," Iris said. "But that is not true. She was interested before Seth ever applied for the Romeo Reels position."

"*Of course*, she was," Hazel exaggerated her agreement. "Because Ashley has changed."

"Yes, I believe she has," Iris confirmed.

Hazel's eyes narrowed, and she swiveled toward Iris with a laser beam glare. "Not where Seth is concerned. And aside from the fact that you've forgiven her for the crimes she perpetrated against you, which I have not done, by the way, this is the same woman who strung Seth along for years before telling him she could never marry *just a fisherman*. Do you recall that little detail that left our brother devastated *for years*, Iris?"

Just a fisherman. Seth almost winced. Interesting, how that still jabbed a little.

"People change, Hazel," Seth pointed out.

"Not that much, Seth, they don't. Not her."

That's when Seth knew he needed to stop this conversation. Ashley was the one topic on which the three of them did not agree. Hazel had a double-barreled reason for despising Ashley; she had bullied Iris all through school. Iris had since forgiven Ashley, who'd moved back to town the previous summer.

Then there was Seth's history with her. After crushing hard on her for years, Seth had given up hope when she'd brutally informed him that she could never marry him, *just a fisherman*, and promptly married someone else. Now a divorced mother of three, Ashley did seem different. In addition to making amends with Iris, she'd apologized to Seth as well, and formally asked for his friendship. A friendship he'd granted, much to Hazel's dismay.

Seth nodded. "You were right about the snakes, Iris."

She grinned. "Of course, I was. I don't make this stuff up. Did you see any?"

"I did. The kid I told you about, Quinn?—

he caught one. It was a rat snake. At first, I thought he was holding a ball of rope, and when I realized what it was, I just froze. And then Quinn—"

"If it's not Ashley, then who has you all tied up in knots?" Hazel interjected, derailing his attempt at a subject change.

"Vic," he confessed, because he couldn't keep anything from his sisters. Not for long anyway. "From Louisiana."

"Vic," Hazel repeated, tapping a finger to her chin. "The dude you're competing with?"

"Yes, except he's not a dude. Vic is short for Victoria."

"Oh," Hazel said, eyebrows darting high onto her forehead.

"Oh!" Iris chirped at the same time, expression in perfect sync with Hazel's.

Then, heads turning toward one another, he watched as his sisters exchanged one of those drawn-out, talking without words, triplet mind melds that Seth knew well. In tandem, they looked back at Seth and crooned, *"Ohhh..."*

"So, you're falling for this woman? While you compete for the same awesome job?" Iris asked.

"Maybe. And yes."

"But there's no way she's as good as you are," Iris stated this as fact. His sister's faith in him was both endearing and well-earned. Last summer, he'd managed to teach her how to halibut fish like a seasoned angler in just a few days in order to impress her boss. "How will she handle losing to you?"

Oddly, her pronouncement produced nearly equal measures of pride and concern. "She is, actually. Just as good. Better in some ways."

Hazel studied him with a puzzled scowl. "Do you honestly believe you can be romantically involved when this is all over?"

"Yes, sure. Why not? But we're not exactly romantic. Not yet, anyway." He was beginning to accept that because he hadn't heard from Victoria, it likely meant he'd gone overboard with this gift. Probably, he should have consulted his sisters first.

"But you want to be," Hazel stated, and he nodded because he knew there was no point in arguing. "What's your plan?"

"Well, I sent her this gift. I sent everyone gifts, and Quinn, too. But now, I haven't heard from her, and I'm doubting myself. She has trust issues, which are totally warranted. I've been trying not to rush things but—"

"Gifts for the whole family?" Iris interrupted.

"Oh, boy." Hazel reached over and squeezed Iris's knee.

"Yeah, you know, like a thank-you for hosting me and everything." Although, the gifts were way beyond what he'd typically extend in a situation like this.

Iris asked, "Was her gift expensive?"

"Not really..." he hedged. "I mean, retail value would be a lot. But Kella gave me a great deal." Kella Jakobs was a local artist whose work had gained international acclaim and fetched top dollar. "Because I supply her with fish. But it's not about that. Vic would see right through some expensive trinket. It's more..."

"Thoughtful?"

"Yes. Okay, here's the situation...?"

He went on to explain, and by the time he'd finished, both his sisters were gaping at him, stunned. Which was understandable; he'd never gone to such lengths gift-wise. "I'm trying to *say* something specific with the gift—you know what I mean?"

"We get it," Hazel breathed softly, still looking a bit stupefied.

"He's gone," Iris murmured.

His sisters exchanged another knowing look that had Seth feeling fidgety and embarrassed.

"Seth." Hazel leaned forward. "You are aware of my list."

Dipping his head, he pinched the bridge of his nose. "Of course, Hazel."

The Romantic Interest List. His sister's list outlined acts and deeds that she was convinced could judge the degree of a man's feelings. The least little infringement could send his sister running. Things like calling or texting more than once a day or asking to meet family members or close friends before it seemed appropriate. The list was long and rather ridiculous, in his opinion, in that it included things like sharing drinks and silverware. Except, now that he thought about it, why did he want his family to meet Victoria? He'd never particularly cared about his family meeting a woman he dated. It was just that Vic was so different than anyone he'd ever dated. So much better and...

Uh-oh.

"Well, in case you've forgotten, thoughtful gifts are one of the biggest indicators of romantic interest. So, I can promise you that whatever you're trying to say to your Victoria, she has now heard you loud and clear."

"I GOT A PACKAGE?" Scarlett asked, peering down toward the boxes stacked just inside the door of the resort's office.

Seated behind the desk, Victoria answered, "Yes, Scarlett, you can have some chips. One package only, though. Gram is making pot roast for dinner and—"

"No, Mama, I'm not talking about the chips…" She knelt for a closer inspection. "I did! I got an actual package!" Scarlett sprang to her feet and did a little dance that made Victoria smile, despite her surprise and suspicion. Then she scooped up the rectangle-shaped box and held it up for Victoria's inspection. "Look, it has my name on it."

The delivery had arrived a few hours before, but a busy Victoria had assumed all the boxes were part of the inventory she'd ordered several days prior. She'd barely glanced at the pile since it was delivered. Quinn, bless him, had appeared out of nowhere and stacked them neatly inside the office for her.

"Who from?" Victoria asked, even though she deduced that it must be from Austin. More evidence of his recent odd behavior.

"You got one, too."

"What?"

"So did Mémé and Gram! It's like Christmas. Except better, because I never get packages in the mail at Christmas."

Victoria stood. No way was Austin playing Santa Claus with the whole family. She crossed over toward Scarlett to see for herself.

"Can I open it?"

"Is there a return address?"

"Nope." Scarlett held it up for her inspection.

"Huh. Yeah, sure. Go ahead."

"Aren't you going to open yours?" She bobbed her head toward a smaller box now stacked on top of what she could see was one of the much larger boxes she'd been expecting.

"Yes, but after you."

"Wait! Should we get Mémé and Gram, and all open them together?"

Ugh. Victoria felt a stab of pride and affection for her daughter, whose kind heart often swept Victoria off her feet. She was like Gram in that way.

"That is extremely thoughtful, Scarlett. Yes, run and get them."

Scarlett disappeared through the doorway and into the breezeway that attached the office to the house. When she'd gone, Vic inspected the packages. Scarlett was right; there was no return address. Strange.

"Now, what is Scarlett going on about?" A harassed-looking Mémé asked a few short minutes later, following Corinne and Scarlett inside the office. "This is some sort of a mistake. I've never gotten a package that I didn't already know was on the way."

Victoria offered up a helpless shrug. "I'm not sure. All I know is that we all got one."

"Yours is heavy, Mémé." Scarlett placed the

package on the desk. "See? It says Ms. Effie Thibodeaux right on it."

"Hmph," she snorted disbelievingly. Mémé came closer to give the package a proper scowl.

"This one is for you, Gram."

"Thank you, Scarlett, honey," Corinne said. "Now, Victoria, do you know who is sending us gifts?"

"Gifts!" Mémé huffed again. "I am way too old to be getting a gift."

"No, Mama, I don't. I swear."

After retrieving Vic's package, Scarlett stood before them and clapped her hands. "So, should we go one at a time? Or everyone at once?"

But it was too late. Mémé was already digging in. Nimble fingers were peeling away layers of paper and bubble wrap, which she let fall to the floor just as an eager Scarlett might.

Scarlett made quick work of her box, too. Rocking back on her heels, she let out a loud gasp and then, "Oh my…" before slapping a hand over her mouth. Removing the hand, she reached into the box and pulled out the gift. "It's a reel."

"A fishing reel?" Victoria repeated. "Is it a Romeo?" Was that it? Had the company sent gifts for everyone?

"No. It's a Dynamo. And it's big, too, like for salmon and steelhead. Wait, and the card says there's a Dynamo rod to match coming in the mail…"

"Of course," Victoria whispered to herself. Their Santa Claus, it was now apparent, was of the Alaskan variety. A Dynamo, she knew, was Seth's preferred rod for catching steelhead. He'd mentioned it when they'd been fishing in the Gulf.

"Do you think it could be from Mr. James?" Scarlett asked, right there with her in figuring it out. "Like for our trip to Alaska?"

"Victoria! It's an ulu." Corinne cried, holding up the traditional Native Alaskan cutting tool. "I asked Seth about them, but I most certainly was not hinting around. And look at this beautiful, fancy handle. This is too expensive. I have to send it back. I cannot wait to see if it works as well as Millie says…"

Victoria barely squelched a laugh because for something she intended to return she sure was in a hurry to try out.

"I found a card!" Scarlett cried. "It *is* from Mr. James."

"Well, if this doesn't beat all…" Mémé muttered, drawing Victoria's attention again. "That child is out of his mind." She sounded almost cross, but Victoria knew her grandmother's nuances very well. It was her *I'm getting choked up but trying to fight it* tone. From the box, she pulled a sparkling glass pitcher and then let out a little gasp. "For my tea."

"Mémé, it's so pretty!" Scarlett exclaimed. "Look at that etching. What does it say?" Mémé held it out for Scarlett's inspection, who read aloud, "'Memories Should Be As Sweet As Tea.'"

Victoria went to work on her small package. Peeling away the layers of tissue paper revealed a silver chain with a jade pendant in the shape of a lovely and intricate symmetrical knot. Her breath caught, her heart melting and twisting because she recognized the symbol.

As long as she lived, she'd never forget it. Or the moment Seth had drawn the exact pattern on the palm of her hand. Even now, she could recall how his touch had electrified her skin. How with one fingertip, he'd managed to warm every inch of her body from the inside out. How her heart had seemed to expand and contract at the same time. Since the moment he'd let go, she'd longed to feel that again.

With trembling fingers, she removed the necklace from the box. A slip of paper tucked inside read, "Crafted for Victoria with love by Kella Jakobs, fine artisan, Rankins, Alaska." Handmade. Special ordered. How in the world had he accomplished all of this so quickly?

"Mama, what did you get?" Scarlett asked.

Victoria stared down at her gift and tried to get her emotions under control. *A promise*, she answered silently. One that she very badly did not want him to break.

"A necklace," she said aloud as Scarlett joined her.

"That's jade," Scarlett said reaching out to touch it. "Alaska's state gem. It's beautiful."

This was all incredibly sweet, wildly romantic, and by far the most thoughtful gift she'd ever received. Her very own Alaskan promise. The only question that remained was, could she trust him to keep it?

CHAPTER NINE

NOT SURPRISINGLY, Seth heard from Scarlett first.

"Thank you, thank you, thank you!" she shouted when he answered the call. "It's the best gift ever!" A satisfying assertion considering he knew she possessed both an expensive tablet and a scooter that she had nowhere to ride, courtesy of her dad.

"I'm glad you like it. It's my favorite for catching steelhead."

"Mama told me. I can't wait to get up there and try it out. She said maybe next summer. For real."

Seth had every hope of moving that trip up a bit, but he knew better than to mention it. Instead, he listened and answered all of Scarlett's questions before she handed the phone off to Corinne and then Effie, who took turns thanking him as well. Then Scarlett got back on the line.

"Mama wants to know if you're busy or if she can call you in five minutes?"

"Yes, of course, she can."

They said goodbye, and Seth waited a very long seven minutes before Victoria's number flashed on the screen. Reaching down, he slid a shaky finger across the display.

"Hello," he said into the phone.

"Hey there," she said. "Sorry about the phone game. I, um, I wanted to talk to you in private."

Seth managed a calm "Okay" even as tension invaded his body. It was too much. He'd gone too far. She was going to tell him to back off. According to Hazel, thoughtful gifts of this extent were second only to an outright declaration of love.

"Thank you for the necklace. It's gorgeous. And hands down the sweetest, most thoughtful gift anyone has ever given me."

He cringed, waiting for the "but."

"I want you to know that I want to accept it. I mean, I love the necklace, and I'm keeping it." At the sound of her lighthearted chuckle, he felt the tightness easing a little. He exhaled.

"I'm glad."

"But." There it was, and he actually squeezed his eyes shut, bracing himself for what came next. "What I'm saying here, Seth, is that I'm already wearing it. And I don't plan to take it off."

Okay. Balling one fist, he solidly punched air while a mixture of relief and joy poured over him. Calmly, he said, "That makes me happier than you could ever imagine, Victoria."

"Good. Me too. So, I'm willing to give this a go. But how are we going to manage it? Compete for this job and…date, I guess? Is that what we should call it? And what happens after, when one of us gets hired? And the other one… doesn't."

"We already spent three days doing exactly that. Managing it, I mean. So we continue doing that. We keep it separate. Romeo Reels on their time. Seth and Victoria on our time."

A pause ensued, and he pictured her brow scrunched, teeth nibbling on her lip, thinking. "Okay."

"Okay?" he repeated.

"Sure, since what I hear you saying is that you'll be fine with me getting the job."

He barked out a laugh. "Seriously, yes, I would. I'm not going to lie and say I don't want it, or that I'm going to let you win. But, Victoria, I already like you enough that I'd want this job for you anyway. I mean, if it can't be me, then I want it to be you. Does that make sense?"

"Me too," she said quickly, so much so that Seth knew she'd already been thinking along these same lines. "I have no problem losing to someone who beats me fair and square."

"Vic?" A MAN asked only seconds after she entered through the rotating doors of the Pike Pier Resort. Romeo Reels had arranged for a car to transport her from the airport. Henry Foster had agreed to meet her when she arrived, and she'd texted to let him know her ETA and that she was wearing a blue jacket and carrying a black backpack.

Victoria smiled a greeting. "Yes, sir. You must be Henry."

"I am. Henry Foster. Welcome to Minnesota." She couldn't help but notice that he didn't bat an eye at the name thing. "I'm delighted to meet you."

Medium height, he had the wiry muscles of a man who took excellent care of himself and probably didn't regularly eat her mama's sugar-dusted beignets for breakfast. Vic estimated him to be about her mom's age, mid to late fifties. Extremely handsome, he had short, thick silver and black hair, a pretty smile filled with even white teeth and a square jaw with a slightly off-center dimple in his chin.

"Thank you, Henry. It's lovely to meet you, too. I've never been to Minnesota before, so it's exciting for me to be here." Victoria indicated around the lakefront resort where they'd be staying for the next three nights.

A woman in a smart-looking suit approached them. "You must be Ms. Thibodeaux?"

"Yes, ma'am, that's me."

"If you'd like to follow me over to the counter, we'll get you checked in. Tony will get your bags." A young man appeared and whisked her suitcase away.

Registration was remarkably quick, and once Vic had her key, Henry asked if she'd like to relax in her room or take a stroll around the grounds before Marissa and Gerard arrived in time for them all to enjoy an early dinner. Their day of pike and walleye fishing on the lake was scheduled to begin very early in the morning.

"I'd like to look around," she confessed. "While there's still plenty of light."

"Is Vic short for Victoria?" he asked, once they were outside and strolling along the path that led to the lake. Victoria did her best not to gawk while drinking in the picturesque scenery.

"Yes, it is, and you can call me either one. It's funny because I don't know how Vic got put on that email that we all received, the one that outlined our fishing schedules and everything. I applied for this position as Victoria, but I've entered a few tournaments as Vic. In the interview, they asked me about that, if it was a nickname. I said yes, so I'm guessing that's it."

"My mom's name was Victoria, and she went

by Vic. So, I was kind of hoping. You know, the possibility was on my mind."

"Seriously? I hope you like your mom," she joked.

"Seriously," he confirmed, and chuckled. "My mom passed away several years ago, but I adored her. She was also a heck of an angler. Single mother who taught me everything I know. Well, her and my nana."

"No way."

"Yeah way. My dad died when I was four years old, and my mom and grandmother raised me. We lived on a lake and fished together nearly every day."

"No, I believe you. I meant *no way* in the sense that in addition to sharing her name, that's another amazing coincidence. Made even more amazing by your follow-up explanation. I also grew up on a lake, raised by my mother and grandmother, who taught me how to fish. Both single moms. My grandfather passed away when my mom was young, and I never knew my father. He left before I was born and died a few years later." Victoria had always known that her mother's supportive role in her life had everything to do with her own experience.

"Huh." Henry shook his head. "Wow."

"I know. And now I'm a single mom teaching my daughter."

"Does she enjoy it? Fishing?"

"Oh my gosh, yes. As much as me, maybe more, and I would never have thought that possible. Scarlett, that's my daughter's name, has aspirations to fish the entire world. *River Monsters* is her favorite show. I often wonder how many eleven-year-old girls have posters of Jeremy Wade lining their walls?"

He laughed. "One of the most important things a parent can do is encourage kids to be whoever they want to be." She agreed, and he said, "Well, we are fellow members of an exclusive club, aren't we? I was a single dad, too, for most of it. My wife died when my daughter was three."

"I'm so sorry."

"Thank you. I don't normally share that information with people I've just met, but under the circumstances, I was compelled. Fishing saved my life after my wife died. I lived for my daughter but fishing also allowed me to have a life of my own. I hope that doesn't sound horrible and selfish."

"Oh, no, Henry, that does not sound horrible or selfish. That's exactly how it was for me when my marriage failed. My husband didn't die, but he nearly ruined me. Crushed my pride and my dreams. Fishing was the thing that kept me from completely breaking apart."

He nodded as if every word made perfect sense. "To be honest with you, I was hoping I'd get sent to Louisiana."

"Really?"

"Absolutely. I've done a lot of fishing in Alaska because I have a brother who lives there. And I've been to Louisiana a handful of times, but every single time, it leaves me wanting more. I believe it's the most underrated sport fishery in North America. Not to mention, it's stunningly beautiful and filled with the friendliest people I've ever met."

As if she weren't already predisposed to liking the man, Henry sealed it with that statement. She beamed. "Hey, you're welcome to come on down any time you'd like. My family owns a little resort, although I always feel the need to add that it's not a resort anything like these standards." She waved a hand around them. "It's a campground and some rustic cabins. It is not flush with fancy amenities, but I can promise I'll get you fish. Any kind you want."

"Gar?"

"You betcha."

"That's on my bucket list. I've heard they're as tricky to catch as muskie. You think that's true?"

"No," she answered quickly. "I've never fished for muskie, which is on *my* bucket list, by the way, so I couldn't say for certain. But

I highly doubt it. With gar, it's all those teeth that make it difficult to *land*. From what I understand about muskie, it's a combination of stealth and presentation, which makes them difficult to *catch*."

His smile was pure approval and Victoria couldn't help but think she'd passed some sort of test. "That is muskie in a nutshell. So, you hosted Seth last week, huh?"

"Yes, I did."

"How did that go? I can't believe I'm asking this, but what did you think of Mr. Alaska?"

Victoria couldn't help but chuckle at Henry's use of the same nickname that she'd given Seth. Unconsciously, her hand strayed to the pendant hanging around her neck.

"Well, we got off to a bit of a rocky start, but in the end, I liked him much more than I thought I would."

"That's good. I was hoping this experience would be just this way, as much about the people we meet as about the competition we're in."

"GROSS," VICTORIA MUTTERED the following week, back at home in Louisiana, and a world away from her thrilling and successful trip to Minnesota. Shuffling through the dirty, tepid water, she tried to splash as little as possible, preferring instead to prepare for the moment when she could confront the offenders responsible for ruining her morning plans to practice for the workshop she'd be teaching at the show next week.

Inside her pocket, she felt her phone vibrate with a text. Her pulse kicked up a notch. She'd never been attached to her phone, but the last couple of weeks had her acting like a teenager in that regard. Or a romantic. Neither of which she minded much once she read a Seth message or heard his voice.

Gingerly removing her rubber gloves, she slipped the phone from her pocket and opened the text:

Hey, what are you doing?

Smiling, she tapped out a response: Ankle deep in water here. Are you jealous?

Of course! What are you fishing for?

So far I've caught six towels, eight plastic bags, and several rolls of toilet paper.

Three aspiring delinquent teenagers had plugged the toilets with towels pilfered from the supply room, clogged the sink drains and the floor drain with plastic bags and toilet paper, and then deliberately flooded the place.

??

Flooded restrooms.

Oh man! I'm so sorry. I wish I was there.

I don't blame you. The life of a resort worker is a glamorous one.

Haha! I meant to help. I wish I was there to help.

She knew what he meant, and her stomach did this little flip because there was no doubt in her mind that he would help without a second thought. Unlike Austin, who'd found almost everything about this life unpleasant.

She answered: Next, I get to kick the aberrant teenaged toilet cloggers out of the park and invite them never to return. THAT will be fun.

I would LOVE to be there for that. Seriously. Call me later if you have time. I want to hear about it. And I want to hear your voice.

Oh. Another flip, even *flippier* than the first. See? This is why she was carrying the dang phone around. These flips were getting addicting.

I will make time.

Good because I talked to Bering and he wants to take us to dinner while we're in Florida if we can fit it in. Hazel might be coming too. I understand if that might be too much for you, but I'd love for you to meet them.

Turned out that Seth's cousin, Bering, the wildlife guide, was going to have a booth at the show promoting his business. Oddly, the notion of dinner with his cousin and sister made her only slightly nervous.

Sounds fun!

Okay! We'll figure out the details later after we get our schedule for the show.

Cannot wait. Talk soon. Fingertip hovering, she hesitated a beat before adding, xox.

Only a few more days, she reminded herself, and they'd be in Florida. Together. Together and competing, she reminded herself. But like Seth had said, there would be Romeo Reels time and Seth and Victoria time. Plenty of opportunity for both.

The Pro Plus Fishing & Outdoor Expo was one of the largest shows of its kind in the world. Officially, the event lasted four days, but their schedule included an extra two days for promotional events. They'd already received a partial outline of activities they'd be participating in so they could prepare. Victoria had spent every spare moment doing just that.

Six days of interviews, photoshoots, panel discussions, workshops, demos, luncheons, parties, "promo events," whatever that meant. And on it went. Marissa's last email said they wouldn't receive the final schedule until they arrived in Florida as they were still finalizing and rearranging details.

Spirits excessively lifted, she got back to work. She was going to have to disinfect the place from top to bottom, but at least she'd managed to identify the problem and remove the offending items, which meant she wouldn't have to call the plumber.

Victoria was furious, although the anger would have to wait. It wouldn't get the mess cleaned up any faster. And she needed to have her temper in check when she confronted the boys and their parents. Angry but controlled. Formidable. At least, she could be positive that the perpetrators were the teenaged boys staying in space B-7. Security footage had caught them breaking into the supply room and entering the restrooms.

They'd been nothing but trouble since they'd checked in. Within hours, she'd had to ask that they turn their music down. The next morning she'd had to "remind them" about the speed limit of watercraft on the lake. Later, she'd nearly called the police when she'd caught them harassing a pair of egrets. Only the intervention of an apologetic father and promises of punishment had stopped her. She also suspected they'd stolen a half case of beer from the store.

With all the water successfully drained and her mop bucket filled with disinfectant, she was roughly halfway through the cleaning process when her phone vibrated again. This time it was a steady buzz in the form of a call. She knew it wasn't Seth, but she pulled it out of her pocket anyway.

Austin. Victoria stared at her phone and considered letting it go to voicemail, but she'd done that once already today. And in light of the consequences from doing so last week, she answered with a flat, "Hello."

"Uh… Victoria?"

"Yes, Austin, who did you expect to be answering my phone?"

"No one. I intended to leave a voicemail. You caught me off guard by answering."

"I took great pains to do so. I hope it's important."

"Is everything okay? You sound weird like there's an echo."

"I'm in the men's restroom. We had a plumbing issue."

"Someone cleaning fish in the showers again?"

Shockingly, the comment made her chuckle as the memory came rushing back. Scarlett was only a few weeks old and her mom had just had knee surgery. Mémé was away visiting a friend in Baton Rouge, so Victoria had been on her own to manage the resort.

Desperate, she'd turned to Austin for help. The one and only time. Together, they'd dug up and cleaned out the line saving the business a huge expense. Only a few days later, she'd discovered the cheating when she'd walked in on him and Amber in their bedroom.

"Yikes. That was a long day."

"One of the longest of my life. My back hurts just thinking about it. Honestly, I don't know how you do it. I've always admired your work ethic."

Okay, what was going on here? First apologies and thank-yous, and now compliments? "Thankfully, this is nothing quite that dramatic. What's up?"

"I just wanted to let you know that I will be picking up Scarlett at four o'clock on Wednesday."

Victoria felt the scowl forming on her face. "Why? Does Scarlett know?"

"Because that is my designated time with my daughter, and not yet, but I will tell her."

"Okay, Austin, stop. Why do you keep referring to your *designated time* in that robot-like attorney voice? And why are you suddenly so interested in spending all this time with her?"

"I am always interested in spending time with my daughter."

"Let's not go over this again."

"Look, Victoria, I know I may have been a bit lax about adhering to our father-daughter time in the past, but you know that's because Amber isn't comfortable having Scarlett by herself. She's always been such an active child. And with the hours I've worked these last few years, it's been a challenge to balance that. But that's all changing now."

Like it wasn't a challenge for her to balance everything? Precisely why she'd chosen to put her dreams on hold while Scarlett was little. His logic was infuriating.

"Austin, I am literally standing in the men's room with a mop and a bucket of bleach. I do not need another lecture from you about how hard you work."

"Of course, you're right. I know what an albatross that place is for you."

"I have never once said that," she countered sharply. Just because she'd wanted to go to college, longed to explore her options, did not mean she didn't appreciate her family's legacy, or enjoy it, or that she wouldn't have come back here anyway. All she'd ever wanted was to know that she *could* achieve something on her own.

"Not in so many words, but you sure as heck wanted something better for yourself."

"Different," she amended. "I wanted something different." *And I'm about to get it,* she almost blurted. A fresh wave of longing hit her. How desperately she wanted it to be true. And yes, a bit of that was because she wanted to rub it in his face that *she* could make something of *herself* all by herself.

"Regardless," Austin said, his tone dropping low and deep in the way it did when he was trying to convey sincerity. "I want you to know that I'm sorry you didn't get your different. You deserve more, Victoria."

Inhaling deeply, she managed to hold her tongue. A miracle, she thought, considering he was responsible for the absence of her different. And he knew it. "Austin, can you get to the point? I need to get back to work, and you said Wednesday was *part* of why you called."

"Oh. Right, yes, um… Consider this your notice, okay?"

"Notice for what?"

"From now on, I will pick up Scarlett at 4 p.m. every other Friday and 4 p.m. every other Wednesday as per the parenting plan. No exceptions. No excuses. Okay?"

"Um, yeah, okay, I guess." As if there was anything she could do about it.

"Great. You asked for a heads-up, so this is me giving it to you."

CHAPTER TEN

FLORIDA. *FINALLY.*

Seth had never experienced time stretching by as slowly as it had since leaving Louisiana. Anticipating and preparing for the show while counting down the days until he and Victoria were in the same time zone again. Soon, they would be in the same room. Soon after that, she would be in his arms.

Seth stepped inside the designated conference room, one of the Florida Maritown Hotel & Conference Center's many options. The place was enormous, and it had taken him longer to travel from the hotel tower to the adjoining conference center than he'd anticipated, which was good to know going forward. Being a few minutes late for this welcome reception didn't seem as critical as tardiness to other events might be.

His gaze skimmed over the banner hanging on the wall, "Greetings, Anglers! The Pro Plus Fishing & Outdoor Expo Welcomes You!" He barely registered the tuxedoed waitstaff smoothly conveying large trays of drinks and appetizers. The clever fish-themed decor was way too subtle for his notice.

There would be time to soak it all in later. He hadn't even taken a moment to look at the final schedule yet. Right now, he just wanted to find Vic. They'd hoped to have a few hours alone together before the show started, but that was not to be. While her plane had gotten in on time this morning, Seth's was delayed. He'd arrived with barely enough time to register, shower away the travel grime and dress for the evening's semiformal reception.

Marissa had added a note specific to this event, advising them to wear what they would to a wedding. But obviously, she hadn't attended many of those in Rankins where khakis or freshly laundered blue jeans were generally suitable. Hazel had advised him, insisting he wear a suit. Via text, Iris concurred. Outnumbered, he'd agreed, and now, scanning the fancy-dressed crowd for Victoria, he was extremely grateful for his bossy sisters.

This preshow party, sponsored by Romeo Reels, consisted of fishing expo personnel, professional anglers, Romeo Reels executives, pro staff, other assorted employees, including all the members of the selection committee, and a smattering of other industry mavens. Many more people than he'd been expecting, he realized, as he continued to search the crowd.

The evening's itinerary included social time with drinks and then dinner, along with the requisite welcome speeches. This would also mark the first time all three contestants were together, so Marissa warned them to be prepared for tons of photos.

"Seth James?" An unfamiliar young woman approached him.

"Yes," he said, smiling a greeting.

"Hi, my name is Molly."

"Hi, Molly, nice to meet you."

"Can I have your autograph?" she asked, producing a glossy booklet, which he recognized as the show's program of events. Flipping it open, she landed on a page that consisted entirely of photos of him. Like the posters of the Romeo Reels finalists hanging in the lobby, these photos had been taken in both Louisiana and Alaska.

His first autograph. Romeo's promotion department had been hard at work. Marissa and Gerard would be pleased. "I'd be honored," he said, and she passed him the program and a felt-tipped pen.

"Molly with a *y*?" he asked.

"That's right," she said and giggled.

He scrawled his name along the bottom of

the photo collage. Before he passed it back to her, he couldn't help but notice the opposite page featured Victoria. He quickly added photogenic to her list of strengths.

Molly asked him about Alaska, then salmon fishing, and they were still chatting when another woman joined them. "Nancie with an *ie*" asked for an autograph, too. After he consented, Molly said, "We're pulling for you." Nancie agreed and included an enthusiastic "Good luck!" The women departed, whispering and giggling as they went.

"Seth!"

The voice belonged to Henry, who approached him along with Marissa and Gerard. Happy to see familiar faces, Seth warmly greeted them all. Marissa flagged down a waitperson and ordered a round of drinks. Last week's venture of hosting Henry in Alaska had been smooth sailing. Fishing with Henry had been like fishing with a cousin or one of his friends. In fact, Henry already felt like a friend. Not surprisingly, he was also a serious contender for the job.

Equal in skill to both himself and Victoria, Henry had traveled more than Seth, but wasn't quite a match for Victoria's natural charm, but then again who was? Although Seth thought Henry possessed a broader knowledge base and a sophisticated polish that he and Victoria both lacked. Seth predicted he would kill it in interviews.

This final round was shaping up to be so much different than he'd anticipated. Funny how he'd initially imagined the experience as some sort of cutthroat, contentious battle for fishing dominance.

Drinks arrived, and they spent a few minutes catching up. Seth tried not to be too obvious in his continuing search for Victoria.

"You guys have an unscheduled photo op in a few minutes," Gerard informed them, glancing at the watch on his wrist. "We weren't sure if Seth would get here in time, so this is great because it's for the feature on *The Angle*. Has anyone seen Victoria?"

"*The Angle*," Seth repeated. "As in my favorite fly fishing show?"

"Yep," Gerard answered. "You guys have a group interview with them in the morning, but the photographer wanted to get some photos first."

Marissa pointed. "Victoria is over by the champagne fountain next to Wyatt. He's sort of been monopolizing her time."

Gerard chuckled. "Why am I not surprised?"

"Wyatt Romeo?" Henry asked, frowning a little.

Seth's curiosity must have been evident because Marissa explained, "Wyatt is Miles Romeo's son. Miles Romeo, as you probably know, is the owner of the company."

That much Seth did know.

"Isn't he married?" Henry commented, his focus now off in the distance.

"Divorced. And I think he might have a little crush on our Victoria," Marissa said.

ALTHOUGH VICTORIA HAD been in Florida for only half a day, it hadn't taken her long to learn that even though the show was about much, much more than who would be crowned the new Romeo Reels spokesperson, their competition was still a big deal. So much bigger than she'd anticipated. Overwhelmingly big.

How could she have been so utterly unprepared for this part of the experience? She'd studied and practiced and planned for all the individual components but had overlooked the... reality of the show itself. Which was rapidly developing into a sensory overload of epic proportions.

Holding tight to her smile, she looked around the vast space crowded with people and wondered if Seth had arrived yet. Knowing they were in this together somehow made her feel better. Now if he would just get here...

Clearly, the company had done an excellent job with the "media blitz" Marissa had mentioned. Her first clue had been the giant, life-sized cutouts of herself, Seth and Henry in the lobby. Photos and posters of the three of them were hanging all over the place. The show's official program contained full-page photo collages and bios. She'd already lost count of how many people had approached her; journalists and bloggers asking questions, members of the public wishing her luck—even a few people wanting her autograph.

Professional anglers, many of whom she admired, were coming up and congratulating her. Tito Benz, one of the most successful tournament bass anglers in the sport's history, told her he was looking forward to her workshop. As if she, Victoria Thibodeaux from Perche, Louisiana, could teach Tito Benz anything useful about bass fishing! Her lungs began to seize up whenever she thought about it.

Not to mention that the grand hall, where the bulk of the show was being held, would each day pack in more attendees than the population of her entire town. Earlier, she'd gotten lost and been late to a coffee date with Marissa and some bigwig executive from a sportswear manufacturing company. Turned out, the woman wanted to discuss the possibility of

Victoria promoting their clothing line. When it was over, Marissa suggested she might need an agent. She'd been smiling when she said it, but Victoria had the distinct impression that she wasn't joking.

But what currently had her in knots was a tearful voicemail from Scarlett. Austin planned to take her to some sort of fancy fundraising dinner on Friday for which she'd need a formal dress, which she did not have, and did she have to go? Because the real problem was that the event was the same night as "the play." Vic was instantly annoyed for two reasons. Why would Austin think that taking his eleven-year-old to a formal fundraising event was a good idea? The second was that with her own mind preoccupied with Florida, and to be honest, Seth, she'd forgotten about the play to which Scarlett had been invited months ago.

When she'd called Scarlett back, she hadn't picked up. She'd then called her mom, who'd told her that Scarlett was with Quinn and his family. She'd tried Austin three times now without success and couldn't help but wonder if he was ignoring her calls as some sort of passive-aggressive payback.

"What do you think, Victoria?" Wyatt Romeo asked, nudging his chin toward the glass she held in her hand. Wyatt Romeo, the son of Miles Romeo, the owner of the company, wanted to know her opinion about the wine. And didn't this illustrate her predicament so perfectly? How could she ever have anticipated that she'd end up discussing wine at a fishing show? Why couldn't he have asked her about monofilament line or roll casting or turtle blades? Or even the weather for that matter? Anything about which she could intelligently speak.

For half a second, she considered trying to wing it. But even if she could pull it off, she hadn't gotten here by pretending to be someone she wasn't. Putting her best foot forward yes, being a fake, no.

Mustering her best apologetic smile, she tipped the glass and gave it a little swirl. "Sorry, but I don't know anything about wine. So, I'll just say what I do like is how it's not too sweet."

"Thank the stars above!" Archie, a friend of Wyatt's, exclaimed, tipping his face toward the ceiling. Wyatt had introduced the man, a former professional basketball player who she'd never heard of, only moments ago. "That means we don't have to talk about wine, right?" Grinning at her, he explained. "Wyatt and my wife can go on about wine for hours." He lifted his glass, which, Victoria noted enviably, contained a beer.

"I don't drink much myself," Victoria confessed. "I'm a single mom, and between my daughter and my family's business, I'm used to being on call 24/7. But when I do, I'll admit I prefer a nice cold beer."

That's when Archie stepped aside, giving her a long view across the room. Right at Seth. *Finally.*

SETH SPOTTED THE champagne fountain just as the tall guy who'd been blocking the view moved. to reveal Victoria. He wondered how he'd missed her earlier because she appeared to him like the only light in the room. So stunningly beautiful that his heart nearly stopped. He made a noise, he realized, and hoped no one else heard the short, sharp intake of his breath.

She was wearing a shimmering dark gray dress. It was sleeveless and hit her at the knees. Snug but not tight. Simple. Elegant. She looked like a movie star instead of a professional angler, or maybe a movie star playing the role of a professional angler. How could Romeo Reels not want to hire her? He'd buy anything she was selling, and he suspected most everyone else in the room would, too.

He wondered if anyone else saw it, the way her eyes locked onto his. It was quick but long enough for him to revel in their connection. But there was a flicker of something else. Something…not happy. And then it was gone. Her face erupted with a radiant smile as her gaze swept over their little group. One hand went up to signal that she'd be right over. Turning her head, she spoke to the man at her side, Wyatt, he presumed. The man nodded, and then they both headed toward them.

Seth tried not to watch her as she crossed the room, but seriously, not an easy task. And it seemed to take forever. He joked with Henry about the monster salmon he'd nearly lost in Alaska and asked Marissa about her dogs. In his periphery, he saw Vic laugh at something Wyatt said, but they were close enough now that Seth could tell that it wasn't her real laugh, the one that made her shoulders shake and her eyes scrunch at the corners. *Too bad for you, Wyatt.*

When they stopped, the first thing Seth noticed was that she wasn't wearing the necklace. The one that just yesterday she'd told him she'd worn every single day since receiving it. *Too bad for you, Seth,* he told himself, trying not to read too much into its absence. Probably, it didn't match her dress, or maybe it wasn't stylish enough?

He was grateful when Henry stepped forward first, allaying his own temptation to sweep her into his arms. They'd agreed it would be best to keep their relationship private for now. Especially when they hadn't even had a chance to define it themselves. They didn't want anything clouding the decision-making process of the selection committee.

"Hey, you," Henry said, releasing her from a friendly hug. "You look lovely."

"Thank you, Henry," Vic said, stepping back but keeping a grip on his elbow. Pretending to look him over, she gave his arm a quick squeeze before letting go. "You clean up pretty well yourself. Although, I think I prefer you in your lucky hat."

Marissa stood on her other side, and Vic started there, doling out hugs around the circle.

Wyatt introduced himself, first to Henry and then to Seth, and engaged them in conversation about the show. Personable in a slick, practiced manner, he immediately rubbed Seth the wrong way. He didn't care for the guy's smirk, either, mainly because it kept snapping back to Victoria as if his eyeballs were magnetized to her dress.

"Well, hello there, Alaska," Vic teased when she made it around to him. "Glad you finally decided to grace us all with your presence." The hug she gave him was irritating in almost every way: platonic, short, and topped off with an added exaggerated clap to his shoulder and no accompanying eye contact. Exactly the opposite of what he wanted. *And perfect for the circumstances*, he silently admitted, watching her joke around and charm everyone. Including Wyatt, who now stood way too close to her. But he already knew she was a better actor than he was, didn't he?

Why was he all ruffled and unsettled? Because he wanted to take her hand, lead her from this crowded hotel ballroom, and be alone with her. And possibly knock Wyatt out cold on the way out the door because why was he rubbing her shoulder like that?

Smiling instead, he quipped, "I wanted to give you and Henry both a chance to make a good impression before I stole the spotlight."

"Photo time," Gerard said, pointing toward the door.

Seth hung back, waiting for the others to proceed so he could bring up the rear. Wyatt, apparently with the same inclination, turned his smirk on Seth and commented, "I'm afraid it's going to be difficult for anyone else to get a slice of the spotlight with Victoria in the room, isn't it?"

GERARD LED THE group through the crowd. Victoria claimed a spot next to Henry and followed them outside onto the hotel's upper terrace, where the photographer was waiting. Standing between Seth and Henry, listening to their good-natured ribbing, she could see that, in direct opposition to her, both men were completely at ease.

The photographer was a pro, too, barking orders in a dry, funny manner that soon had everyone laughing. For the first batch of photos, he used the gulf as the backdrop, the next set was taken in front of a large expo sign, and the last on a wide set of metal stairs. Victoria managed to fake her way through it.

The following hours continued with the same gale-force whirlwind. They were whisked back inside to a smaller room for dinner where they were seated at a large round table and served a steak and seafood meal. Everyone said it was delicious. Victoria's may as well have been cardboard and plaster; anxiety had disconnected her taste buds. One speaker followed another, including a welcome by Miles Romeo. Victoria, Seth and Henry were introduced and asked to stand to a flurry of applause and camera flashes.

When dinner was complete, a lull ensued while coffee and dessert were served. Taking advantage of the opportunity, Victoria slipped out to call Austin.

This time he picked up. "Hello, Victoria."

"Austin, what is going on? Scarlett called me, and she's distraught."

"Yes, I gathered that."

"The Duquettes invited her to this play months ago and—"

"Yes, I know. Unfortunately, this isn't negotiable. I want her with me on Friday."

"Austin, please, this is extremely important to her. Scarlett does not ask for much." She wanted to add that before his recent renewed interest in parenting it wouldn't have mattered.

He sighed. "Well, Vic, I'm sorry, but this is extremely important to me."

"Okay, so you see the solution, right? Scarlett has something important to her, and you have something important to you. She does her thing, you do yours. You can keep her longer on Sunday to make up for it."

"No, that's not it. I want my family with me at *this* event."

The statement bristled her already-frayed nerves. "What event? Why? How could it possibly matter if Scarlett is there? You guys go to stuff like this all the time."

"Because it is *my* event, Victoria. A kick-off fundraiser for my campaign. All my years of hard work, the long hours, weekends—the time I've sacrificed with Scarlett—it's finally paying off. I'm running for district attorney."

CHAPTER ELEVEN

VICTORIA ENDED THE CALL. A mix of anger, frustration and disgust churned inside of her like a frenzied whirlpool. Deep down, she'd known something was up with Austin. She'd been too distracted with her own life to put the pieces together. The sudden adherence to the parenting plan, the family portrait, the apologies, the compliments, the thank-yous—it all made perfect sense now.

He'd been laying the groundwork, trying to get on her good side.

But using Scarlett as a prop in his picture-perfect campaign family was over-the-top. She would not allow it! Scarlett would not become another victim in Austin's self-centered quest for political greatness. She'd already paid that price for the both of them.

"Victoria?"

Startled, she turned to find Seth standing before her. "Seth, hi." Despite her state of mind, or maybe partly because of it, she wanted to launch herself into his arms. Like she needed his arms around her to feel normal again. She was craving his hugs now—was that normal?

"Hello," he said softly, his gaze traveling over hers, which sent her pulse racing and made her head buzz in a different way. A good way. "Finally."

"Finally," she repeated, affection for him supporting the smile she did not otherwise feel.

Locking his eyes on hers, he tipped his head. "Are you all right?"

No, she wanted to scream. She nodded instead. "Yep. Just a little issue back home with Scarlett."

"Everything okay?"

"It will be." She would make it be okay.

"Do you want to tell me what's going on?"

Staring at his face, seeing the concern, she did want to. Desperately. She wanted to tell him everything. "It's nothing. Just a disagreement with Scarlett's father."

"Okay," he said. But she could tell he wasn't buying it. "It doesn't seem like nothing. You seem pretty shaken."

Victoria didn't respond. She couldn't. Not without giving herself away. She needed a minute. Several, probably.

"I hope you know you can talk to me about anything."

The problem with that was they'd specifically laid down ground rules, which included keeping Romeo Reels time separate from Seth and Victoria time. She'd even removed her necklace, deciding to wear it only when they had "their" time. Another problem, and one she could address.

"People know who we are, Seth. Marissa told us there was going to be a media blitz, but I wasn't expecting *this*." Arms up, palms out, and fingers spread wide, she did a little half twirl before letting them fall. "Were you? This is…intense."

"Maybe not quite to this degree," he answered, but the casual shrug of one shoulder told her he wasn't surprised. Making her feel even worse. As if he could read that on her face, too, he quickly qualified, "But remember, I've been to these types of shows. I've been to this one before."

Victoria hadn't ever attended anything like this. She'd questioned Seth about what to expect, watched YouTube videos of various events, including countless workshops in preparation for hers. She'd formed an accurate mental image of what it would look like to attend the show; she just hadn't anticipated how it would feel to *be* the show.

And she absolutely did not know how to separate it all, her growing affection for Seth, her problems at home, the encroaching feelings of inadequacy. She couldn't shake the notion that she didn't belong here. Pressure formed in her chest, tightening her lungs, and her skin felt prickly and raw.

Seth smiled and added, "I will admit that Romeo's promotion team has done a heck of a job. I can't imagine what their budget must be. I got asked for my autograph."

"Yeah, me too. I think I'm just a little overwhelmed."

He glanced toward the doors. Vic followed his gaze and saw Gerard walking through. Lowering his voice, he said, "Let's talk about this later, okay? Maybe I can help."

Help. The offer was like a trigger. Because she knew he could help, just talking to him about everything would help. But where would it stop? How could she explain her issues where Austin was concerned? Confiding in Seth would require a level of trust that she didn't know if she'd ever reach again. And no doubt, due to Austin's resurgence in her life, simmering anew in the back of her mind was the incident that she couldn't share with anyone. Ever. And none of this was Seth's problem. Nor should it be. She had to tackle this alone, just like she always had.

"No," she interrupted. "You can't. It's too

much, and I don't… You know what? It's probably best if we just concentrate on what we came here to do." But what she really meant was *you*. Seth needed to focus on doing what he could to get the job. She did not have the luxury of setting her personal problems aside.

She needed to give him the freedom to do that.

SETH NOTED THE stubborn set of her jaw and the hardness in her eyes. Dread swept through him because this behavior reminded him of the Victoria he'd first met. The one who didn't like him. She was having second thoughts. Already had them, if opting not to wear the necklace meant what he now suspected.

"Victoria, I don't know what's going on, but I think if we sit down and talk—"

"Seth, have you seen the schedule?"

"The schedule? Uh, no, not the final one."

"There is literally no time for talking. We should get back in there."

"What are you saying?"

But she was gone, already walking away. And he knew what she was saying. Stunned, Seth headed the opposite direction. Because if he followed, he couldn't trust himself not to do something reckless. Like beg her to reconsider.

What had happened to change her mind so quickly? He needed to get out of here and…

But then he looked up and saw Gerard deep in conversation with a woman named Monica, another Romeo Reels employee who could very well be a member of the selection committee. What was he thinking? This was his future. He couldn't give up his dream because Victoria had decided to brush him off. In this sense, he needed to take a lesson from Victoria: set his emotions aside and do whatever it took to get this job.

Steeling himself, he headed back in the right direction. On the journey, he made a joke that left Gerard and Monica laughing. Once inside, he was relieved to find that dessert was being served buffet style, which meant that no one would notice his delayed reentry. People were milling around, getting coffee or drinks from the bar, or choosing dessert from a long table set up along one edge of the room.

Reluctantly, his gaze homed in on Victoria, where she stood with a group of unfamiliar faces save one, he realized as tension gripped his body. To go from a quasi-breakup to watching her laughing and talking with Wyatt Romeo made him want to punch the wall. Or Wyatt. Mostly Wyatt.

Racking his brain, he couldn't think of anything he'd done to deserve this. He thought about the last text he'd received from her, sent early this morning after she'd arrived, while he was still en route. It was the first thing he'd seen after landing: This place is WOW! But also kind of yikes. Can't wait for you to get here. xox.

"Hey," Henry said, interrupting his reverie. "How're you doing?"

"Great!" He exclaimed, taking a cue from Victoria and dialing up the enthusiasm. "I'm great! Isn't this great? How are you?"

"Great!" Henry mimicked. "If this gig doesn't work out, maybe you could get yourself a tiger suit and peddle breakfast cereal."

Seth chuckled and shook his head. "That was too much, wasn't it?"

"It was a lot of greats, buddy. Are you okay? You're not doing drugs, are you?"

"Funny." He scrubbed a hand across his jaw. "I'll be fine. I'm just a little tired. Jet lag?" he offered unconvincingly.

"I suppose," Henry conceded, sounding doubtful. "Or," he offered brightly, "maybe you screwed up with Victoria, and you need to figure out how to fix it?"

Seth narrowed his gaze at the older man. "Excuse me?"

Henry grinned. "I didn't get this far in life by being an idiot. In my own highly esteemed opinion, one of my strongest traits is my keen powers of observation. No detail is too small for my notice. And one of the things I've noticed about Vic is that she always wears a certain necklace. The interesting thing, to me, about this necklace is that the pendant is jade, the most precious of Alaska's gems. When she was in Minnesota, I asked her about it, and she said it was a gift from someone very special. That it meant the world to her."

Seth swallowed and glanced away. "Yeah. I *thought* it did."

"Well, what did you do?"

"I have absolutely no clue."

"Hmm. She was wearing the necklace this morning when she arrived. But tonight, no necklace. That should give you a timeline to work with."

Meaning whatever this was about had transpired in a matter of hours.

While they watched, Wyatt slipped an arm around Vic's shoulder for a photo. Seth gritted his teeth. "Before I got here but after she met that guy. Maybe I'm being traded in for a better model."

"Pfft," Henry snorted. "Vic is not interested in Wyatt Romeo."

"Yeah, of course not," Seth agreed dryly. "Why would she be? Rich, educated, good looking, smooth talking, snappy dresser." He hated how his thoughts turned to Ashley, that stomach-churning notion of not being enough.

"Because he's not genuine. She was already married to one of those. Victoria wants a man she can count on, one that she trusts."

Seth looked at him sharply. "She talked to you about this stuff, about her ex and trust?"

"A bit." Henry shrugged an easy shoulder. "I asked. I don't know all the details, but it wasn't difficult to piece the highlights together."

"I don't know what to do."

"Just remember how new, and how different, all of this is to her than to you and me. She's never been to a show like this. The biggest city she's ever seen is New Orleans. She's barely traveled outside the south. Did you know that Minnesota is the farthest she's ever been from home?"

THE CROWD BEGAN dispersing soon after dessert. People were grouping together in pairs and bunches, making plans to go dancing or out for drinks. A piano bar was the destination of a crowd that included Marissa, Henry, Seth and a bunch of other Romeo Reels staff. Victoria, on the other hand, couldn't wait to get out of there. It made her achy inside to watch a laughing Seth move off with the group even as she knew he'd be foolish not to go. At this point, they should be taking any opportunity that arose to make a favorable impression with the selection committee.

And likely, this was why Marissa approached her. "Are you sure you can't come with us?" she whispered conspiratorially. "I wouldn't be quite so outnumbered, and I know Wyatt will be disappointed."

"I would," Vic lied with an easy smile. "But I need to call my daughter before it gets too late." No way was she going to admit that she needed some time alone. To regroup. Breathe. Get her head on straight.

That determination lasted all the way up the long elevator ride, down the hall and into her room. Victoria turned on the light, kicked off her shoes, and sat on the bed. Where she was met with the glaring sound of her own struggle and failure. A sob formed right in the middle of her chest. Bringing her hand up in an effort to will it away made it worse, because it reminded her of the necklace she wasn't wearing, and Seth, who she'd pushed away. Why had she done that? Why had she blown him off when she needed him the most?

She'd never longed for the comfort, the companionship, of another person in this way. But when he was standing right in front of her, offering exactly what she needed, she'd gotten scared. The idea of trusting him terrified her, but the idea that she'd lost him was much worse. The sob broke free, and tears began to fall.

"No, no, no..." she whispered, swallowing the next round and bolting to her feet. She hadn't cried in years, not for herself anyway. She saved them all for her daughter. In this situation, tears felt like giving up. "Crying is not going to fix this."

Up and moving, she changed out of her dress, washed her face, and brushed her teeth. Then she put on her necklace and checked her phone because she'd only half lied to Marissa. She was waiting to hear back from Scarlett, and she wanted to answer if her daughter needed her.

And she was glad she did because there was a text and three photos: Quinn made me go fish my troubles away. Check out this bass I caught! Chunky is almost as wide as she is long. Show Seth! Tell him I used the crimson dabber that I told him about.

Victoria smiled at the photo of her holding up the fish. Quinn, who'd taken the shot, was next to her grinning goofily. "Thank you, Quinn," she whispered, "for being my daughter's friend." Which caused a fresh and painful wave of longing for Seth. She'd gotten a taste of this type of friendship and was addicted. How would she get through this without him?

The next image showed both kids with french fries and milkshakes:

Dr. Duquette took us to Dairy Daisy for dinner. It's a banana caramel shake kind of day. Love you a billion. Ps: I'm sorry I bothered you about daddy's stupid dinner. I'm fine. Quinn made me laugh and laugh.

Vic checked the time and smiled because she knew Corinne was letting her stay up past her bedtime, and then typed out a response:

You are NEVER a bother. Anytime, anyplace, it does not matter. There is nothing more important than you. I will work this out with your dad. I'm so glad you're having fun! Jealous of that shake. Good night, my favorite daughter. Love you a billion x 2.

Gratitude sank into her at this reminder of what was truly important. No matter what happened, she had Scarlett. And Quinn. And Mama and Mémé. They would all still love her if she returned home without this job. That would be the worst part, though. Scarlett seeing her do everything right, treating people with consideration and respect, and still failing. While Austin looked out for himself, used everyone in his path and then succeeded.

The phone was still clutched in her hand when another text came in and made her jump. From Seth. Heart pounding, she read his message:

Can I please come in? I'm standing outside your door.

She ran to the door without a second thought. "Hi," she said, opening it and waving him inside. "Hurry, Marissa's room is right across the hall."

"Don't worry. She and Henry were queued up to sing a Billy Joel duet when I left the bar."

That vision had her smiling through the bout of happy, fizzy nerves his presence was causing. "What are you doing here?"

"I was thinking about what you said earlier, right before you told me you didn't want to see me anymore."

"That's not what I—"

"I know. I was talking to Henry, and I realized that you said there was no *time* to talk, not that you didn't *want* to talk to me. Can we please talk now?"

"Yes, but before you say anything, I want you to understand how much this…" She paused to wave wildly around. "All this show stuff caught me off guard. I knew we'd be busy, but I thought we'd be able to, you know, sneak away for a coffee, and you could come to my room, order a pizza, and we could just hang out or whatever. I know that probably sounds stupid, but we don't have pizza delivery back home. I *never* get to order pizza, so I was looking forward to that more than I care to admit." Jeez, she sounded like her eleven-year-old rambling in her own defense.

Pausing for a breath, she continued, "We agreed to keep Seth and Victoria time separate from Romeo Reels time, and that seemed like the perfect idea." Without thinking, her hand came up again to touch the necklace. "But then, after I got here, I realized we weren't going to have a chance for Seth and Victoria time. We weren't going to have time to do any of those things, much less a first date, or even a first kiss. I feel like we're being watched. Not in a creepy way, but in like it might get *noticed* if we spend time together in that way.

"And then Scarlett called and… I didn't, I *don't*, want to lay all my problems on you."

SHE WAS WEARING the necklace.

Seth felt relief and affection mix in this odd way inside of him, like a chemical reaction bubbling over and making him want to laugh. But he didn't. He'd never want Victoria to think he was laughing at her. Because he wasn't. It was pure relief. And joy, because he couldn't help but fixate briefly on the looking forward to things she'd listed. Like their first pizza, first date, first kiss…

Nodding slowly, he tried to process all this information. Good news, mostly. If he hadn't talked to Henry, he might never have ended up here tonight. He owed Henry huge.

But first, he and Vic needed to clarify a few things. "That is very thoughtful of you," he said carefully.

"I'm glad you understand." She gave him a weak smile. "I have a lot of baggage, and that's not fair to you to have to pack it around with me. It's better this way. You need to focus on putting on the best performance you can."

"Hmm. So, if you were to talk to me about all of this, would that somehow take away from you turning in your best performance?"

"No, of course not. The opposite, I think. At least, that's how I felt…before. In fact, I couldn't wait for you to get here."

"Before what?" he asked, liking that last part an awful lot.

"Before I talked to my ex. I was already struggling with feeling overwhelmed and insecure about the show. And then he tells me this thing and, *boom*, it was like being slingshotted backward to our past. There's a lot there, Seth. Things I can't talk about. And now he wants to use Scarlett to help him get what he wants, just like he used me, like he uses everyone. And I can't be there for Scarlett right now. The timing is so terrible that I would accuse him of doing it on purpose to sabotage me if I thought he was that clever."

"I see. Well, I still think I should get to decide whether listening to my girlfriend's problems, supporting her, maybe offering to help or at least provide some comfort, would affect me and my performance."

"Girlfriend?" she repeated, her expression softening, her body visibly relaxing.

He shrugged. "You put the necklace back on. That suggests to me that you still have feelings for me, right?"

Tears were shining in her eyes. "Seth, I have all the feelings. In fact, I might have too many feelings. The reason I took it off was because I wanted to follow the rules we established and keep everything separate. But I don't think I can do that, which is why I told you that we should just focus on our Romeo Reels time. When this is over, maybe we can… Try again."

"Try again? Is that what you want? Or is that what you think is best for me?"

"Best for you," she answered immediately. "Because, Seth, look at me, I am a hot mess. That's not an easy thing for me to admit. I pride myself on always being prepared. Composed. But today was like a perfect storm of everything going wrong, and I... It's been a struggle, a struggle that I don't want to drag you into."

"If that's all that's going on, then no."

"No?"

"I don't like this plan. I should get a say in this, too. And I want to try *still*. Not *again*. I want to be with you whenever I can. I don't care if it's five minutes in the evenings, or seventeen seconds in the morning, or touching your hand under the table, or passing you in the hall where I can just look my fill, or texting and calling if that's truly all we have time for. But I want to know that you're mine. Because I want to be yours, Victoria. Whatever that means right now. When I said that to you about keeping the time separate, I didn't know I was going to fall for you as hard as I have. Or that our schedule would be quite so packed."

"Oh."

"We can carve out space for some of the things you were looking forward to. We just need to plan, yet also be spontaneous. Take advantage of opportunities that arise."

She nodded, looking relieved and agreeable and so beautiful that he could not wait any longer to touch her.

"Like our first kiss, for example. Maybe now would be the perfect moment to cross that off your list."

CHAPTER TWELVE

Because I want to be yours, Victoria, played over again in her mind followed by, *Whatever that means right now.* And by not pressuring her, by giving her as much space as she needed, those words meant everything.

"Well," she said, smiling even as her heart became a frantic bass drum beating inside of her chest. "First kiss is definitely not on the schedule, but I suppose in keeping with your call for spontaneity, we could make time for it."

Eyes sparkling, mouth hinting at a smile, his expression held both joy and satisfaction.

Intending to close the remaining distance, she stepped toward him. But he was moving now, too, and met her halfway. She brought her arms up, winding one around his shoulders and using the other to grip the back of his neck.

Securing his hands around her waist, he stared down at her for a few seconds, heightening her anticipation. Then he dipped his head until his mouth hovered just above hers. She could smell the minty sweetness of his breath as he whispered, "First kiss. Finally."

"Finally," she repeated, just before he pressed his lips to hers in a kiss so gentle, yet so intense that it took her breath away. She had to close her eyes. If she'd been overwhelmed by sensations earlier, now she was overcome. And awed. But in the best possible way.

Like she was hyperaware of her own body, and his, and every incredible sensation flowing through them. The crazy fast beat of her heart, the rush of blood through her veins, the heat of his skin, his silky smooth hair sliding through her fingers, and the soft sounds coming from the back of his throat captured her from head to toe.

Being in his arms was so completely perfect, and how had she existed her entire life without this feeling? She'd had a child with another man and never experienced anything like this kind of connection.

When he deepened the kiss, her thoughts shifted, and she also realized how incredibly good he was at this. And how she was not… quite as experienced. But my goodness, that didn't seem to matter one bit.

He pulled away enough to look down at her. "Vic, I…" His brown eyes were dancing with emotion, and she loved everything she could see there, like her own thoughts were shining right back at her. And it must have been true because he kissed her again, quickly, and said, "I need a second." Then he tucked her in close and held her in his strong arms. He was trembling, and she was heartened that he at least seemed as shaken as she felt. The sensation of being comforted and appreciated and adored was just…sublime.

"Wow," she said after catching her breath. "You might be even better at that than you are at fishing."

"Thank you," he said and chuckled. "I think."

"Definitely a compliment. Maybe I should be jealous of someone, several *someones* probably, but instead I'm just grateful that they were preoccupying you while I was out on the water. It goes a long way to explaining why I'm so much better at fishing than you."

Arms snug around him, she could feel the laugh reverberating in his chest, and she liked that, too. So much. He slipped a hand around the back of her neck, entwining his fingers into her hair.

"Speaking of fishing and you feeling like you don't belong here, the Romeo people know you haven't been to this type of show before—you heard Marissa and Gerard say it. They're taking everything into account. Anyone can accumulate experience. It's the other stuff that matters. That *it factor* people are always talking about—personality, charm, style, looks— although Henry is a close second to you in that department. All of that, you either have, or you don't. And you have it, Victoria. An excessive, unfair amount, if you ask me. Seriously, if I were the one making the decision, I'd hire you right now."

"Seth." Emotion clogged her throat. "That is so nice."

"Even your voice is perfect."

"My voice?"

"Yes, your voice is like, I don't know, the finest buttery maple syrup for the ears."

She laughed. "You've lost it."

"Seriously, just relax. You've got this. If today you were a little off your game, I can guarantee you that no one noticed. Personally, I fear what you'll be like when you're on."

"Thank you. That means…everything to me right now. I'm a little embarrassed that I needed to be talked down."

"You're welcome." Narrowing his eyes, he peered at her intently, but she could see the humor and affection shining in his gaze. "You would do the same for me, I know it. But you do realize that just because I've admitted all of that, does not mean that I'm going to let you win? I have *plenty* of charm and good looks and…stuff of my own."

"That you do," Victoria agreed with a laugh.

THE FOLLOWING MORNING had the three finalists together. They went to "casting practice" and "interview prep." Then they were combed and fluffed and powdered before heading into a series of interviews, including the "most exciting coup" of the week, according to Marissa.

Somehow, she'd gotten them an appearance on *Morning Wire*, the second-highest-rated cable morning show in the nation. The coanchors, Janina Redfield and Jeb Lufkin, were the biggest reason for that success. A witty, handsome, adventure seeker himself, Jeb was continually scouring the sporting news in some of the more underreported arenas searching for interesting people to feature or stories to tell. Everything from endurance athletes to regular people accomplishing incredible feats.

The week before, he'd showcased a competitive cyclist who'd abandoned his first-place lead in a grueling road race on Vancouver Island to save a young girl and her dog from an attacking cougar. By all accounts, he'd saved their lives, destroying his bike in the process, which he'd used to fend off the cat. Good stuff.

Janina was widely acclaimed for her comedic talent, ability to connect with people and her interviewing skills. Popular with viewers, she came across as caring and interested in her guests with a dry but kind humor. She also had a penchant for going "off script" in hilarious ways that the audience had come to expect and adore.

Jeb introduced the three finalists, talked briefly about the extensive selection process, and how they'd been chosen from among thousands of applicants. He followed that up with a smattering of typical but entertaining questions: what they most liked to fish for, what fish they preferred to eat and what they enjoyed doing when they weren't fishing. Jeb told a story about how he'd once encountered a great white shark while diving the Hawaiian Islands.

"So, enough about the fly fishing versus spearfishing or fishing for shark compliments or whatever it is you're doing, Jeb," Janina joked after he finished. "I want to talk about what people are really looking forward to, and that's seeing you guys in action in an event called the casting competition. That's you three competing against each other by seeing who can score the most points by making all these wacky casts. Let's check out this video of you guys at target practice this morning, so the audience knows what we're talking about."

The promo for the competition showed each of them hitting—and missing—various targets laid out in the huge pool that had been constructed in the expo's largest showroom. Set to upbeat music, and interspersed with comments from each of them, Victoria was impressed by how well it had come together.

"That looks like a ton of fun," Janina said when it ended. "And you're all playing for your favorite charities, so that is very inspiring, too. So tell me, honestly, who is going to win this thing?"

"That would be me," Seth said. Beside him, Victoria's hand shot up.

Henry's arms went wide in a helpless shrug. "Hopeless, both of them. Although I find their confidence cute. I can thread a needle with my fly rod, and they both know it. They've seen me in action."

"Ooh," Janina gushed, "It's getting *reel* right here in our studio, folks. Get it?" Chuckling, she mimed a fishing reel. Then, wincing, she said quickly, "Sorry! Couldn't help myself. But this is just what I was hoping for! And, in a fun little twist, I have permission from the Romeo Reels people to make this event even more interesting. How about a friendly wager among the three of you?"

"A sporting wager?" Jeb interjected. "Now, you're speaking my language."

"What do you say, guys? Are you in?"

Chuckling and smiling, they all agreed because, really, what choice did they have?

"Any ideas on what the loser should have to do?"

"Loser eats a live worm or a minnow?" Victoria threw out the suggestion as if Scarlett were sitting right beside her.

That produced simultaneous head turns from Seth and Henry.

"That's disgusting," Seth said.

"What are we, in middle school?" Henry commented dryly.

"Seriously?" Victoria gaped at Janina. "Can you believe these wimps. How is that any different than eating sushi?"

"Heartbeat, for one." Seth held up a finger. "And the fact that it's alive leads to another dangerous possibility—one where it gnaws through my gut. No way."

"I said minnow, not piranha," Victoria quipped.

This garnered laughs all around.

"Okay, I like it. So eating live bait is officially *on the table*," Janina said. "Unless you two wimps—oops, I mean guys—can come up with something better?"

"How about a swim in the gulf?" Henry suggested.

"Oh, sure," Seth said with an eye roll, and a thumb hitched toward Henry. "Mr. Triathlon here takes a polar bear–style swim every morning where he chips the ice off a Minnesota lake and busts out three miles of crawl stroke before breakfast. It's all part of his 'training'—" Seth exaggerated the word with a set of air quotes "—that he professes to love. But the truth is he just wants us all to suffer along with him."

"You're not sounding very confident, Alaska," Henry shot back. "It's like you're already gearing up to take that swim."

"Ouch, he got you there, Alaska!" Janina teased. "Seriously, it's so great how you three all seem like friends when there's so much on the line. Then again, there's probably a lot of common ground among you."

They all agreed. That truly was the most surprising aspect of this for Victoria. Not surprisingly, Henry had been the one to predict it.

"You know what, though?" Jeb said. "Henry might be on to something. How about the losers walk the plank off the end of the pier? Pier 3 is right outside their hotel."

"Wearing mermaid suits?" Janina suggested brightly. "Or maybe one loser pushes the bigger loser into the water? We'll figure out those details later."

"And we'll be there to film it," Jeb added.

"Good news!" Janina grinned and clasped her hands together. "We're getting the thumbs-up from Marissa Rivas, our point person at Romeo Reels. She's over there in the wings, literally giving us a thumbs-up. Can you guys see that?" The camera panned toward Marissa. "I don't know about you people," Janina shrugged at the audience, "but I, for one, cannot wait to see who walks the plank."

The interview wrapped up with further silly but surprisingly interesting questions. Seth understood the duo's appeal and thought it was cool how they seemed just as nice off camera as on.

"You three were just complete…greatness." Marissa gushed when they were heading out of the studio. "Vic, Seth, I could literally see sparks flying while you two were bantering. Then along comes Henry with the trash-talking. That was utterly superb, Henry, because you don't look like a trash talker. And, Victoria, the minnow suggestion! Pure brilliance! I can guarantee that this interview is going to be the talk of the show. Just in time for the casting competition. I'm predicting it's going to be standing room only.

"So, after we get back to the hotel, you guys have your individual Q&A sessions, then an hour and a half free for lunch. Then your workshops, followed by…"

Seth heard the part about free time for lunch and quit listening. He pulled out his phone to check the schedule because he would have remembered if there were ninety free minutes where the possibility of hanging out with Victoria was an option.

"I thought we had a lunch meeting today with the, uh, product development department?" Victoria asked, taking the question right out of his mouth.

"Oh shoot, did I not email that update? Thank you for bringing that to my attention, Vic. That meeting has been moved to tomorrow afternoon, after lunch, before your afternoon workshops. The new-product people thought it would be better if you weren't all sitting there eating. You know, so that they can show you the stuff, and you can move around and try out the new products."

"Works for me," Henry said. "Playing with fishing gear sounds like fun."

Seth had to agree. He was also elated about the gift of time they'd been granted. He texted Victoria: Time for lunch?

"CAN YOU TELL me what's going on with Scarlett?" Seth asked over plates of fish tacos. They'd walked along the waterfront, checking out menus at the beachside cafés and bistros before settling on one as much for the view as the food. Luckily, the tacos were delicious.

"It's a long story, but the highlight is that Austin is insisting that she go to this event with him on Friday, but she already has plans to go to a play with Quinn's family, plans that were made months ago. And Austin's event is a boring fundraising dinner, nothing that a kid would enjoy."

Victoria hadn't talked specifics about her relationship with her ex-husband. But she'd said enough for Seth to conclude that Austin wasn't the most engaged of fathers. He was trying not to judge the other man, but if he had a child, he would never miss his appointed time outside of a full-fledged emergency. Especially if that child was a daughter as awesome as Scarlett.

"Is it during his visitation?"

"Yes, but he hasn't ever stuck to the parenting plan. Until recently."

"What changed?"

"He's running for district attorney."

"Ah. And now he wants to project a certain image to the public?"

"Exactly, and Scarlett is old enough to see

through this. She hasn't mentioned it yet, but it seemed inevitable. This fundraising dinner is the first time she's balked at having to go to her dad's. But I knew it would happen. It had to. He only wants her at his convenience."

"That is bad."

"You have no idea. His image, his reputation, has always been the most important thing to him. He will do whatever it takes without regard to anyone else to make sure it remains intact. His goal is to be governor someday. Or more."

"Wow."

"Yeah, he's a piece of work. His dad and their cronies wield a lot of power in western Louisiana and are always wanting more."

"Am I in danger of being arrested on some trumped-up charge when I come and visit you guys?" he jokingly asked.

But Victoria didn't laugh. "I honestly don't know what the man is capable of. But you're safe where dating me is concerned. There is no love lost between us. I can promise you that. Especially since I put my foot down about this dinner. She's going to her play and he is not happy."

"I don't get it. I cannot imagine why he let you go."

"He didn't have any choice."

"So, you ended it?"

"Well, it was mutual," she answered with more than a hint of sarcasm. "In that I didn't want to stay married to a man who was sleeping with someone else who he actually did want to marry. And not because she was pregnant." *And because he wanted to keep her quiet.*

"Oh, wow."

"I know. It's humiliating." She wanted to add that it was all part of a larger, worse experience she'd suffered at Austin's hands. But that was a story that she was even less proud of, and one she couldn't ever tell. To anyone.

"It shouldn't be. Not for you anyway."

"Thank you for saying so. Enough about me. Is there anyone in your life who I should know about?"

"No. As I mentioned before, I've never been married. Never been engaged. Had a few girlfriends. There was one I was hung up on for a lot of years. You should know that because someone will probably mention her at some point."

"Years?"

"Yeah. It took me a while to realize that I could never be what she wanted."

"Are you kidding me?" Victoria gestured

at him. "What else could she possibly want?" Leaning forward, she reached under the table and squeezed his hand. Seth marveled at the way her touch sent his pulse racing. Then she sat back and looked at him expectantly, waiting for an answer.

"Money, status, a lifestyle that I couldn't give her, and wouldn't even if I could. Ashley likes nice things, and I'm not exactly a crystal and china type of guy, you know?"

"Ha. Yes, I think I do." Reaching over, she picked up her glass of lemonade, and raised it in a toast. "It sounds like Ashley would be a perfect member of Team Triple A. That's what I call Austin, wife Amber and daughter Avery. As if they needed another way to exclude Scarlett from their circle, they named their daughter an '*A* name' to match theirs. Austin is all about appearances, money and what you can do for him."

"Yes, it sounds like she would. There's a bit of irony about my situation now. Ashley told me that she didn't want to be married to *just* a fisherman."

Victoria grinned. "That is funny. Does she know that you're in the running for this job where you will be like a superstar fisherman?"

"She does. We are sort of friends now. We had lunch last week."

"Hmm, you're nice to be friends with her, which leads me to my next point. How she could ever believe that you are *just* a fisherman is an absolute mystery to me."

CHAPTER THIRTEEN

"GOOD AFTERNOON, ladies and gentlemen. Welcome to the Romeo Reels casting competition!" Marissa's voice boomed through the sound system. The crowd erupted with cheers and applause. Victoria, Henry and Seth waved from where they stood on a dais making them level with "the pond." Marissa took a moment to let everyone settle in.

The enormous indoor pool had been constructed for angling demos and fun challenges where show-goers could try out products, test their skills or play games. Now, people were gathering around it shoulder to shoulder to watch the event just as Marissa had predicted.

Victoria wasn't nervous. Bolstered by Seth's pep talk the night before, a good night's sleep, Scarlett's happiness at being allowed to go to the play, and then a successful morning of interviews and appearances, she drew energy from the crowd. A voice in the back of her mind cautioned against depending on Seth too much. Only to be countered by another, pointing out that he truly cared about her. Not to mention the fact that he believed she deserved to be up here standing next to him. And that all felt so good.

Marissa was speaking again, explaining how the competition would be scored. A series of targets had been arranged around creative obstacles, each worth a point value determined by their level of difficulty. One hundred points for the simpler casts, increasing in increments of a hundred up to one thousand. There was a single, impossibly difficult target valued at three thousand points. Each of their "lanes" had been set up with the same configuration.

Different targets than their practice session, but the same idea. Studying the course now, Victoria felt confident that she could hit some of the more challenging ones. And she knew she could kill it with the easy casts. Leaving her pondering whether it would be better to rack up a bunch of the lower scores quickly or attempt the more difficult ones and hope her aim was as good as she thought? No matter what, this was going to be a blast and probably a very tight competition.

"And now," Marissa said, "time to meet our competitors. As most of you are probably aware, these three talented anglers are also the finalists in Romeo Reels' current search for our next pro staff team member and company spokesperson." She motioned to them and then gave the audience another moment to cheer.

Once they'd quieted, she began the introductions in an impressive, booming style reminiscent of a boxing bout or a professional wrestling match, "And now, making his stand in the far lane, I'd like to introduce ice fishing enthusiast, fly rod Jedi, and a man who is rumored to have once hooked the biggest muskie ever to get away in the Land of 10,000 Lakes. Hailing from Flat Rock, Minnesota, please welcome Henry Foster." The crowd went wild. Henry grinned and did this cute, shy wave. Victoria stepped over and gave him a high five.

"Ready for battle in the middle lane, we have a bass angling virtuoso and gulf water wizard who, according to her grandmother, was jigging for sac-a-lait before she could walk. From Perche, Louisiana, give it up for Victoria Thibodeaux." More cheers and applause. Victoria waved. Hearing her name shouted from the crowd evoked a thrilling combination of excitement and adrenaline, along with just enough embarrassment to keep her humble.

"Our third contestant, locked and loaded, is a grayling guru, steelhead slayer and all-around salmon sovereign who once hooked a halibut so huge it pulled his boat all the way from the

Bering Sea to Kachemak Bay. From Rankins, Alaska, I present to you, Seth James."

The roaring crowd went mute. Or at least, in Victoria's world it did. The scene shifted into slow motion while a woman hurried up the stairs and onto the dais. She then rushed toward Seth, threw her arms around him, and planted a kiss on his cheek. He looked surprised but not upset. While the woman continued to cling to him, he angled his head and whispered in her ear. The move looked so familiar and intimate that Victoria felt herself wince. Adoring smile in place, the woman produced a scarf from her pocket, then reached up and wound it around his neck where she tied it neatly in place.

"Surprise, Seth!" Marissa's voice cut through Vic's haze. Toward the audience, she announced, "A very special friend of Seth's by the name of Ashley has flown all the way from Alaska to cheer him on. Several members of Seth's family are here, too." She pointed into the crowd, but Victoria didn't look. She couldn't. She'd gone numb.

Ashley? The woman he'd loved. The one it had taken him *years* to get over, and that he'd lunched with just last week. Here. Kissing him on stage. Kissing him for years, apparently, while she'd been busy fishing and raising her daughter. What was she supposed to do with this? She didn't even know how to feel.

And then suddenly, Henry was by her side, sliding one arm around her shoulders and pointing at something that she knew meant nothing. "Smile," he whispered near her ear.

"Henry, I can't..." But he squeezed her arm, so she forced a smile.

"Oh, yes, you can," he encouraged gently. "You get it together right now, young lady, you hear me? I don't know what is going on over there with Alaska, but right now, you and I, we are going to make him walk that plank. All you need to do is cast, which we both know you can do in your sleep. Can you focus on that right now? If you can, then he's going down."

She bobbed her head in agreement.

"Good. Let's do this," Henry murmured, but before he moved away, he added, "And it won't be our fault if he drowns."

PANIC MODE. That's where Seth was and he had no idea what to do next. What was Ashley doing here? He'd asked, of course, those very words, "Ashley, what are you doing here?" And all she'd said was, "Surprise. I came with Bering. He needed help. We'll talk later. Good luck!"

Glancing toward the audience, in the general direction that Marissa had pointed, he saw Bering and Tag wave from the front row. Hazel stood beside them, scowling. He hadn't known his brother was coming either. He wasn't surprised by Hazel's presence, just that she'd arrived without letting him know.

Back to Ashley. For the life of him, he could not conceive what he could have said or done that would make her think that flying all the way here from Alaska was a good idea. Especially the storming the stage part. Seth had made it very clear at lunch last week that he was over her. Thanked her, even, for not reciprocating his affection all those years ago.

None of that changed what had just happened, what Victoria had seen. What was she thinking? Whatever it was, it could not be good. If Austin had stepped on the stage and hugged and kissed her, he probably would have thrown the guy in the pond.

She was holding it together remarkably well. The stricken expression on her face had lasted only seconds but would haunt him forever. Thankfully, Henry had stepped in. Whatever he'd said seemed to have helped because now they were smiling and joking.

Marissa was talking about the rules, but Seth had no idea what she was saying. Beside him, Henry got into position, so he did the same.

The buzzer sounded. Game on. Seth tried to set his reel, but his fingers felt thick and clumsy. Every move felt sluggish like he was slogging through a vat of thick syrup as he fumbled with his line.

Henry's movements, on the other hand, were nimble and efficient, casting approximately five times to every one of Seth's attempts. Somehow, Seth managed to land a five-hundred-point target keeping him from being completely skunked.

Marissa's voice penetrated his fogged-over brain. "Victoria is off to an early lead with a high-dollar cast into the bucket hanging from the rock ledge. But Henry isn't far behind, and my goodness his hands are like lightning. Another five-hundred points for Henry! Oh! And that's another high pointer for Seth. He's catching up…"

On she droned, and Seth felt like the round was never going to end. All he wanted to do was talk to Victoria, to explain. What exactly he was going to say he had no idea.

A glance at the scoreboard told him that Marissa was being kind. They were nearing the halfway mark, and while he'd gained some ground, Vic was still ahead. But only barely; she and Henry were now neck and neck. Resisting the urge to lay his pole down and be done with it, he flicked the line without aiming and then watched, spellbound, as it landed in the tiny plastic cup in the far end of the pond. Pure dumb luck. He did it again.

Marissa let out a whoop. The audience cheered. "That's six thousand big ones for Seth right there. Oh boy, this competition is suddenly a three-way fight again."

Miraculously, he'd pulled close to Henry. Time was running short so he decided to play it safe and see how many short casts he could accumulate. With only seconds to go, the crowd erupted again, even louder.

"Another ringer! This time for Henry! Three thousand for Henry on top of a thousand right before that one puts him securely back into the lead. Oh! And there's another thousand. Henry is on fire!"

The timer sounded. "And that's game over."

Henry looked right at Seth and gave his head a little shake. Waving and smiling at the cheering crowd, he glided toward Seth and commented in a low tone, "I suspect that's true in more ways than one for you, Alaska."

Seth offered a weak, "It's not what it looks like." He didn't know what else to say, and could only hope Henry's comment wasn't true. He could not lose her over something like this. And after she'd just confided in him about her history with Austin. The timing literally could not have been worse.

Marissa announced that Seth and Victoria would be "walking the plank" in a few hours and invited everyone to gather at Pier 3 to watch it go down. "*Morning Wire* has a big surprise lined up for the losers, or maybe I should say a *tall* surprise?"

Up until this point, Seth hadn't wanted to let himself think about not winning because he had a slight fear of heights. Okay, more than slight. But hopefully, all it meant was walking off the end of the pier and how far down could that be, ten, fifteen feet? Twenty at the most. He could handle that. Probably.

They descended the dais. He didn't know what to do first, find Victoria and try to explain, or talk to Ashley. Victoria disappeared into the crush of the crowd as Hazel materialized in front of him, saving him from having to decide.

"Seth!" she hissed and dragged him behind one of the huge potted trees that lined the room. "What is going on? What was that?"

"I was hoping you could tell me."

"I have no idea! I flew in separately. She came with Bering and Tag. I guess Bering wanted another person to work the show so he could do some networking, and he and Tag could take a charter boat fishing one day. Tag volunteered Ashley, although my guess is Ashley volunteered herself. And Tag, being our clueless big brother, agreed. Iris swears she knew nothing about it."

"Hazel, this is a nightmare. Victoria and I just got to this really great place where we—"

"I know! You wrote me and Iris a long, flowery text…*book* about it, remember?"

"Yes. I don't know what to do. I can't think straight."

"Right now, you need to go find her and just… I don't know, tell her you think that she's *crazy cool* or *superpretty* or whatever. I believe those were two of your key phrases. Pick one. No, pick several."

"I don't know where…" Seth gazed helplessly around the crowded room.

"I heard her tell Henry she was going up to her room."

"How did you—"

"Really?" she interjected with an eye roll. "You want me to detail my eavesdropping technique, right now?"

"No, I'm going."

"Hurry." She pushed him away, but then pulled him back by one sleeve. "She is superpretty, by the way. And she's way better at casting than you. Although, you were seriously off your game."

"I am aware."

"And now you have to walk some sort of plank?"

"Right off the end of the pier."

"What? And you agreed to do it? You know what, never mind, we don't have time to discuss what you were thinking. Go!" She pushed him again, and this time he took off through the crowd.

Seth caught up to her just as she was about to get on the elevator. "Victoria!"

"What?" She stepped inside.

"I can explain." He followed her.

"Can you?"

"Actually, no, I can't, but I can tell you—"

"Seth!" a breathless, giddy Ashley leaped into the car, threading her arm through his. "There you are, big guy!" He let out a groan. This was like a bad sitcom. "I'll go up to your room with you and we can—"

Reaching out, Victoria pressed the button for the top floor. But before Seth could process her intention, she tapped the door-close button and slipped out.

"THAT WAS A pretty slick move," A voice called out from behind her. Victoria knew it had to be directed at her. Face flushing with embarrassment, she pretended she hadn't heard the remark and beelined for the stairwell. Maybe several flights of cardio would help calm her down and clear her head.

The voice followed, saying, "You are a very fast walker. Seriously, you've got like a world-class stride. Although, I can't blame you for wanting to get away from that."

Victoria stopped and turned toward the voice, intending to make a polite excuse, only to find herself face-to-face with Hazel James.

For a few seconds, all she could do was gawk. She realized her mouth was hanging open when she muttered, "Hazel, hi." Both of her hands reached out to grasp one of hers. "I am thrilled to meet you."

Despite what Seth claimed about them not looking alike, she could see the resemblance. Their eyes might have been different shades of brown, but the shape was similar, and they sparkled with the exact same vibrancy.

"You *do* know me." Hazel's smile, too, was reminiscent of Seth's with an irresistible mix of confidence and mischief. The kind that made you want to smile back.

"I do. I think I am what might be considered a superfan."

"Seth said you follow my blog, but I didn't

know if that meant you'd read it one time, or you actually followed it. It's wonderful to meet you, too. This is interesting because I feel like I already know you."

"Same. I'm sorry about ignoring you just now. I didn't know…"

"I know." She grinned. "That elevator bit truly was fabulous. I wish I'd done it so I could write about it. The part that isn't funny, though, is why it happened. Just so you're aware, my brother didn't know Ashley was going to be here."

"I can believe that." The shock on his face was evidence of that. But Austin had worn a similar expression when she'd caught him cheating, so how could she truly know for sure if he was surprised by her presence or surprised that he got caught? After all, he'd stood there and let her kiss him and even whispered in her ear. "But does it really matter if he knew or not? I mean, you saw it, too. Anyone could see that they're…close."

"But they're not! That's the thing. It's a long story that we don't have time for right now, but I can tell you that my brother is crazy about you. He talks about you all the time. And he's never talked about a woman he's dated. Ever. Other than in passing."

"Not even Ashley?" Vic blurted and instantly hated how jealous she sounded.

"No." Hazel sputtered out a laugh. "Especially not Ashley. They only dated in high school, and Ashley and I were not friends. We have never been friends. He would never talk about her to me."

"So, you can't be sure how he feels about her then?"

Hazel grimaced, realizing how she'd made Victoria's point. "No, I can. I'm positive. My brother and I are so close. We have this connection." She held up her hand and pinched her thumb and fingers together, just like the gesture Seth had made when they'd gone sac-a-lait fishing. "We're triplets, but we're not identical or anything, so I can't explain it away with biology. Our sister Iris is close to us, too, but it's not the same as with Seth and me. It's like… I just *know* how he feels. Like my emotions are tuned in to his, and vice versa."

"Hazel, I'm trying to understand this, I am. But the fact is that Ashley is here and obviously believes differently. It's difficult to accept that's not founded on something. I know that part of my reaction is because of my own relationship history, but that doesn't change what happened."

She didn't want to say too much so she went

with, "Look, I appreciate you pleading his case, Hazel. Truly, I do. I'd like to think I would do the same for my brother if I had one. Unfortunately, I have to get going. We have to walk the plank, and there's a solid chance I may punch your brother and knock him cold before I push him off the top."

Hazel grimaced. "Oh, please, don't do that!" The sincere, underlying agony overlaying her tone gave Victoria pause and she added, "That's why I wanted to talk to you. I'll leave it to Seth to clear things up about Ashley. Because I *know* he will." With a deliberate look, she paused to let that sink in. "Right now, I need to tell you something else."

"Okay?"

"Seth is terrified of heights."

Good, Vic thought, *a true punishment then*. Maybe it would—

"And before you decide that's a good thing or that he might deserve a little misery right now, I need to explain."

Victoria waited, feeling both a little guilty about her uncharitable thoughts and astounded that Hazel had seemed to read her mind. The way Seth often did.

"My brother is not just *afraid* of heights. I'm not talking about a case of a little anxiety here. He has a clinical phobia."

"Why would he…" Victoria started to ask why he would agree to this wager then, but she already knew the answer; he never expected to lose.

CHAPTER FOURTEEN

SETH STARED AT the impossibly high platform and couldn't decide which was going to be worse, the climbing or the jumping. If he could even climb that high with his arms and legs already turned to gummy worms. A ball of ice was growing in the pit of his stomach, and even with the warm tropical breeze, his skin felt clammy and chilled.

Morning Wire had taken the walking the plank notion and run with it. Instead of the "easy" drop from the end of the dock Seth had envisioned, they'd borrowed a portable ten-meter-high dive from a local university swim team and set it up on the end of the pier. Staff members from the show were swarming around getting ready for the shoot. Spectators lined the boardwalk and gathered on the beach.

So many spectators. All here to witness his humiliation and probable demise. Soon to be aired on television and posted all over social media. It would probably go viral when the first responders were called in to rescue him from the platform like a frightened cat hanging on for dear life. They'd have to call for special tools to pry his hands from…

"Seth!" Hazel found him. "You can't go through with this. You're not doing this, are you?"

When they were ten years old and taking swim lessons, a way-too-brave Seth had attempted a flip from the pool's diving board. In an epic fail, he'd slipped, hit the back of his head on the board, and wound up unconscious on the bottom of the pool. The lifeguard had rescued him while an ambulance was called. A trip to the hospital revealed a concussion and resulted in twelve stitches. His fear of heights was born that day and had been festering ever since.

"Thanks so much for your faith in me."

"Of course, you *can* do it, but I don't think it's a good idea." Reaching out, she wrapped her hands around one of his. "Your hands are like ice."

"Yeah, I can't feel my fingers."

"Listen, you need to make up a lie, say you aren't feeling well."

"That wouldn't be a lie. I think I might puke. Hazel, this is all so…bizarre. Today started out as the best of my life. Today at lunch with Victoria, I had everything. I was securely in the running for my dream job, and I truly believed I'd found the woman of my dreams. And now, a few hours later, the wrong woman makes an unprecedented grand gesture, I make a fool of myself at a casting competition, I've lost Victoria and now I'm going to die."

"Hey!" She jerked his hand to get his attention. "You are not going to die, not today, cowboy! Not on my watch. And you did not lose Victoria. Have you talked to her yet?"

"Cowboy?" he repeated flatly.

"Yeah, well, *You are not going to die today, fisherman!* doesn't pack the same punch, does it? I thought about *soldier* but since you haven't been one it felt disingenuous."

"I haven't been a cowboy either."

"Will you stay focused on the conversation, please? Have you talked to Victoria?"

"Yeah, definitely, I'm the one who is going off topic," he droned sarcastically. "No, there hasn't been time for talking since she ditched me in the elevator. How can I explain what Ashley did? I don't even understand it myself. I keep thinking about what I told Vic at lunch today about how I was hung up on Ashley for so long. Years—I said *years*, Hazel. And then she shows up here! If Vic's ex would have done what Ashley did, I don't think I'd even want to hear her excuse."

"I don't believe that," Hazel said. "You would listen. You would listen because you love her. Seth, you are not responsible for another person's actions. Give Victoria a little credit. She's a reasonable, intelligent, lovely person who happens to like you. Did you talk to Ashley?"

Seth ignored the love comment. He couldn't think about that possibility right now. It would only make losing Victoria worse. "I tried to talk to Ashley. But she seems to think we're destined to be together."

"Are you kidding me?"

"Nope. She says she'll do whatever it takes to prove it to me."

"The woman is delusional. I'll talk to her."

"She doesn't understand why you don't like her."

"Oh, please. Did she tell you that?"

"She did."

"She does. Trust me, she knows."

"Seth!" An excited Marissa hustled toward them. "Here you are! Ready? This is going to be so incredible! Thank you for agreeing to do this. You guys are so far beyond what we could have even hoped for as finalists. This kind of free publicity is priceless. It's not going unnoticed by the powers that be, by the way. Miles Romeo is here!"

An attractive blond woman joined them. "Seth?"

"That's me," he answered blandly, reluctantly. He'd never been so disappointed to be himself.

"Hi, I'm Maggie, it's nice to meet you. I'm a production assistant here to give you instructions on how we're going to proceed. So, we're going to have you and Victoria walk…"

Seth tried to pay attention. He truly did. But with every trigger word out of her mouth like *ladder* and *platform* and *jump*, his head went lighter, and his lungs squeezed tighter until he thought he might pass out. Somehow, he'd have to follow Victoria's lead. That is, if she'd even look at him right now.

Glancing around, he spotted her with Hazel, their heads bowed together, chatting like old friends. Victoria appeared utterly unconcerned about the disaster that lay before them. Likely that was true. Seth knew his phobia was irrational, but that didn't make it better. He had little difficulty flying in planes and helicopters or even riding rollercoasters. The problem occurred when there was nothing but dead air between him and the ground, especially when that ground was water. Like from the top of a high dive.

"Hey, loser," Victoria said in a much lighter

tone than he anticipated, coming over to stand beside him. "You ready?"

"Mmm," he managed.

Maggie shouted something. Victoria looked at him and said, "That's our cue." She started walking, so Seth did, too.

"Smile," she said, giving his shoulder a playful nudge. "Cameras are rolling."

Seth smiled.

"*Is* that a smile, though?" she teased. "It looks more like a snarl. Like a cranky tomcat."

Shockingly, that made him chuckle, and he realized that just being by her side was easing his lungs from their crushing constraints. At least enough for him to address his other major problem. "Victoria, I am so sorry about Ashley. She doesn't mean anything to me anymore. I had no idea—"

"Shh. We are *not* talking about that right now."

Seth acquiesced because the high dive was now looming over them. Like gallows. He stifled a hysterical laugh as they glided into the dark shadow it cast like two condemned convicts of old. He could feel the scar on the back of his head throbbing.

Once they reached the bottom of the ladder, Victoria turned and faced him. "Hey," she said, tipping her head a little to snag his still-distracted gaze. "Look at me." The firmness of her tone startled him enough that he did. She reached up and placed one hand on his shoulder, gripping it tightly. Lowering her voice, dazzling smile in place, she said, "Hazel told me everything. Here's our plan. I am going to go up first, and once I get up there, I'm going to make sure you can see me. Then you start climbing up and just focus on me, okay? Climb and focus. And then, when you get to the top, I'll take your hand and walk you through it, and we'll jump together. I'll be with you the entire time telling you what to do. Easy-peasy."

A lump clogged his throat, and he could only nod. Humiliating to be this close to tears. She clapped him on the shoulder as if they'd been joking around. Angling her head so that her mouth was close to his ear, she whispered, "Relax. You've got this, Alaska."

FROM THE TOP of the platform, Victoria watched Seth climb the ladder and felt her already-softening resolve melt further. Even if Hazel hadn't warned her about his fear of heights, she would have known that something was wrong. He was way off. The tightness around his mouth and the tension in his jaw was bad enough. What really had her worried was how his sparkle was gone. How those insanely beautiful brown eyes that were usually full of life and humor were now flat and glazed. He was truly terrified.

She would get him through this. He'd talked her off her proverbial ledge when she'd been ready to quit and go home. It was the least she could do for him.

"Almost there," she said. A few more rungs and he was at the top. "Okay, cool. Good job. Don't look down," she cautioned once he'd gotten to his feet. "There's a camera out there on that boat, so you need to smile, too."

He did, or at least he managed not to scowl. She took his hand and entwined her fingers with his. Then she lifted their hands. "Wave with your other hand," she instructed. He did. Thankfully, the sturdy-looking "plank" was plenty wide enough for them both. Victoria had worried it might be a narrow pliable diving board. "Now, we're going to walk out there together. It's only a few steps. We'll jump on three. Hazel told me you're an excellent swimmer."

He nodded. Squeezing his hand, she took a step, urging him to come out beside her. "Probably not as good as me, though," she teased in an effort to distract him. "But we already know I'm better than you at almost everything. Don't look down," she reminded him again.

"Just focus on the horizon and think about what you want to do when this is all over. I'm thinking I'd like to grab some ice cream and maybe check out the vintage gear that Romeo has on display." They reached the end of the plank. "Here we are. It's almost over."

"Victoria?" Seth's voice was a ragged whisper.

"Right here," she said, giving his hand another squeeze.

"Thank you," he whispered. "I can't believe you're doing this for me."

"Yes you can. Ready? One…two…three."

Together, they jumped.

WHEN SETH HIT the water, he thought his heart might explode. But not from fear. That was gone. It felt amazing to be alive. Like intoxicating. Breaking the surface, he discovered Victoria already there. Waiting. Grinning and hanging onto one of the life preservers that the *Morning Wire* crew had supplied for them.

"Look at you," she said with a proud grin. "You survived."

"I did." He thought his own smile might split his face in two. Two strokes and he was across from her, gripping the opposite side of the floatie. "Thanks to you."

"Please. I didn't do anything but offer a little encouragement."

"We both know that's not true."

"I'm proud of you," she said. "Hazel told me what happened when you were a kid. That's so awful. I don't think I would have gone through with it if I'd been that scared."

"Hmph," he said, rolling his eyes dramatically, and then lying through his teeth, "I wasn't scared." She laughed, and he went on to confess, "I probably wouldn't have done it if Henry had been my losing partner. He's awesome and all, but somehow I don't see him holding my hand and guiding me through all of that."

That made her laugh again. He needed to tell her that he loved her. Because he absolutely did. Hazel had known before him, of course, which meant he had known too and not yet acknowledged it. But there was nothing like the fear of death to catapult important sentiments to the forefront of your mind. And truthfully, Ashley's appearance had cemented the notion. Because these feelings were so different than the childish infatuation he'd experienced years ago.

Victoria already felt like a vital part of his existence. If she were no longer in his life, he wouldn't function the same. He kept having these flashes of a future with her that he'd never even dreamed could be possible. And maybe what he was about to do was partially due to the timing and circumstances, but he didn't care. It didn't make it less accurate. He had to say it.

"Victoria?"

"Yes, Seth?"

"I love you."

"Shut up." She splashed him in the face.

"No," he said, chuckling and sputtering, and then smoothing the water from his face. "I'm serious. When we were up there, you told me to focus on what I wanted to do when this was all over, and all I could think about was how I didn't want to die without telling you how I felt. Victoria, I swear, I don't have feelings for Ashley. I can't. It's not possible because everything inside of me belongs to you. There's nothing left for anyone else. I am in love with you, and no matter what happens job-wise, I think—"

"Seth, adren—"

He cut her off midword and finished it for her, "Adrenaline. I know what you're thinking—that this is the adrenaline talking, the aftereffects of my near-death experience. But it's not. Maybe saying it right now at this moment has a little to do with that, but my feelings are real. It's not like anything I've ever experienced. And I hope you feel it, too."

Soft green eyes searched his before giving him a little nod. That was enough for now.

"You don't have to say anything. I know we have more to talk about, but right now, we better get out of this water before my sister calls the coast guard."

ONSHORE, THEY WERE immediately met with an assemblage of enthusiastic chaos. Cameras, microphones, Henry, Hazel, Gerard, Marissa, Wyatt and Miles Romeo, and a mob of other people all greeting and hugging and congratulating them. Seth quickly introduced Victoria to his brother, Tag, and cousin, Bering. Ashley, she noted gratefully, was nowhere to be seen.

Janina and Jeb and the *Morning Wire* crew descended upon them for a quick interview. Seth wisely made a joke, mentioning but downplaying his fear of heights, and giving Victoria credit for "coaching him through it." After kudos from Miles Romeo and additional photos, they headed back to the hotel with just enough time to shower and get ready for dinner.

And for her to ponder Seth's admission. The sweetest, most romantic declaration of love ever. Which suddenly had her laughing with unbridled joy because the man didn't do anything halfway, did he? Seth loved her.

Reining in her giddiness, Victoria forced herself to think rationally. Seth *said* he loved her. But how could she *know* for sure? She'd trusted

Austin with those words once, too. Closing her eyes, she replayed the conversation searching for flaws, any indication of insincerity. All she could see was his beautiful face and the love reflected there; all she heard was the truth in his tone.

Words are cheap, Victoria. It's actions that are costly. That's what Mémé would tell her, and that's what she would go by. A glance at the time told her she needed to get moving. At least the evening's schedule called for casual attire and a crowd of people among who Victoria expected to feel comfortable. She slipped on a long sleeveless sundress, applied some light makeup, and arranged her still-damp hair into a quick updo.

Checking her phone revealed a message from Scarlett. She smiled at the accompanying pic of her and Mémé with the canoe they were building. Vic sent a quick response and included the information about their news story set to air the next morning. Grabbing her bag and phone, she headed for the elevator.

Halfway down the hall, her phone went off again. Warmth rushed through her when she read the text from Seth:

Google tells me the effects of adrenaline last about an hour. In case you weren't keeping

track it's been one hour and twenty-nine minutes since we jumped. And I still love you.

The seafood buffet was being held in another large banquet hall. Attendance included
an eclectic mix of pro staff from all the angling
companies and assorted industry professionals. In other words, lots of fishing enthusiasts.
Victoria entered the room to a vibe that was
electric, almost celebratory. She was greeted
warmly and was chatting with a well-known
trout fly tier she'd met the day before when she
spotted Henry.

"Vic!" Henry waved at her.

Excusing herself, she joined him. "Hey, you.
How's it going?"

His grin seemed a bit enigmatic as he answered, "Pretty good. We have a table. Seth
and I saved you a spot." Peering at her closely,
he said, "But I wanted to make sure everything
was okay between you guys before you head
over there."

Victoria felt a fresh wave of affection for
him. Impulsively, she hugged him. But he
seemed to expect it, hugging her right back.

"Thank you, Henry, for getting me through
that. For everything." Secure in his arms; she
wondered how she'd gone from no men in her
life to two of the best ones she could ever have

dreamed up? Stepping back, she said, "We're fine. Or we will be. His sister explained a few things. Congratulations, by the way, you've got mad skills. And thanks to you, that was some sweet vengeance. At least, at the time."

"True," Henry agreed, and chuckled. "I'm going to get a beer. You want one?"

"That would be perfect, yes."

He pointed. "We're over there."

Across the span, she could see the round table where Seth and his family were already seated. The event, she recalled, included a plus-one for every person invited. As a vendor, Bering was likely on the guest list, which explained his and Tag's presence. Hazel had already told her she was attending as Seth's. Vic felt herself relax because that meant maybe Ashley wouldn't be attending. She certainly wasn't going to offer up her plus-one.

Exhaling a relieved breath, she started that way when she heard a voice behind her. "Excuse me, Victoria?"

So much for that hope, she thought, her stomach pitching wildly because she knew before she even turned around who she'd find. Tacking on a serene smile, she faced the unavoidable. "Hello. Ashley, right?"

CHAPTER FIFTEEN

"Oh, hi, you know me? Of course, you do. After that display, who doesn't? Can I talk to you for a minute?"

Up close, Victoria could see that Ashley was very pretty. Flawlessly applied makeup accented her wide expressive eyes. She wore a red sparkly form-fitting dress too nice for the occasion, but she was classy in that perfectly put-together way that Victoria would never be, didn't want to be, truthfully. She had too many other things to do.

Victoria glanced toward the table to see if Seth or Hazel might save her, but a crowd of people now obstructed her view. "Uh, well, I don't have a ton of time…" she said, bracing herself for a confrontation.

"It won't take long. No drama, I promise," she added, accurately translating Victoria's hesitation.

Best to get it over with, and maybe in a room full of people, there would be less chance of a scene. "Sure."

"Great." Ashley puffed out a little breath, and Victoria realized the woman was nervous. "I just want you to know that I know that I made a huge mistake in coming here."

That was not what she expected. "Oh."

"Seth had *no* idea. He's been a good friend to me since I moved back home to Rankins. Nothing but a friend. But lately, I've been thinking about my life, the mistakes I've made, and I realized that I let a really good man get away. I got fixated on the idea that I could undo one of those mistakes. With Seth. It was stupid and impulsive, and I'm so embarrassed."

Victoria had to hand it to the woman; she was brave. It took a lot of courage to own up to your mistakes. Unfortunately, there were some mistakes that you couldn't undo. They seemed to be the ones you paid for forever, too. She knew that better than anyone, didn't she? But this wasn't one of those. And for some reason, she couldn't let her believe it was. How could she blame this woman for wanting Seth?

"Why was it stupid?"

"I didn't listen to what he told me last week. We had lunch together, and I can see now that he was trying to put distance between us. But I had this fantasy, and I thought... It doesn't matter now. The point is, he's in love with you."

"How would you know that?"

"Hazel told me. And in the elevator. The things he said about you… He never talked to me like that, never loved me like that. Not even when we were silly teenagers. No one has ever loved me like that."

Wow. She couldn't deny that it felt good to be the one to be with Seth. But she knew how it felt to be the one passed over, too. "Thank you for telling me all of this."

"I'm sorry if I messed anything up for you guys."

Another glance and Victoria saw the crowd had shifted to reveal a perfect view of Seth. Head bowed, he appeared to be on his phone.

"You didn't." Attention on Ashley again, she said, "And for what it's worth, it took a lot of guts to fly all the way here and wave your heart around on that stage like you did. And then to come to me and explain. I admire that."

Pausing for a beat, Ashley studied Victoria as if gauging her sincerity. "That means a lot to me, thank you."

Vic realized her phone was still gripped in her hand when it vibrated with a text. "I'm sorry. I'm going to check this in case it's my daughter."

"Of course." Ashley gave her a knowing smile. "I'm a mom, too. My son texted seven times today to ask me if we were out of peanut butter. The eighth time I didn't answer. Fifteen minutes later, my mom calls to say he cut his finger while slicing some cheese and needs stitches."

But the message wasn't from Scarlett. It was Seth:

One hour and forty-two minutes. STILL in love. I think that settles it. Everything ok?

Lifting her head, she looked his way, and this time her gaze collided with his. And there it was, that invisible link of chemistry and affection connecting them, binding them. It felt so powerful, strong, unbreakable. Inevitable, too, she suddenly realized. There was no point denying it anymore. Unable to contain her smile, she tapped out a quick reply:

Well, that does it then. Who am I to argue with science? Everything is just perfect. I'll be right there.

"THIS SEAT IS for Victoria, right?" Hazel tipped her head toward the vacant chair between her and Seth before gesturing to the empty spot on her other side. "I'm like an island here. Why is there an extra seat at our table?"

"That's for Cricket," Bering answered.

"Cricket?" Hazel repeated rather sharply, tossing looks over one shoulder and then the other. "Cricket is here?" If Seth didn't know better, he'd think she was displeased by this information. But that couldn't be, Cricket was their family's oldest friend. "Why is Cricket here?"

Why was her voice about two octaves too high? Seth shot her a look that asked the question, or at least the gist of it, which she ignored. And that made him even more curious.

"Who is Cricket?" Victoria asked, slipping into the seat beside him.

"Tag's best friend," Hazel said.

"A friend of the family," Seth explained.

"Hannah's business partner," Tag added.

Seth chuckled at how he and his siblings sounded like a chorus, all chiming in at once.

"He is all of that," Bering said after a chuckle of his own. "And possibly my partner as well. If things proceed as planned."

"Yours?" Hazel said to Bering, now more composed, but still tense enough for Seth to note. "You're taking on a partner?"

"I'm expanding," he said. "I think. Maybe."

"Where? To what?"

"I'm considering adding a tour option to my guide service. Or possibly it will be a new business. Not sure yet. Cricket is interested in a partnership. I'm surprised he hasn't mentioned it to you yet. We were hoping to sit down with you and talk about it. Get your perspective on it and the travel industry in general."

"What types of tours?"

"Specialized ones that hit the major Alaskan highlights, or portions of them, like Denali, glaciers, wildlife viewing, but also with stops in the cities for museums and cultural events. With optional excursions for the more adventurous."

"Like group tours?"

"There he is," Seth said as Cricket appeared at their table, beer in hand.

Sliding into the seat beside Hazel, Cricket answered like he'd been privy to the conversation all along, "Sort of, but smaller and supercharged. We'll use vans, boats, ATV's, possibly horses—whatever the terrain and situation calls for. As well as our planes and maybe helicopters, too. We're early in the planning phase, so we'd love to hear your thoughts on the concept, Hazel."

"I'd be happy to give you my thoughts, Cricket," Hazel replied tightly.

Seth took that opportunity to introduce Cricket to Victoria and Henry.

"So, Victoria," Bering asked once that small talk was out of the way. "Next to Alaska, I've heard that Louisiana offers some of the best fishing in the world."

Victoria's smile was radiant, and Seth wanted to believe he had a hand in it. The Ashley incident seemed, if not forgotten, then at least not weighing on her. She hadn't said she loved him yet, but her last text had come close. At the very least, it was a clear acceptance of his declaration. And acceptance meant she was open to someday returning the sentiment, right?

"I can't speak to fishing in Alaska as I've never been, but I can brag a bit about the fact that in Louisiana, we can fish year-round." When Bering started to interject, she joked, "Without chipping ice off of something to do it."

He laughed. "I grant you that our weather can be a bit more inconvenient."

Victoria said, "Louisiana is still pretty underrated on the global and even national stage, which can also be a bonus. Not in our respective businesses, obviously, which rely on tourists. But there's still a surprising amount of 'undiscovered' space in Louisiana." She added air quotes to imply that she meant the term to be relative. "You know, places that haven't been ruined with an Instagram hashtag yet."

"I totally get it. It's kind of a catch-22 for those of us who make a living capitalizing on the great outdoors, right? We want tourism dollars, but we also want to keep our environment as pristine as possible. But what does that mean exactly? One person's careful is another person's reckless."

"It is a very tricky balance. As I mentioned earlier, my family runs a small resort and..."

The conversation continued to unfold, and Seth was impressed by Victoria's choice of topic where Bering was concerned. The environment and everything that went along with it was his cousin's passion. The James and Thibodeaux families may have hailed from vastly different parts of the nation, but growing up in the country established a kind of common ground, and love for the literal ground, that was unshakeable.

Before long, Bering was offering her a job as a fishing guide. Maybe that would convince her to make a trip to Alaska this summer.

"I would love for you to meet my wife, Ally," Tag said when Victoria mentioned her grandmother. "Her grandfather and your grandmother would make a great pair." Seth also loved his brother for inadvertently helping his case.

Now that he thought about it, he couldn't have chosen better than Tag and Bering for this first introduction to his family. Tag was probably the most easygoing of all his siblings. People said he had a knack for making everyone feel noticed and included. And it wasn't contrived; his brother was a genuinely kind and generous human. Everyone liked him. Victoria appeared to be no exception.

Hazel, he knew, was the real test. She was his sister, triplet companion, best friend, confidante and all-around bearer of his soul. They could communicate without speaking and agreed on nearly everything, from political views and religious beliefs to movie preferences and food choices. Except where his romantic companions were concerned. He knew very well that just because he was crazy about Victoria didn't mean Hazel's feelings would automatically follow. They'd spent more than a decade at odds over Ashley.

The fact that his sister had been unusually quiet all through dinner did not escape his notice. He was too enthralled by all things Victoria to realize that it should have also caused him concern. Once dessert was served, he was riding high on a tsunami-style wave of hope regarding his and Victoria's future.

But then Hazel, who'd been poking at her cheesecake, laid down her fork and cast a probing gaze first at him, and then Victoria, before settling on him again. "So, how are you guys going to work this out long-term? I keep running through all the scenarios in mind. Seth, are you going to move to Louisiana?"

"We haven't—"

Shifting her attention to Victoria, she said, "I don't see a scenario where you can move to Alaska. Your family is in Louisiana, not to mention the business. I can see how important that legacy is to you."

Beside him, Vic tensed, and Seth tried to make light of her comments, "We should wait and see who gets the job before we start making any decisions."

"You guys have a lot to consider, so—"

"Hazel," Cricket broke in with a low serious tone. "Their relationship isn't anyone else's business."

Hazel's eyebrows pulled up as she deliberately swiveled to stare at Cricket. The table went stone-cold quiet as she delivered him a long, slow blink. "You don't think my brother, who I love more than anyone else on the planet..." Clearing her throat, she started again, "You don't think Seth's happiness is any of my business?"

"They're adults. They'll work it out."

Nodding knowingly as if she'd just solved a complicated riddle, she said, "That's your problem, Cricket, you don't think anyone else's happiness is your business, do you? If you don't have an *opinion*, then you won't upset anyone, right?"

"Sometimes one person's version of what constitutes happiness isn't the same as another's," he returned smoothly. "And I have opinions. I just don't feel the need to share them when it isn't my place."

"Not your place," she repeated flatly, and Seth knew the conversation was no longer about him and Victoria. What had happened between these two? Inhaling a deep breath, Hazel tapped a finger on the table with a slow, steady beat. Uh-oh. Counting. That meant she was struggling to hold on to her temper.

Seth noted eight long beats before she made eye contact with him. "I'm heading up to bed. I'm disgusted." Eyes going wide, she snorted out a laugh and clapped a hand over her mouth. Composing herself, she corrected, "Exhausted, not disgusted. Or—" she said, with a sidelong glance at Cricket "—maybe I'm both. I don't know. But we'll talk about this later, Seth."

Turning a smile on Victoria, she said, "Victoria, please forgive me if my inquiry in any way sounded intrusive. I like you *tons*. I feel like we're already friends. I want this to work out for you guys. That is why I'm asking. I want you both to be happy. If there's anything I can do to help, I'm here for you."

"Of course, Hazel," Victoria said quickly. "I feel the same. And thank you. I hope you get some rest."

"Yes, yeah, we'll talk later," Seth rushed to say. They'd also be discussing how in the world Cricket had gotten under her skin. What was up with the tension between them? But he had enough sisters to know that it wasn't a good idea to ask at this moment.

Cricket, on the other hand, did not have sisters. A fact that he'd shown tonight. Although, he'd been around the James women enough that you'd think he'd know better than to tell one to mind her own business, especially where her family was concerned. Particularly Hazel, where extra caution was required when any combination of her triplet siblings was involved.

THE OCEAN SPRAY felt delicious on Victoria's sun-warmed skin, the salty breeze revitalizing her after so many days trapped indoors. She enjoyed the feel of the boat, too, as it cut a path through the flat, turquoise water of the Gulf. The brilliant blue sky was attractively overlaid with patches of cloudy white lace. Another gorgeous morning had dawned on this, the last day of the show. Made even better by the surprise fishing trip Romeo Reels had arranged for the three finalists.

With their show commitments now officially complete, the selection committee was meeting to make the final decision. The new spokesperson would be announced at the evening's closing ceremony. Undoubtedly, the Romeo people thought that a morning out on the water would be a nice distraction from the agonizing wait. Which appeared to be working for Seth and Henry at least. Victoria observed them, where they were seated in the middle of the boat, chatting and sipping coffee. Two old friends without a care in the world.

She, on the other hand, was sitting in the stern and stewing about what Hazel had said. What was going to happen to her relationship with Seth? If she was hired, she feared that Seth might look back and resent the distraction she'd been for him. If he was hired, would she always wonder if she would have done better without him constantly on her mind? But then again, either of them getting the job meant a long-distance relationship. How would they manage that?

Of course, Henry getting the job was also a real possibility. On the surface, that would solve a lot of their issues, at least the internal ones. And there might be other opportunities to pursue if she didn't get offered this job. They'd all been approached by other companies.

The boat began to slow. Henry stood and went to speak to the captain. Victoria knew he had some thoughts on red snapper strategies, which they were going after today.

"Hey," Seth said, moving to sit beside her. "You okay?"

"Yep," she said. Because what would it solve by voicing her concerns? There was no point in speculating about the myriad of circumstances that could play out. So why couldn't she stop thinking about them?

"Nervous?"

"A little."

"Me too. After tonight, everything is going to change."

Victoria forced a smile. "Is that supposed to make me feel better?

Mouth curling at the corners, he scooped up one of her hands with his and laced their fingers together. He lifted the bundle that was their hands and kissed her knuckles. The first public display of affection to occur between them. If cruising on a boat in open water could be considered public. She could get used to it, she decided as her anxiety immediately began to ease. Amazing how he could calm her mind with just his touch.

"I'm sorry about Hazel going off the rails last night. I could tell it bothered you."

"It did a little, but don't be sorry! Your sister loves you and cares about you. Her point was valid."

"To a degree, it was valid. But something else is going on there. She and Cricket had an argument or something."

"I wondered about that, too. The tension between those two. Wow. Is there a history there?"

"No! Not like that. I mean, they've known each other forever. It would be more like a sibling fight. He's Tag's age, so he's always been like this older brother figure for us."

"Hmm." Victoria did not see it that way but wasn't about to say so. She didn't have a brother, and Seth knew them both much better.

"But I have been thinking about the logistics, too, and I'm relieved this is almost over. Because no matter what happens now, at least I'll be able to kiss you whenever I want."

"That is an excellent point. I was just thinking something similar."

"Victoria, no matter what happens, we will figure this out. There's too much…feeling between us for it not to. I am all in."

Fortified by those words, his conviction, she nodded. He was right. It would. It had to. "Me too." Now would be a good time to tell him she loved him. That no matter what happened, she was committed to making this work. She could no longer see a future that didn't include him, not a happy one anyway. "Seth, I—"

The engine went quiet. "Snappers!" the captain cried. "Oh, yeah...schooling right here. Folks, I can tell you right now this is going to be a very good day."

Victoria and Seth exchanged eager grins. Because *fishing*.

"Yes," she agreed. Keeping a tight hold on his gaze, she hoped Seth could see all the love she felt for him shining in her eyes, the same way she could see it in his. "It already is."

CHAPTER SIXTEEN

A JUBILANT VICTORIA practically skipped off the elevator, hustled into the spacious lobby, and scanned the space for anyone who might be a pizza delivery person. It might seem a small thing to someone else, but the fact that Seth had remembered about the pizza had her feeling extremely warm and fuzzy inside. The fishing trip had been a total blast that reinforced the camaraderie among the three of them.

The ceremony didn't start until eight, and they were officially on their own for the afternoon and evening.

They hadn't even made it back to the hotel before Seth sent a text: How about we knock that pizza order off your list tonight?

Victoria had nearly kissed him on the spot. Refraining, she'd casually texted a reply: Sausage and anchovies?

Looking up at her, he'd made a face and mouthed "Anchovies?"

And when they got to Seth's room where, still smelling like fish and sunscreen, she'd followed through with that kiss. Seth, steadfastly rejecting the anchovy option, had ordered two pizzas, four different flavor combinations.

A young woman wearing a uniform, including a hat with the appropriate pizza logo, stepped through the doors. Victoria waved and approached, paid and included a generous tip. Even that part was fun, she decided, when the woman thanked her with a sunny smile.

She was on her way back to the elevators when Henry exited from the area and into the lobby looking freshly showered and extremely handsome. Stepping to one side, he frowned down at the phone he held in his hands.

"Henry," she called out a greeting. His head snapped up, and his expression looked alarmed like maybe she'd startled him.

She stopped in front of him. "Hey, are you on your way out? Do you want to come up to Seth's room and have some pizza with us? Mine has anchovies, but Seth—"

"Victoria," he interrupted, glancing around uneasily. "Are you alone?" That's when she realized that not only was Henry not smiling, he also looked troubled. In all the interviews and events and appearances, she'd never seen him anything but poised. All week, his performance had been pretty much perfect. His daughter was supposed to be flying in this afternoon for the reception. She hoped nothing had way-laid those plans.

"Yes. Are you okay?"

Shifting on his feet, eyes boring into hers, he asked, "You haven't heard anything?"

"About what?" He was unmistakably un-settled, which prompted a rash of nervous thoughts. Had the committee decided to an-nounce the winner early? Or maybe word had been leaked out. Or… Oh, no. Was this about her and Seth? Had they been outed? She couldn't imagine how that could matter now when the decision had been made.

"Oh, Vic…" Raking a hand through his hair, he stared down at his feet. "I do not want to be the one to tell you this."

"Henry. Tell me what? You're scaring me."

At that moment, and for the first time in her life, she understood the term "blowing up a phone." Because that's what suddenly began happening to her cell where it was securely tucked into the back pocket of her jeans. It felt like it was going to explode.

She reached for it, and Henry said, "Don't. Don't look at it. There will be nothing good there."

That didn't help her anxiety any. "Henry, what?"

Lightly gripping her elbow, he guided her

over toward a small sitting area. Then he looked her solidly in the eyes again and asked, "Victoria, do you have a criminal record that you didn't divulge when you applied for this job?"

Faster than a lightning strike, her entire body went cold and then numb as if she'd been flash-frozen where she stood. The pizzas slipped from her grasp. Henry caught them and set them on a nearby table. A rush of blood echoed loudly in her ears. She could see Henry's lips moving, but she couldn't hear his words. Was she going deaf? Possibly she was having a stroke.

Strong hands cupped her shoulders. "Vic, look at me."

That she heard. So she did. She concentrated on his face, specifically his mouth, while he repeated the question and a few others, which included words dredged up from the nightmare that was her past: *arrest, conviction, criminal record*. Then he repeated a version of his first question, "Victoria, have you ever been convicted of a crime?"

"Yes, but…" *No, no, no…* Those records had been sealed. Then expunged. But had they? Had she been lied to? Austin and his dad had sworn this information would never see the light of day. She could still see Linus's smug face, hear his vaguely threatening tone: *Victo-*

ria, honey, you need to do this, do you hear me? For Austin. This is for your baby's future. It's just your signature on a piece of paper. That's all it is. No one will ever know. I promise this will never see the light of day. You're a minor and... Even before this moment, that had never been true; it had been haunting her forever. Because she'd never truly trusted them.

"I didn't..." *Do it.* Her throat was suddenly too dry to continue, her heart too sick to try.

That's when the first reporter found them. "Excuse me, Victoria Thibodeaux? Can I have a word?"

Through a fog of confusion and dismay, Victoria turned her head toward the voice but could only stare blankly. She needed to get out of there, but she still couldn't move. Even her arms hung limply by her sides. Could *shock cause a stroke?* she wondered absently.

The reporter took her passive silence as a yes. "My name is David Belt. I'm a sports and outdoor reporter for the *Florida Navigator.* Did you divulge the details of your wildlife violation when you applied for the position of spokesperson for Romeo Reels? How do you think it would look for one of Romeo Reels' highest-paid brand ambassadors to have a criminal record?"

An "Um," and some slow blinking was all

she could manage even as something began to wake up inside of her, a voice telling her to move, to talk, to do something!

"I…"

Henry advised, "Don't answer, Victoria."

Another person walked over to join them. "Ms. Thibodeaux, my name is Olivia Wallace with Gulf States Law Dog, an online news site devoted to the political happenings in our southern region. Would you care to comment on the details of your wildlife conviction? I understand you were young at the time. Is it true you were married to Austin Galbraith? I assume you are aware that your ex-husband is running for district attorney? Can you tell our readers what role Mr. Galbraith played in that dark chapter of your life?"

Austin. Victoria felt her stomach twist painfully as she began to think this through. Definitely, he had some hand in this. It was the only explanation that made sense, even though it made no sense. That was the only good thing about their arrangement. She'd never had to mention it, but they both knew that if the truth ever came out, he had more to lose than she did. Until now. Was he jealous of her success? Unlikely, she hadn't even really had any yet. Angry that she'd allowed Scarlett to skip his dinner? That was the only explanation she could come up with at the moment.

Henry's fingers wrapped around her elbow with a firm grip. "I'm sorry," he announced to the small crowd now gathering. "Victoria can't comment right now. As you all probably know, our schedules are jam-packed, and we have another engagement that we're already late for." Pizzas forgotten, he led her to the elevators.

SETH STEPPED OFF another elevator with a full heart and an empty stomach. Victoria should have been back up to his room by now. His texts asking her what she wanted to drink had gone unanswered. A quick scan of the lobby didn't reveal her presence either. He rechecked his phone. Nothing.

Walking further into the space, he spotted Hazel seated on one of the leather chairs in a far corner. Face set in concentration, head bowed over her phone, scrolling away and muttering to herself. Completely engrossed in the task, she didn't even flinch until he was standing right in front of her.

"Hey, what are you doing down here? Have you seen Victoria?"

Her head snapped up, troubled eyes latching onto his. "Seth." One word, that's all it took. Something was wrong.

"Hazel, what's wrong? Are you okay? Did you and Cricket get into it again? Do you want to tell me what happened?"

"This isn't about me," she answered elusively. "Or him." Expression steady and intent, she asked, "Victoria isn't on Twitter, is she?"

"What?" The question threw him off. "Uh, no. She doesn't do any social media. And by any, I mean she doesn't even have accounts. She barely tolerates her phone."

Hazel exhaled with a series of quick, shallow nods. "Good. That's good. I've just been checking your accounts, and right now, I'm very glad that you are so inactive. When you don't respond, it won't be as weird. For now, I don't even want you to get on there to check your notifications, okay?"

"Why?" Hazel knew all his passwords. Most of his accounts she'd set up for him years ago, and he'd never bothered to change passwords. He mainly used them to keep up with the angling world, rarely posted, and never anything very personal.

"Seth, you are about to face a social media storm of epic magnitude."

"Did someone find out about us?" Seth asked in a hushed tone.

"Not that I know of. I hope not. That would

be even worse for both of you. Because, Seth, this is… Do you know where Victoria is?"

"Not at this exact moment." He explained about the pizza. And then, searching the lobby again, he muttered, "I thought I might see her down here…"

"Okay, so you have no idea what's going on? Of course, you don't. You wouldn't be standing there all calm if you did."

"Hazel, this is getting irritating. Are you going to tell me what's going on?"

"Sit."

He took a seat next to her. "What is this about?"

"This is about you. Well, technically, it's about Victoria. So you, too, by extension. This is really bad." Tapping the display on her phone, she began reading aloud: "'Hey @RomeoReels how does someone with a wildlife conviction get considered for a pro angler job? Victoria Thibodeaux needs to go back to the swamp that she crawled out of. She's nothing but #alligatorbait #poacher #VictoriaThibodeaux #ProPlusFishingOutdoorShow.'

"Here's another one: 'All you have to do to score a chance at a six-figure spokesperson salary with @RomeoReels is have a pretty face and get away with a major fishing violation.

Well done Victoria Thibodeaux! #LousianaOut-
law #rewardthecriminal'

"And then there's, '@RomeoReels has
hooked a real winner! #VictoriaThibodeaux
revealed to be a champion all right. A champion poacher. I'll be buying their products real
soon. NOT! #boycottRomeoReels'

"It goes on. There are tons more. It's on other
platforms, too. Did you know about this?"

"No. They've got the wrong person. That's
all ridiculous."

Sweeping his gaze around the lobby again,
he was struck with a new urgency. He needed
to find Victoria so she could straighten this
out. That's when he saw the pizza boxes. On
a table adjacent to the doorway leading to the
elevators, they were just sitting there with no
one around. Pushing to his feet, he crossed
the room, his pulse pounding nervously. Once
there, he stared down at the boxes while his
stomach knotted tight with dread. Reaching
down, he lifted the cardboard top, and the smell
of anchovies hit him with full force.

WHEN THE ELEVATOR dinged and the doors
opened, Victoria half expected to be met by
police or security guards even though she knew
that was ridiculous. The reporters had made her
feel like a criminal. Trekking down the long

hall, she willed herself not to cry and forced herself to think.

Her phone, still buzzing wildly in her pocket, erupted with Scarlett's ring tone.

"My daughter," she told Henry. With trembling hands, she answered the call. "Scarlett, hey, honey."

"Mémé and Gram have been calling and calling you, and Daddy is trying to reach you, too. He says it's an emergency. A reporter guy came here, and Mémé shooed him away. People are calling here and asking for you. Mama, are *you* okay?"

Victoria was so far from okay that she didn't know how she was still standing. It took effort just to breathe through the severe tightness in her lungs. But she managed to reassure Scarlett because that's what she had to do.

"Okay, well, call Daddy. Gram wants to talk. I told Quinn I'd go out searching for snakes later if he'd fish with me tomorrow. But I'll take my phone, so you can call me and tell me when you win."

"Sounds fun. Be safe, and I will definitely talk to you later."

A brief conversation with her mom only revealed a more detailed version of what Scarlett had reported. Ending the call, she found herself inside Henry's room. Not surprisingly, it was neat and tidy in that way that didn't look like it had been cleaned for company. There were no splashes of fabric peeking out of drawers or smashed shoes showing under the edge of the closet door. And why would there be? A bubble of bitter laughter welled up from deep inside of her. Doubtful that he could have anticipated that he'd be harboring a fugitive. Besides, this neatness was totally in line with his personality. And clearly, she was redirecting her thoughts, so she didn't have to face what was happening.

Henry must have suspected so, too, because he suggested, "Why don't we sit down, and we'll figure this out."

She did. With the shock wearing off, tears began to pool in her eyes. She blinked them away, but the emotion migrated to clog her throat so that when she spoke it was a raspy likeness of her usual voice, "I don't know what to do."

"Can you tell me about it?"

Could she? She'd never spoken the words aloud to anyone. Not even to Mama or Mémé. Austin and Linus had been adamant about that detail. One word, and they'd sue her for custody of Scarlett. She realized now that Scarlett was older, and Austin was a terrible father, and with the records to prove it, that likely wouldn't happen. But at the time, it easily could have.

Henry, looking somber and concerned, retrieved two bottles of water from the fridge, passed one to her and took a seat in an adjacent chair.

Trying to think this through, she opened the bottle and took a drink. She hadn't even realized she was thirsty until the cool water soothed her dry-as-paper throat. Too bad there was nothing to soothe the humiliation and despair now burning her from the inside out. She could see no good outcome here. Turning her thoughts to the facts, she acknowledged that somehow the story of her arrest and conviction had gotten out.

"You don't have to tell me anything at all. But if you want to talk, I promise it will stay between us. Victoria, I know it sounds odd, but I adore you almost like you were my own daughter. I want to help. There's nothing you could tell me that would change the way I feel about you."

All she saw was sincerity, concern and patience, as well as a complete lack of judgment as she studied Henry's face. It did something to her. Maybe it was because she'd never had a dad, but if she did, she'd want him to be just like this man. Or maybe it was because she couldn't stand the thought of him believing the worst, or of *someone* not knowing the truth.

"I was seventeen when Austin and I started dating. Austin was twenty-three. We'd only been together a few months when I found out I was pregnant." She winced. "I hadn't even told him yet. I hadn't told anyone. I wasn't exactly in denial. I just wasn't ready to talk about it yet. I needed time to process the fact that I was going to be a teenaged mom. And figure out how to tell my mama and grandma.

"That day, I was really sick, pregnancy sick, and I didn't want to go out with him because everything made me want to puke. Especially smells. Even the smell of fish, if you can believe that one."

Henry offered a sympathetic smile.

"But Austin showed up anyway with his friend Gordy. They wanted to go fishing and needed a boat. I let them use one of ours. I had no idea what they were planning. A few hours later, they came racing back to the resort. Austin came and got me, all frantic, and dragged me out to the dock. When Fish and Game showed up a few minutes later, I still didn't know what they'd done. But the game wardens did. The idiots had the live well full of illegal fish.

"We were all three taken in for questioning. They were facing huge trouble. The boys both knew not to say a word. Austin and Gordy were both in law school. Gordy's dad was a judge. Austin and his father, Linus, convinced me to take the blame. Since I was a minor, if I pleaded guilty, the documents would remain sealed. Forever. If Austin had this on his record, it would hurt his career, and ruin his dreams of a political future.

"I resisted. He begged. I told him I was pregnant and didn't want my child to have a convict for a mother. He knew how badly I wanted to go to college. Austin and his dad told me that if I agreed to do this, Austin would marry me. I'd have all the financial help I'd ever need. Then, when he finished law school, I could go to college. And they'd pay for it all."

She paused and shook her head. When she went on, her voice cracked on the words, "This is still very humiliating."

"It doesn't sound like you did anything wrong."

Pulling herself together, she exhaled sharply and continued, "I agreed. I signed the statement. And then... Scarlett was only a few months old when I discovered he was cheating with his high school girlfriend, Amber. Had been all along. She was the woman he wanted, the one he'd intended to marry. I was just a... distraction. A mistake. And then his get out of jail free card. Such a cliché, stupid poor girl falls for rich boy and ends up pregnant."

Henry's composed expression had gone cold, unreadable. "You are not stupid, Victoria. You were a girl, yes. But not a stupid one."

"Their family is very old-school. Linus told me that if I divorced Austin, the college deal would no longer be valid. I had a choice—I could stay married knowing my husband had a mistress he was in love with and go to college, or I could divorce him and get nothing.

"When I threatened to expose them, tell everyone what really happened, they laughed at me. Why would anyone believe me? They mocked me, ridiculed me, pointed out how I'd just look like the scorned, bitter woman that I was. I still had to live with myself, so I chose divorce. And of course, there was my daughter. It didn't matter, I told myself, because out of the ashes of that flaming mess, I got to keep Scarlett. He didn't even try and fight me for her. My mama and grandma were so supportive. Mémé, she… She never said I told you so after she warned me about Austin. And, oh she sure could have…" Trailing off thoughtfully, she brushed a tear from her cheek.

"Anyway, they dove right in with helping me raise this incredibly amazing child. And gave me time to pull myself together. I forgave myself for being weak and stupid, told myself that it didn't matter. I might not have a college degree, but I could still have something that was my own. That *I'd* accomplished. And I figured out how to do that. I still can't believe I'm here…"

"I can," Henry said. "You are exceptional, Victoria. And everything you've been through and now accomplished should reinforce that."

She would have smiled at that, but fresh tears got in the way. "And now, the one thing I wanted, he's taken from me. Again. I'm not saying that I think they were going to choose me, Henry. Losing to you or Seth fairly, I could handle. I was at peace with that. You both deserve this job. But this, having it *taken* from me, this feels like losing to him all over again."

"Because it is," Henry agreed. "That's exactly how I would feel, too. What if you told your story now?" he suggested. "Expose this despicable piece of trash for what he truly is."

Victoria gave him a sad smile. "I still have the same problem. I have no proof. I confessed. Linus Galbraith is still wealthy and powerful. Who would believe me?"

"Reality and perceptions are often at odds. Let's take a minute to consider your options."

But there was only one option, and she knew it. Victoria had no choice but to withdraw her name from consideration. The job application had included her signed promise that she'd never been convicted of a crime. She'd turned in the paperwork believing that her juvenile record had been stricken and no longer mattered. The realization was like a painful blow. But not nearly as much as the one that came next; she and Seth could no longer be together. This would follow her forever. And him, by extension.

If the company discovered they were dating, it would undoubtedly affect his chances. At the very least, his judgment would be doubted. At worst, his honesty and integrity questioned. She hated how her mistakes could rub off on people she cared about.

Henry! She shouldn't even be here. "I'm so sorry, Henry. I shouldn't have told you all of that because now I have to ask you to lie for me if anyone…"

"Hey, stop that. It's your story. It's nobody else's business."

"But this could look bad for you."

"I can take care of myself. But I think you should consider talking—"

"No, Henry. I appreciate you wanting to help. And just finally telling someone the truth, having *you* know that I'm not the person they're saying I am means so much to me. But the truth doesn't matter. I know what I have to do. And right now, I have to get out of here."

A FEW MINUTES LATER, after Henry escorted her to her room, shockingly without being accosted, Victoria was stuffing clothes and belongings into her suitcase and backpack.

Taking a deep breath, she composed an email to Marissa and then quickly hit Send before she could overthink it. Next, she tapped out a text to Seth, immediately deleted it, and started over again. Three more texts, three more deletes. Working on a fourth when a check of the clock told her she needed to get moving. *Delete.*

Henry, bless him, would be going to meet Seth right now so that she didn't have to worry about running into him. After a quick study of the hotel map, she rode the elevator to the third floor, where one of the restaurants was located. From there, she did her best to casually stroll through the place. She descended a set of stairs and exited onto the street. Then she opened an app on her phone and requested a ride. Four minutes later, she was on her way to the airport.

CHAPTER SEVENTEEN

"YEAH. I KNOW she's gone." Seth frowned at Henry. "I've been texting and calling and waiting for her to show up." He assumed she'd left to take a walk or get some air. "But she needs to get back here so we can straighten this mess out before the ceremony."

Henry had texted, asking if he could meet for a drink in a bar near the hotel. Hazel had been with him, so he'd brought her along because he could barely think straight.

"She probably got the job. I don't know about you, but if I were the one doing the hiring, I would give it to her. No offense."

"None taken." Henry smiled, but it was a little weak, sad. "I'd give it to her, too."

"Seth," Hazel said, glancing up from where she'd been studying her phone's display. "What Henry is saying is that Victoria will not be attending the ceremony."

Henry confirmed this when he exchanged a pointed look with Hazel. There might have been something else in the glance as well, but… Wait, she was *gone*?

In tune with Seth's thoughts, Henry clarified, "She's withdrawn her name from consideration. She's on her way back to Louisiana."

"Why would she do that? That seems extreme." As did her leaving without telling him, talking to him, allowing him to help or at least… Be with her. Be there for her.

"When we applied for this position, we signed a statement declaring that we'd never been convicted of a felony or a wildlife violation."

"Yes, but…" Seth hadn't yet considered that the accusation might be valid. "Henry, are you saying you believe this is true?"

"She told me it was."

"She *told* you?" Seth asked, unable to keep the hurt and disbelief from his voice. What else had she told him?

"Yes. But, Seth, it was because I ran into her downstairs in the lobby. She had just picked up your pizzas and had no idea the story was out there. I felt like I had to tell her what was going on, so she wasn't completely blindsided. I only managed to barely accomplish that because approximately one minute later, she was approached by two different reporters. I got her out of there, and we went up to my room, talked briefly, and then she insisted she had to leave."

Seth wanted to ask what they'd talked about, what things she'd told him, but he shouldn't have to. Didn't he deserve the same consideration as Henry? Or more. They were in a relationship. One where they'd agreed to be together, to see each other exclusively and as often as possible. He'd told her he loved her. No, she hadn't said the words, but he knew she felt them. Or, at least, he believed she did. Her actions suggested she did.

But he also knew what a great actress she was, didn't he? She'd proven that time and time again. Uncertainty and frustration crowded their way in. Was it possible she wasn't who he believed her to be? That would mean everything she'd said, and done, was a lie. Seth refused to accept that. He needed to hear the words from her. Innocent until proven otherwise, right?

"I was afraid of this," Hazel said, madly clicking and scrolling around on her phone.

"Afraid of what? That she was some sort of criminal?"

"No! I was afraid that there was a reason why she bolted. Maybe it is as simple as she did it. But I'm leaning toward the possibility that there's another explanation. I've traced the

Tweets back to Louisiana. The story broke online in a local newspaper. I just found the original article."

"What's the site?" Henry asked.

Hazel told him, and now that Seth was accepting the reality, questions rushed in, "But why would someone do this? Who would do this to her?"

Hazel answered, "I'm working on that. Someone jealous, maybe? Even the smallest taste of celebrity can bring out the worst in people."

Hazel reached over and gave his forearm a squeeze. "Hopefully, this article will give us some answers. In the meantime, it's important that you don't give anything away regarding your feelings for Victoria. If people discover you're in a relationship, they won't want to believe that you didn't know about this. And even if they do believe you didn't know, they'll criticize you for not knowing. Or for being ignorant, or for getting duped. You can't win this, so you need to stay quiet."

"Hazel, that's…twisted. And wrong."

She shrugged an agreeable shoulder. "That's social media."

"Are you saying that I'm supposed to pretend like Victoria means nothing to me?"

"For now. The good thing about social media

is that it's a fickle beast with a short attention span." Cocking her head as if considering her own statement, she qualified with the assertion. "Usually. The key is not to feed the monster. At all. Stay silent. Act surprised."

"I am surprised!"

"That's good. Fortunately, and unfortunately, you three have made a lot of fans. Whoever handles social media at Romeo Reels has helped to make you guys stars, in the fishing world at least. Their Twitter account has over five-hundred thousand followers, which means a ton of comments and opinions. Sometimes those can take on a life of their own. You need to wait for this to die down. See how the dust settles."

"You mean leave Victoria to deal with it on her own?"

"Seth, I know you want to help. But she handled her life just fine before you came into it. Let her do this. At least, for now. Until we have more information."

He knew what Hazel was implying, that he thought he could rescue Victoria, take care of her. But that wasn't it at all. What he had with Victoria was balanced, equal. They were like a team. He was there for her; she was there for him. That's how they rolled.

He was better *with* Victoria, focused and prepared, and yet she kept him grounded. And he helped with her confidence, provided perspective and kept her calm. But his thoughts were also bouncing all over the place, and he felt conflicted now that she'd left and would not communicate with him. Maybe he'd read it all wrong.

"Seth, I'm ninety-nine percent certain that Victoria has already reached this same conclusion. Why do you suppose you haven't heard from her? She's keeping her distance from you for the same reason. She doesn't want any of this scandal to touch you."

"That part I can confirm," Henry said.

"But I don't want to—"

"What good will it do for you to ruin this for yourself?" she asked. "If you don't get this gig, you'll get another offer. You've already been approached by various companies expressing interest if Romeo doesn't hire you. No matter what, a relationship with Victoria hurts you right now, hurts your chances of getting a pro staff, or some other cool fishing job. Victoria's thinking of what's best for you, Seth."

BUYING A TICKET, getting through security, navigating the terminal, finding her gate, walking, and doing all the mundane travel details made it easier for Victoria to stave off the pain. But all along, she felt it. Like there was a knife being held to her heart just piercing the edge, waiting for her to stop moving. Waiting until there were no distractions so that it could properly slice its way inside and deliver maximum impact.

Now, strapped into her seat at thirty-some-thousand feet above Florida's gulf water, there was nothing to do and nowhere to go. Nothing to stop the knife. Unlatching the tray table, she folded her arms, dropped her head to rest there and let the searing white-hot blade do its damage.

Not getting the job was bad enough. A terrible disappointment for sure. But like she'd told both Seth and Henry, she'd been prepared for the possibility of losing to either of them. To even be considered in the same league as them was an honor. To have made it that far was her greatest personal triumph to date. A dream come true. She'd made connections, gotten a glimpse of other opportunities that might be available if this job didn't pan out.

It was how it was ending that was killing her. Forfeiting in shame elevated her failure to a completely new level. She'd finally gotten a taste of a different world, a life of her choosing, only to have it disintegrate around her. Taking all those options with it. Another nightmare come true, courtesy of Austin. And she hadn't thought anything could be worse than what he'd already done to her. How wrong she'd been.

Because even all of that was bearable compared to losing Seth. No matter how she thought and considered and strategized, she didn't see a way forward for them. This would stick with her forever. Her career was over, but his was just beginning. If he got this job, or even another job in the industry, being with her would only reflect poorly on him. She couldn't let that happen. She would not let Austin ruin another person's life. Especially not Seth's.

Thinking about him, about all she'd lost, drove the knife deeper. It hurt to breathe. Sitting up, she flattened one palm against her breastbone, braced the other on the window beside her, and squeezed her eyes shut.

Why hadn't she told him how she felt? At least he'd know how incredible she thought he was, how truly wonderful he was with Scarlett and Quinn, how much the kids adored him, how no one had ever cracked Mémé's shell of suspicion as quickly. *I love you.* Why couldn't she have just said the words?

"Excuse me, miss?" Victoria heard the voice and felt a tapping on her shoulder. Opening her eyes, she discovered a flight attendant standing in the aisle.

"Are you okay?"

That's when she realized how she must look. The hand on her chest was gripping a fistful of shirt with the other still pressed to the window.

Muttering an embarrassed, "Oh, yes, I'm fine," she folded her hands in her lap.

"Are you sure?" The woman's face held nothing but kindness and concern. "Is there anything I can get for you?"

Victoria tried to blink away the tears, but there were too many. Eyes overflowing, they spilled onto her cheeks. Smiling weakly, she whispered, "I'm sorry. I lied. Clearly, I am not fine, but I will get it together. I promise."

The flight attendant handed her a napkin. Victoria took it and used it on her face. Hands moving efficiently, the woman grabbed, opened, and poured some liquid into a glass. Then she leaned in and whispered, "Honey, I am so sorry for your loss, whatever it may be. I know there's nothing I can say to take away the kind of hurt you're feeling." She passed over the sparkling beverage. "This is my favorite wine. Maybe it'll take the edge off." With a sympathetic smile, she included, "On me."

Victoria was comforted by her thoughtfulness, if not the wine, and managed to gather the courage for what she had to do next.

Once on the ground in New Orleans, she retrieved her car from long-term parking where she'd left it. She made only one stop. At roughly halfway to home, she pulled into a truck stop where she filled up with gas. The attached convenience store was well stocked, and she purchased a large black coffee, a bag of pretzels and a disposable cell phone. She made a quick call home, learned nothing new, gave her mama the number, and told Scarlett she loved her.

Staring at the phone, she desperately wanted to contact Seth. But she knew it was best for him if she didn't. That way, if someone asked if he'd heard from her, he could truthfully say no.

From there, she drove straight to Austin's sixteen-acre estate that bordered his parents' even more substantial property. They'd gifted him the land upon his graduation from law school and built him a house. Victoria had been secretly thrilled when he and Amber had opted for the construction of a completely unoriginal colonial-style monstrosity set in the middle of a vast expanse of emerald green lawn.

The house sported a mix of white-painted siding and neat red brick. Austin was so proud of the portico out front and the "genuine Italian marble" he'd had imported. Victoria had snickered to herself the first time she'd seen it because the columns appeared way too large for the roof they supported. The front door looked tiny amidst its grandeur, too, and the black ornamental shutters were literally too small for the windows. Leaving the place with a wildly ostentatious yet exaggerated appearance. Like a cartoon house.

Immaculate overgroomed trees, perfectly symmetrical shrubbery and a decorative half fence contributed to the house's overall lack of personality. It was no place Victoria would ever want to live.

Amber answered the door, looking as pretty as usual. And uncharacteristically relatable: no lipstick, pronounced lines around her eyes, expensive clothing a bit rumpled.

"Victoria, hello. I told Austin you might show up here. Please, come in."

Victoria bit back every sarcastic reply, and there were many. She always did her level best to be civil to Amber. Her issues were with Austin. Mostly. So instead, she smiled politely and accepted the invitation into the grand parquet-floored, chandelier-lit entryway.

"Thank you, Amber. I assume he's home."

"He is. I'll go—"

"Victoria." Austin shuffled out of a doorway near the end of a long hallway and strode toward them. "I've been trying to reach you."

"I turned my phone off and don't plan on ever turning it back on again. I stopped listening to my voicemail after the second threat to drown me in whatever swamp I crawled out of. I'm going to have to get a new number."

"Victoria, I am so sorry. I don't know—"

She interrupted with a stop sign hand. "Please, don't say things you don't mean. I'm just here for some answers."

He frowned and said, "But I do mean it. Will you come into my office and sit down so we can discuss this?"

Amber said, "Victoria, I know you've been traveling. Would you like some tea or a glass of water?"

"No, I'm fine, Amber, but thank you."

Following Austin into his office, she took a seat on the small sofa. He settled in an adjacent wingback chair.

Forgoing small talk, Victoria got straight to the point. "There are so many things I could say to you right now but whatever your logic was, I did not deserve this. If this is because I wouldn't allow Scarlett to go to your fundraising dinner, I—"

"Victoria," he interrupted, appearing genuinely shocked by the accusation. "I did not do this. It was Rod Eyers."

"Rodney Eyers?" It took her a second. "The man running against you for district attorney?"

"Yes. He's denying it, of course. But it was someone from his campaign."

"But why?"

"Did you read the article?"

"What article?

"The article that started all of this. It was about me. Our unfortunate episode was only a mention in the context of my ex-wife being a criminal. It's taken on a life of its own."

"What, why?"

"Politics can be a dirty business. You know that. Anything can be twisted to make a person look bad."

"But this makes *me* look bad. I don't get how this hurts you. We've been divorced for more than a decade."

"It calls my character into question."

Victoria shook her head. She literally had no words for that degree of irony.

"The story is evolving. It's been leaked that I was there that day, the day that we were, uh, apprehended. My role in the matter is being scrutinized."

"How…?" But Victoria was thinking quickly now because this made a perverse sort of sense. "Linus promised me that it was just my signature on a piece of paper that no one would ever find out."

"I know. Believe me, we are working on that. What are you doing back here already? Your mama said you'd be in Florida until tomorrow evening. Did you get the job?"

"No. I withdrew."

"Why?"

"When I applied, I signed a form saying that I'd never committed a felony or a wildlife violation."

"I see. Well, under the law, a violation as a minor shouldn't count."

"I am aware of that, Austin. That's what you and your daddy promised me, remember? That's the only reason I signed that confession. I saved your hide and now I'm being punished. *Again.* For something we both know that I did not do, and I—"

"Victoria," he interrupted, "calm down. How do you think I feel? This could be very damaging to my campaign."

"Your campaign," she repeated flatly. Anger flared inside of her, hot and intense. Clenching her fists in her lap, she forced herself to inhale. "Austin, you ruined my life. This job was—"

"That's a little dramatic. This isn't an offense that warrants—"

The jarring ring of her new cell phone startled them both. Only her family had this new number. Reaching into her bag, she retrieved the phone and answered the call.

And that's when her world truly fell apart.

CHAPTER EIGHTEEN

MARISSA AND GERARD found them in the relatively out of the way bar. Seth didn't ask how but noticed that neither Henry nor Hazel seemed surprised to see them either. It felt inevitable.

"Did you guys know about this?" Gerard asked, gesturing for Marissa to take a seat while he snagged a chair from a nearby vacant table.

"No," Henry said firmly. "I found out from my daughter, who has been following the show on social media. She called and asked me about it. I was checking it out when…" He went on to explain how he'd seen Victoria in the lobby and warned her. Seth noted that he didn't mention how Victoria had essentially confessed her guilt to him. If he hadn't already thought the world of Henry, this sealed it. Even as much as it stung that it wasn't him, Victoria had confided in a worthy man.

Seth felt Marissa's eyes on him, and he wondered if she knew about him and Victoria. Or suspected? Would she believe him when he said he hadn't been aware of Victoria's past?

All she said was, "Seth?"

"She didn't say a word to me."

And yet the truth had never made him feel worse. Despite Hazel's claim about Victoria's radio silence being for his protection, he wasn't sure he bought it. He certainly didn't like it. It hurt that she didn't trust him enough to confide in him, but she'd talked to Henry. And maybe he needed to accept that their relationship wasn't as strong as he believed it to be. But the simple fact remained that he still loved her.

Gerard nodded thoughtfully.

Marissa sighed. "What a mess. The selection committee is reconvening right now with the legal team to reevaluate their decision in light of Victoria's withdrawal. According to all the legalese, if an applicant withdraws, the position will be filled from the pool of remaining applicants. But no one can agree what to do when the situation involves a fraudulent claim of eligibility. Meaning another qualified applicant could have had Victoria's spot, etcetera.

"We have no idea how they're going to proceed. Miles is furious. This was shaping up to be the most successful PR event in the company's history. And now all anyone can talk about is how Romeo Reels almost hired a poacher."

"Have you spoken to Victoria? Do you have any information about the actual event in question?" Hazel asked.

"No. All I have is the email stating that she was withdrawing her name from consideration and apologizing for any inconvenience it might cause."

Gerard huffed out a laugh. "Inconvenience? She lied on her application. She committed fraud. Romeo Reels could seek legal action."

Seth resisted the urge to protest. Besides, he couldn't say anything in her defense, could he? He didn't know anything. He looked at the one person who did.

Henry started to speak when Hazel said, "I don't think so." He almost smiled because his sister had nothing to lose by defending Victoria, did she?

All attention shifted her way.

"Technically, she didn't have to disclose it."

"Excuse me?" Marissa said with a small shake of her head.

"I've been doing some research, including reading the original article from the Louisiana newspaper that broke this story. For some reason, people are overlooking the fact that even if it is true it was an offense by a juvenile. A juvenile's records are sealed. For a purpose. And often expunged. The records are nonexistent from what I can discern. Again, if it is even true, she was likely and truthfully told that as an adult she could honestly say it never occurred. Google is very knowledgeable about Louisiana juvenile law.

"It appears that this reporter, Olivia Wallace, is basing her story on an anonymous source and unconfirmed police reports—not on actual formal documents like notes from an arrest or court proceedings."

"That's strange," Marissa commented. "Why would a reporter take that kind of risk? And if it wasn't true, why would Victoria withdraw? Why wouldn't she stay and fight? I would have taken her for a fighter."

"Good questions, Marissa," Hazel said. "And ones we should be asking. I'll start. Who stands to gain by taking Victoria out of the running?" Lifting both hands, palms up and out, she motioned toward Seth and Henry at the same time. "These guys do."

Tipping one hand toward Seth, she said, "Seth is a hard no. This man is my brother, and I know him better than he knows himself. It would never occur to him to probe into his opponents' backgrounds and dig up dirt to get this job. He only wants to win based on his skill and merit. Fishing skills. Where he is unmatched. At home in Alaska, where everyone fancies themselves an angler, Seth is a legend." Slowly cocking her head to one side, she paused a beat before adding, "Casting competition notwithstanding. He mucked that up for reasons we don't need to get into right now."

"Thanks for pointing that out, Hazel," Seth commented wryly.

Lifting one shoulder, she went on, "What I'm saying is that Seth would be happiest if you just had a derby and let that be the deciding factor. Let the most skilled angler rule the day!"

Everyone laughed because they all knew him well enough to know she spoke the truth. Seth shrugged and faked a sheepish smile. "What can I say? I like to win."

Hazel grinned and went on, "The good thing about that trait is that if he were to get this job, he would apply that same competitive drive and work ethic. He'd be an excellent spokesperson because he would become an expert with every product and master each task assigned to him. He won't settle for being less than the best."

"Um, thank you for real this time, Hazel."

She acknowledged him with a smile. "That leaves Henry." With her other hand, she gestured in his direction. "Now granted, I don't know Henry nearly as well, but I have observed quite a bit this week. And I can assure you that he has both the smarts and the ingenuity to conceive of a strategy like this and—"

"Hazel, I don't—" Seth interrupted.

"Let me finish," Hazel countered with a scowl. "*And* pull it off without anyone being the wiser. But he wouldn't. No way. Henry's integrity is above reproach. He strives for excellence in all areas of his life. He wants to be, excuse the cliché, his best self. Throughout this whole process, he's proven that time and again by helping and advising both Victoria and Seth when *not* helping them would have been to his advantage. He's not only one of the most intelligent and interesting people I've ever met, he's witty, thinks fast, and when he talks people listen. No offense to Miles Romeo, but Henry could rock this job *and* run the company in his spare time."

Henry smiled, looking both pleased and embarrassed. He shook his head as if he couldn't quite believe her assessment. Or, more likely, he couldn't believe that she'd said it out loud. Honest, insightful analysis. That was Hazel.

"It sounds to me like you should be on the selection committee," Gerard quipped.

Hazel's shrug conveyed her agreement. What she said was, "There's something fishy about this whole thing if you ask me."

Marissa picked up her phone and tapped

the display. To Gerard, she said, "A text from Miles's assistant. The selection committee is asking to see us right now."

Gerard pushed back his chair and made to stand. Then, seeming to think better of it, he frowned thoughtfully at Hazel. "Before we go, what would you say about Victoria if someone asked you?"

Hazel nodded. "Victoria might not be the best all-around angler. If that's what you're looking for, then both Seth and Henry probably have her beat. But that's just experience. Besides, the job is about more than that, isn't it? And Victoria wants *this* job more than either of them. I would say she *needs* this job, but that feels a bit dramatic and would maybe be overstepping on my part.

"Honestly, she's better suited to it, and the job is better suited to her. She brings this passion and energy to everything she does. She's just…magnetic. If anyone who is even remotely interested in fishing watches her or listens to her for three seconds, they'll want to *be* her. Just that voice of hers alone is hypnotic, right? But it's more than that.

"You've seen the way people take to her. They want to know her, be her fishing buddy. She makes the whole pro angler fantasy real and accessible because she's so gracious and genuine and approachable. It means folks will buy whatever it is she's selling."

Several silent seconds followed as everyone appeared transfixed.

"Wow," Gerard eventually muttered.

"Yep, nailed it," Marissa said, pushing to her feet. "Come on. We need to go."

Quick goodbyes followed, and they hurried away. Henry and Seth both got on their phones to read the article.

"Finished?" Hazel asked them a few minutes later when a frowning Seth looked up.

"Yes. The story isn't even about her. This is a hit piece on Victoria's ex-husband."

"Did you know that he's running for district attorney?"

"Yeah," Seth confirmed. "Victoria is collateral damage in a political campaign."

"That's the way it appears to me, too," Henry agreed.

They finished their drinks and continued to discuss the situation. Marissa texted to let them know that reporters were camped out in the lobby and the conference area. When it was time to go, they paid their bill and headed back across the street to the hotel. To avoid the main entrance, they used a keycard and went through a side door and rode an escalator up to the conference area. Only to discover that Marissa was right; it was packed with people.

"Reporter," Henry said quickly as one particularly alert man noticed them and broke away from the crowd.

All smiles, like they were old friends, he approached and said, "Henry, hi. Nice to see you again. You must be Seth James. My name is David Belt, with the *Florida Navigator*. Can you gentlemen spare a moment for a quick chat?"

"Afraid not," Seth replied in a not-quite-as-friendly tone. "We have to get to a thing."

Seth kept walking. Henry was one step ahead of him. With Hazel flanking him on the other side, they managed to skirt the crowd still clustered in front of the elevators. Where the hallway narrowed, a bottleneck of people halted their progress. Two security guards were keeping the mob at bay. Upon spotting Seth and Henry, one of them waved and stepped forward to meet them.

That's when someone else realized who they were. Questions were shouted, and cameras flashed, but not for long as they were swiftly escorted inside the room. Where there were more newspeople. Seth braced himself, but they all kept a respectful distance.

Under the right conditions, Seth would have

taken the time to appreciate the elegant atmosphere, including the vintage-inspired angling gear decorating the space. It felt wrong to indulge without Victoria there.

In addition to the three finalists and their respective guests, the head table was slated to include the Romeo family, Marissa, Gerard and other key company people along with their partners or guests. Henry remained near the door, waiting for his daughter to arrive. Bering had texted to say that he, Tag and Cricket were standing in line and would be seated at a nearby table.

"Do you really believe all of that?" Seth asked Hazel once they'd found their places. "About Victoria possibly being innocent?"

"I don't know what to believe yet. I need more information. Which I'm going to get. And even if Vic did make a mistake as a teenager, something I think most of us on this planet can relate to, and even if it was a crime, she doesn't deserve the treatment she's getting. That Olivia person—I don't even want to call her a reporter—deserves to be called out."

"I agree with that. What can we do?"

"I'm working on it."

There was no time to discuss it further because the Romeo Reels people were now filtering into the room. Soon they gathered around the table, and greetings and small talk ensued while everyone settled into their places. Henry and his daughter arrived, taking two of the final three seats. Everyone was smiling and laughing, but to Seth, the atmosphere felt forced. There was an underlying tension and he knew he wasn't the only one who felt it.

Then Marissa appeared and, standing between him and Henry, leaned in to say, "The CEO will be making an announcement."

Three people were bunched near the podium as if gearing up to start the proceedings, but the room was still buzzing with conversation when Seth's phone, tucked inside the pocket of his jacket, vibrated with a call. Making him cringe a little, both because he realized he'd forgotten to silence it and also because he didn't want to silence it in case Victoria called. While his fingers fumbled to find the right button to silence it, he saw Quinn's smiling face lighting up the screen.

Which gave him pause. Why would Quinn be calling now? A text wouldn't be unusual, but a call felt off. He very much wanted to answer, but now a man stood behind the podium, fiddling with the microphone.

Seth silenced the call and began tapping out a text. Before he could finish, a message popped on the screen. And for a horrifying moment, the world stopped spinning. If anyone else he knew had sent the same two words, he wouldn't have a clue what they meant, but from Quinn, that was all it took to communicate a tragedy: Scarlett. Cottonmouth.

Bolting upright, he nearly toppled his chair.

"Good evening, and welcome, everyone," Microphone Man said at the same time.

"Awfully confident there, aren't you, James?" Wyatt joked. "They haven't announced the winner yet."

Seth ignored him as he attempted to absorb the news, the repercussions; Scarlett had been bitten by a cottonmouth snake.

"Seth?" Hazel tugged on his sleeve. "What's wrong?"

Head shaking, he sat again, handing her his phone so she could read the message. How quickly could he get there?

"Oh no!" she whispered before passing it to Henry.

Henry paled. "She's only eleven," he said aloud, blatantly ignoring the man at the microphone.

Seth looked at him. "I have to go."

Everyone at the table was staring curiously at them now.

"Of course, you do," Henry agreed. "Do you want me to book you a flight?"

"Hazel can do it. She's like a professional."

Hazel, already on her phone, started nodding. "It's already done. You're flying to New Orleans because that's the only direct flight leaving anytime soon. I'm getting you a car, too. Don't worry about packing all of your stuff. I'll do that. Just grab what you need and go. Get moving. I'll text you all the information you need."

"Keep us posted," Henry said and then a more urgent, "Seth!"

Seth met his gaze again.

"We'll get this straightened out. All you need to do right now is be there for them however you can."

"Seth!" Marissa, who was seated next to Henry and listening to the exchange, had gone wide-eyed. "You're going somewhere? Where are you going?"

He stood again. "I'm sorry, but there's an emergency. I have to go. My sister and Henry will explain."

"Can't you wait a few more minutes?" she asked.

"No," he said. "I can't." Turning away, he added softly, "I never should have waited this long." He should have gone after Victoria the moment he'd realized she'd gone.

Seth hurried out the door and into the hall.

Pausing, he looked right and then left, trying to decide which direction would give him the best chance of avoiding people and reporters.

He went left, remembering there were stairs down to the lobby. From there, he could take a different set of stairs up a few flights, grab an elevator, and hopefully avoid…

"Excuse me?" a woman's voice called out. Seconds later, she caught up to him. Stretching out a hand, she said, "Seth James, right? It's nice to meet you. My name is Olivia Wallace from Gulf States Law Dog. Any chance I could speak with you about Victoria Thibodeaux?"

Seth stopped so quickly that the woman nearly stumbled, trying to keep him close. "Olivia Wallace," he repeated. "You've made quite a name for yourself with this story, haven't you?"

"Thank you. Would you care to comment on the situation?"

"That wasn't a compliment. What situation would that be? The one where people are now repeating bits and pieces of your *story* that is only *part* of a story? An unsubstantiated one at that. Go back to journalism school and retake your ethics course, and then I'll consider giving you a comment."

"Excuse me?" Olivia looked affronted. "What are you accusing me of exactly?"

"I read your so-called article. You reported that Victoria Thibodeaux committed a crime, and you did so without any evidence to corroborate the claim. What you did was unconscionable."

"I cited a source. The fact that she even has a sealed record indicates criminal activity."

"Do you personally know for a *fact* that she has a sealed record?"

"I don't... Um."

"And isn't outing a sealed juvenile record illegal?"

"Well, in certain cases—"

"And you have an anonymous source with no documentation."

"Who is extremely credible," Olivia said defensively, although Seth could see she was losing steam.

"Here's an actual real tip for you from a person who isn't an anonymous coward. What's the real story here, Olivia? Do you even know? That's the one you should be chasing. And I'm going on record stating that Victoria Thibodeaux is being unfairly maligned. By you. If you want to go after Austin Galbraith, go after him. Leave Victoria alone."

CHAPTER NINETEEN

"WITH SUCH DISTINCTLY delineated fang imprints we are confident it was a full-impact bite."

Fang imprints. Full-impact bite. The words were like dialogue from a horror film. Victoria had lived her entire life in the South. Much of it outdoors where snakes reigned supreme. Showing respect and exercising caution was second nature, all the while knowing an altercation was always a possibility. Quinn's presence in their life added additional knowledge and awareness. But it wasn't something she dwelled on. A fact she was incredibly grateful for at this moment because the reality was so much worse than she could have anticipated.

Victoria's stomach churned but her focus remained razor sharp as she listened to the doctor.

"It was definitely a cottonmouth and a large snake, not huge, but your daughter is thin and light. That can mean a high ratio of venom. The photo and details from your daughter's friend, Quinn, were very helpful. Dr. Duquette was wise in calling ahead and luckily Dr. Larkin was available. He's our snakebite guy, one of the leading experts in the country. He's administered more antivenom and is in with Scarlett now. We won't know the extent of damage for a while."

"But she's going to live." Victoria didn't ask. She stated it as a fact. Because her daughter had to live. Scarlett was her heart, her soul, the best parts of her and the only thing that truly mattered.

"I am very confident on that count. Cottonmouth bites are rarely fatal. Barring an infection or a reaction to the antivenom, which so far has been smooth sailing, she should have an excellent long-term recovery. However, she is in an incredible amount of pain, which we're attempting to manage."

Victoria blinked away tears. Mémé squeezed her hand. Her mama exhaled a relieved breath. Immediately shifting beyond relief about Scarlett's prognosis, the next concern had her recalling one of Quinn's many lessons. *The pain of a cottonmouth bite is like a searing red hot poker beneath your skin. Except it doesn't stop. It just keeps burning and burning...* She would give anything if she could take it and bear it in Scarlett's place. No doubt, poor Quinn was thinking about that, too.

Her heart twisted with anguish and love

for the boy, too. She worried about the guilt he'd feel because they'd been out searching for snakes. But Victoria knew it could just as easily have occurred when they were fishing, bird-watching, exploring, working around the resort or any of the other myriad activities they got up to on a daily basis.

Right at dusk, they'd been on their way back to Quinn's house when Scarlett had spotted a frog. Moving closer for a better look, she hadn't realized that hidden in the reeds something else was stalking it, too. Without warning, unusual for the species according to Quinn, the cotton-mouth had struck her forearm.

Because he knew it could be important, Quinn had snapped a photo of the snake before scooping Scarlett up in his arms and sprinting for home. Somehow, he'd managed to call his dad Griffin who'd met the kids in the driveway, loaded them into the car, and then raced to the local hospital. Being a doctor himself, he'd had the foresight to call ahead. They'd given her a dose of antivenom and loaded her into a helicopter and flown her to Baton Rouge where Dr. Larkin had been waiting.

"What about her arm? Will she be able to use her hand?" Austin asked, which irritated Victoria, even though she knew that wasn't fair. Thorough, meticulous and detail oriented, those were some of the man's only positive traits. He'd want to know all the statistics.

"I can't predict anything yet. The swelling is significant. And, as I mentioned, tissue damage begins with envenomation. Muscle damage is inevitable but the antivenom halts the progression. It'll be days before we have an idea."

Victoria had had enough medical talk for the time being. There would be bridges to cross no doubt, but for now she needed to be with Scarlett. "Can I see her?"

"Of course. But we're going to do one person at a time for now." A nurse appeared and led Victoria to Scarlett's room.

Seth wasn't fazed by the fact that it was the middle of the night when he landed in New Orleans. He found several texts waiting, including one from Quinn relaying that Scarlett was in a hospital in Baton Rouge. Another contained his rental car information, thank you, Hazel. After picking up the car, he drove straight to the hospital. A quick stop at the information desk told him where the waiting room was located. His plan consisted of camping out there until Victoria or her mom or grandma appeared. If no one showed by morning, he'd text Quinn and make a new plan.

Walking through the main lobby, he no-

ticed two people on a sofa. A man was reading with a kid curled up beside him. The kid's
face was half-covered by his arm but he recognized Quinn.

Approaching the man, Seth whispered, "Dr.
Duquette?"

The man smiled. "You must be Seth."

At Seth's nod, he said, "Please, call me Griffin." They exchanged handshakes and Seth
took a seat in an adjacent chair.

"Do you know how Scarlett is doing?"

Seth expected a complicated summary seeing as how the man was a biologist. But that
wasn't what he got. In layman's terms, Griffin
explained the severity of the bite, but that Scarlett had received multiple vials of antivenom to
which she was responding well. In the doctors'
opinions, and his, she was out of the woods, or
at least through the most dangerous part.

Seth felt a surge of relief at the news. Nudging his chin toward Quinn, he asked, "How is
he?"

"Worried. Guilt-ridden. He refuses to leave."
Griffin scrubbed a hand across his jaw. "He
says he's staying as long as Scarlett has to stay.
This is one of those parenting moments that
leave you completely baffled. Do I force him to
go home and get some proper sleep and food?

I don't know. I wouldn't want to leave either. I don't want to leave.

"Scarlett means so much to Quinn. To my wife and me, too. These two kids are like…" He shook his head. "Soul mates? No, I don't like what that implies." He slipped Seth a small smile. "They are just simpatico—you know what I mean? Since they were this tall." He held out a hand a couple of feet from the floor. "I've never seen anything like it. I've certainly never had a friendship like theirs."

Seth agreed. They acted like siblings, the kind who genuinely liked each other like him and Hazel. "I can't imagine anyone blaming him."

"No, of course not. The Thibodeauxs are the best people I know. My wife and I work a lot. Too much, if I'm being honest. She's a doctor, too. Microbiology research. I probably wouldn't work as much if Quinn didn't have Scarlett and her family. When he was little, I offered to pay them because he was there so much." Chuckling at the memory, he added, "That did not go over well with Ms. Effie."

Seth smiled. "I can imagine."

"They've always treated Quinn like part of the family. The kids are over there more often, but we treat Scarlett the same way when she's with us."

Quinn stirred and then popped upright. "Seth!" He shot off the sofa and into Seth's arms. "You came."

Seth hugged him. "Of course, I did. You got my back, kiddo, I got yours. That's how this works."

Quinn stepped back and nodded somberly. "This is good. Victoria is going to be so happy."

Until that moment, Seth hadn't realized just how much he wanted that to be true.

"SETH IS HERE?" Victoria stared at her grandmother and tried to process this next revelation. Revelations comprised her life right now, didn't they? One soul-shattering shock after another. Admittedly, this one wasn't nearly as traumatic as the last few. Even though it might not be a good move on his part, she couldn't deny the mix of happiness and relief blooming inside of her.

"That's what I said. He was in the waiting area when I came through. We talked a bit." Effie moved around the hospital bed where Scarlett was sleeping. Leaning over, she pressed a soft kiss to her great-granddaughter's cheek. "Our poor baby."

"How? Why is he here? What do I say?"

"From what I understand, Quinn texted him last night and he caught the first flight he could get. Been here since early this morning, with Quinn who still refuses to leave, and his daddy. As for that second question, I don't think you'll have to say much at all. For now, anyway." Mémé gave her a pointed look and Victoria knew what it meant. She wanted her to "make this right." But there were things her grandmother didn't know. Victoria could only imagine what she would say if she knew the whole story. She didn't want to think about that now anyway. It no longer mattered. Scarlett could have died.

But Seth mattered.

And yet, Victoria stayed put, trying to get a handle on her emotions and thoughts. Who had gotten the job? She wanted that for him, even as she'd be sad for Henry. If he had gotten it, he *definitely* should not be here but now that he was, she realized how much she wanted him to be. But…

"Victoria!" Only her grandmother could manage to make a whisper sound stern.

Turning her head, she met the scowl she knew would be waiting. "Hmm?"

Mémé's features softened along with her tone, "Stop thinking so hard and go talk to the man. You don't have to resolve everything right now. There *will* be time for that later, however.

Because, Victoria, I know there's something you're not telling me."

"Mémé, I don't—"

"Shh. We'll talk about it later. Seth is worried about our peanut here, too. And Quinn. Those two boys are peas from the same pod. Just... let him be here for you." Her grandmother nodded toward the table. "There's your coffee. Now take it and get."

"Yes, ma'am." Standing, she picked up the drink, walked around the bed and kissed her grandmother on the forehead. "Thank you for the coffee," she whispered, but they both knew the words encompassed so much more.

In the waiting room, she was surprised to discover Seth perched on a sofa by himself watching a cooking show on a muted television. It didn't take him long to spot her. He stood, and then watched as she crossed the room to him.

"Seth..." Shaking her head, she blinked away fresh tears.

"Hey," he said, his voice soft and brimming with sympathy and love. And because she craved the comfort she knew she'd find there, she absolutely could not resist walking forward the last few steps. He reached out, took her into the circle of his arms, and held her close. Victoria laid her cheek against his chest right in that sweet spot she loved. Squeezing her eyes shut, she tried to memorize every sensation: the perfect pressure of his strong arms, the warmth of his skin, the delicious scent of him mixed with a hint of coffee and peppermint. She'd thought she'd never have this chance again.

"Seth," she breathed him in. "I…" *I love you.* The words escaped from her heart but then got jammed in her throat. She needed to tell him how she felt, but she didn't want him to think the declaration was due to gratitude or exhaustion or some other extraneous emotion. Waiting for the right moment would be better.

"I'm so glad you're here."

"Me too." Another long soothing moment passed before he asked, "How is she?"

Victoria liked that his first question was about Scarlett. Staying wrapped in his arms forever was incredibly tempting. Unfortunately, being a grown-up was more important so she stepped back enough to see his face. Keeping her hand in his, she gestured toward the sofa. He followed her lead and they sat together, side by side, and that felt amazing, too. Having him here with her felt so…right. She knew she should send him away, but she didn't have the strength.

"Good, considering. I mean, she's going to live through this so…"

"That is the best news. Any idea how long they're keeping her?"

"Dr. Larkin says a couple of days at least. In case of infection or complications. It's so ugly, Seth. I'm no doctor but it looks bad. I'm worried she'll lose her hand."

He gave her hand a reassuring squeeze. "Okay. Well, let's let the doctors worry about that for now. Quinn's dad says she has the best doctor."

"Yes. Extragrateful for Dr. Larkin and to Griffin for knowing to call him. All the doctors and nurses have been amazing."

"What can I do?"

"You can tell me if you got the job?"

"Oh, that's right, you don't know..." He raked a hand through his hair. "So, after I left last night they announced—"

"Wait, you left before the announcement?"

"Yes, when Quinn texted, we were all at our table waiting for the ceremony to begin. Anyway, the CEO announced that they were holding off on making a decision until they could do an investigation into your situation."

"An investigation?"

"Their legal department isn't sure how to handle these circumstances."

Oddly, the news felt like a disappointment. She'd accepted her fate. All an investigation would accomplish was more misery, more time for her name to be dragged through the mud.

"But I withdrew."

He shrugged a shoulder. "Apparently that didn't satisfy them. That's all I know. You should be expecting a phone call from Marissa. They know about Scarlett, so it probably won't be soon. Do you want to tell me what really happened?"

In her mentally overwhelmed state, the temptation was nearly irresistible. But the facts hadn't changed and confiding in him would only involve him. And possibly cause him future harm. She'd confessed to Henry in a moment of weakness and now could only hope that he remained unscathed. A possibility that seemed more likely since she and Henry weren't the ones romantically involved. She didn't want to risk Seth's future, too. She wouldn't send him away, but he had to know what he was facing.

"Seth, you know you shouldn't be here, right? An investigation isn't going to change the outcome for me. The decision is still going to come down to you and Henry. Just being here with me could hurt your chances."

"It's my decision to be here. I want to be here, if you want me."

"I do. Of course, I do. I'm so glad you came."

One arm was already around her shoulders, and now he looped the other around her body and pulled her close. "Good. Me too. We can talk about the rest later, whenever you're ready. Right now, all you need to do is concentrate on Scarlett."

LATER THAT DAY, they moved a stable Scarlett out of intensive care and into a room on the fourth floor. With plenty of people to tend to the patient, Seth tried to figure out the best way to help. Overhearing a conversation between Effie and Corinne as they devised a schedule for working at the resort and spending time at the hospital gave him an idea. One that might be the answer for him and someone else.

He found Quinn and his dad in the new waiting room.

"Hey, buddy, how you holding up?"

Quinn's cheerful smile was a bright contrast to the bluish crescents beneath his tired eyes. Poor kid looked dead on his feet. "Sitting with Scarlett for two hours was great. We had milkshakes and french fries and watched a movie until she fell asleep. It was awesome. She's going to be okay."

"That is awesome," Seth agreed. "She's doing really well, isn't she?" At Quinn's nod, he said "I have a plan I wanted to run by you."

"Sure."

"So, I'd like to make things easier for Victoria and everyone. There's not a lot I can do here at the hospital, but I've been thinking there's quite a bit I could do at Bayou Doré. Right now, Effie and Corinne are planning on taking turns driving back and forth. But they're already tired, and Victoria isn't going anywhere. She shouldn't have to. But maybe I could go and hold down the fort."

Quinn nodded, as if he agreed this did indeed sound reasonable.

"Problem is, I don't really know what I'm doing. You still planning on sticking around here until Scarlett is released? Because I could seriously use your help. Maybe we could work it out so your dad or I could bring you back here for visits."

Quinn's forehead crinkled. Seth could tell he was thinking it over. He glanced at Griffin. "What do you think, Dad?"

"It's totally up to you, Quinn. I told you I'd stay here at the hospital as long as you wanted. But I think Seth is on to something. Imagine what a relief it would be to all of the Thibodeauxs if they knew the resort was taken care of so they could just focus on Scarlett. I am certain they'd feel better about trusting Seth with the task if you were there. You know the place as well as they do. And Seth is right, I'll bring you back to visit whenever you want."

Quinn agreed with a solemn, "I'll do it. Let me make sure it's okay with Scarlett first. I told her I was staying."

FOR THE NEXT four days Seth and Quinn were acting comanagers of the resort. Quinn worked harder than Seth had ever seen a kid work. They were up before dawn to clean and stock the restrooms. Each day brought a new adventure of checking in new guests, saying goodbye to others, answering the phone, answering emails, answering questions, making reservations, canceling reservations, rearranging reservations, renting boats and equipment, selling supplies like soda, ice and countless bags of chips and marshmallows. They also cleaned the cabins, made beds, picked up garbage and performed every other task that was required no matter how big or small.

Some they had to manage more creatively than others, like the guy who had them stumped when he came into the office and demanded to move campsites because his had too many mosquitoes.

Studying the reservation list, Quinn, in a brilliant move, suggested, "Okay, B-7 is available. It's further from the lake so that ought to do the trick."

A completely illogical solution, but they didn't see the guy again until he checked out the next day, a happy camper.

A couple of afternoons, Griffin drove Quinn to the hospital. When the evening chores were finished, Seth would wait for Victoria to call. She'd update him about Scarlett's condition, express her concerns about her recovery, and tell him about her day. Seth never pressured her to discuss her past or their future. Instead, he did his best to lighten her mood with funny stories about his and Quinn's exploits as comanagers. Then he'd fall into bed, exhausted and satisfied that he was doing what he could to make her life easier. And hopeful that he might finally, truly, earn Victoria's trust.

WITH MÉMÉ SITTING with Scarlett and Mama off getting takeout, Victoria found a quiet spot outside in the hospital's courtyard to take care of the correspondence she'd been neglecting. First, she texted Henry with an update about Scarlett's condition. She was careful not to reference her "situation" or the investigation. She didn't want any kind of record floating around out there that could be hacked or stolen and-or misconstrued.

Moving on to email, she tackled the resort's messages first as they'd be the easiest to manage. She'd given Seth a lesson in how to handle reservations and respond to common inquiries. Anything else that he wasn't sure about she instructed him to leave in the inbox for her to handle. There was only one message on behalf of a family interested in renting the whole place for a reunion. She felt a welling of gratitude toward Seth and Quinn for watching over the place.

In her personal inbox, she found an email from Marissa inquiring after Scarlett's condition and asking that she call as soon as she felt comfortable. She and Gerard had already sent Scarlett flowers. Victoria was touched, and in the process of responding when she heard someone approach.

"Excuse me, Victoria?"

Victoria looked up and into the face of Olivia Wallace. "Are you kidding me?" She started to stand.

Olivia thrust out a hand. "Please!" She cried, and then fired off a barrage of words, "Wait! I know I am the last person you want to see right now, but I need to talk to you. It's important."

"You actually think we're going to have a conversation?"

"I am so sorry," she said, as if Victoria hadn't

refused her request. She placed an envelope on the table in front of her. "This is a written apology. Law Dog will be posting this along with a follow-up story soon."

Victoria sighed. "That's nice. But the damage is done, isn't it?" Victoria wanted to accuse her of ruining her life, but Olivia Wallace wasn't responsible for that. She was just the messenger. An irresponsible one, yes, but not the underlying cause. That didn't mean she wanted to have a chat with the woman, however.

She began gathering her things even as Olivia took a seat across from her. "You know what the weird part about all of this is? That story isn't even about you. It's about your ex-husband. He's the one who is supposed to be suffering the damage."

"Yeah, well, he's rubber and I'm glue."

"What?"

"You know that old kids' saying 'I'm rubber, you're glue. Whatever you say bounces off me and sticks to you'? That's the way it works with Austin. Everything bounces off him and then sticks to me."

"Me too," Olivia said and barked out a sharp laugh. "He's getting me fired." Then, turning serious, she eyed Victoria thoughtfully. "It's true, isn't it?"

"What are you referring to?"

"My source, who ghosted me, said that Austin was the one who committed the crime. You were innocent. He said that Austin implicated you somehow. But your name is in the notes as 'admitting to everything' and 'taking a deal,' so I printed that. Irresponsible, on my part, not to research that more thoroughly. Should have left your name out of the story."

"Someone else would have found it," Victoria pointed out. "Our relationship wasn't a secret."

"I know," Olivia agreed. "I just wish it hadn't been me."

"Who is this source?"

"I don't know. That's the problem. The guy assured me that if I printed this story it would be Austin who was raked over the coals. The veracity of Austin's account would be investigated. And there were others, hc claimed, who would come forward. But that didn't happen, and my source disappeared. And then it got picked up but *you* were the story. Probably through searches because of the outdoor show. Romeo Reels made you a hot ticket. Then I got caught up in *that*, and literally chased my own story. So dumb. I'm not proud of this. Seth James was right about that part."

"Right about what?" she asked, her pulse

shifting into overdrive at the mention of his name. "When did you talk to Seth James?"

"Oh, I didn't talk to him—he talked to me. Told me off is more like it." Olivia explained how she'd found Seth in the hall and how he'd defended Victoria. Causing a fresh outpouring of love on Victoria's part because she'd left him without a word, and he'd still believed in her.

"That's when I realized I was slamming you when I should have been defending you because if you have a juvenile record that has been sealed and or expunged, no one should even know about it, much less write about it.

"But listen, you already know all of that. And I know nothing I say is going to help you now. Not like you need. But what I can offer you is the chance to tell your story. If you want to. I recognize you have no reason to trust me, other than the fact that I've also been...*glued* by Austin Galbraith."

Victoria chuckled at that.

"I'm a firm believer in karma and the idea that bad people will eventually get what's coming to them. But I've also noticed that sometimes karma needs a little nudge."

CHAPTER TWENTY

THEY KEPT SCARLETT in the hospital for three more days. Seth and Quinn had hung a huge "Welcome Home Scarlett" banner across the porch railing. Inside, they had flowers and cupcakes waiting. Twinkle lights and streamers decorated Scarlett's room. A pile of books they'd ordered online sat on the nightstand, and a giant plush fish pillow lay across the head of her bed.

Seeing her smile as she took it all in made Seth's heart squeeze in a particularly sweet way. As did the hug she gave him when he presented her with a card along with several lures he'd picked up for her at the show.

And her expression was pure gold when she studied the card. He'd signed, "Mr. James," then crossed that out and replaced it with, "Seth."

Grinning, she held the card up for Victoria's inspection. "Mama, can I please call him Seth now?"

Victoria chuckled and shook her head. "Yes, you may, Scarlett."

"Thank you. And thank you, Seth. I can't wait to try 'em out."

Scarlett wore out quickly from all the excitement. Soon Victoria and Corinne got her settled in her room to rest and have a nap.

Seth waited nervously while Effie walked around, inspecting the house, the yard, the office, and even taking a stroll around the campsites. Finally, standing outside the office, hands on hips, she frowned at a flowerpot beside the door. After plucking a wilted bloom, she studied Seth for a long moment. "Well, you boys have certainly done a passable job, haven't you?"

Seth wasn't sure what to make of her statement, but Quinn was elated, assuring him that "passable" was the highest of compliments where Ms. Effie was concerned. So Seth accepted the commendation with an optimistic satisfaction that lasted another two days. Because that's how long it took him to accept that he and Victoria were never going to get the happy-ever-after he'd been wishing for.

SETH HAD JUST finished giving Victoria a hand with prepping the bass boat for a guided trip she was conducting the next morning when he paused to admire the sky. A swirl of clouds and color were teaming up to present a show-stopping sunset. Victoria followed his lead, and in silent consensus they walked over and sat in the same spot where he'd settled that first afternoon he'd arrived there and watched Scarlett land the bass. He felt so comfortable with this family, and in this remarkable place that it was difficult to believe only a month had passed since then.

And yet the comfort extended only so far where Victoria was concerned. He needed to acknowledge the painful truth.

Like she could sense that he was going to broach the difficult topic of their future, she took his hand and said, "Seth, I am so grateful for everything you've done for us. For me, for Scarlett, looking after the resort. And Quinn. I was so worried, thinking he'd never get over the guilt. I thought it might drive him and Scarlett apart. But if anything, it seems to have brought them closer."

"I agree. I'm happy about that, too."

Capturing his gaze, she finally said the words he'd been waiting for, longing for, "I love you."

But now they were like a bittersweet arrow to his heart. He almost wished she hadn't said them because he knew it no longer mattered. Not in the way he needed it to.

"I should have told you that ages ago. Even before I quit and came home. On the airplane

I was so sad that I hadn't told you how I felt. Then, I wanted to say it when I first saw you in the hospital, but I didn't want you to think I was saying it because I was grateful you were there or something. But I do, I love you, Seth. I've never been in love before. Not like this. And so, I kept waiting for a big moment so I could share my big feelings." She let out a bright little laugh. "I don't want to wait anymore."

It hurt too much to look at her face. Nodding slowly, he let his gaze wander across the brilliant colors, now beginning their dance across the surface of the lake.

"Thank you for telling me," he said, knowing at that moment that he would never get over her. She would always be the one, the face he saw before he fell asleep at night, and his first thought in the morning. "I'm convinced it's my lot in life to fall in love with women who don't love me the same way I love them."

"What do you mean? I do love you."

"But not like I need you to. You still don't trust me enough to tell me."

"That's not it!" Seth was glad that she didn't pretend not to know what he was talking about. "It's not that I don't trust you. It's more complicated than that. I *can't* tell you. For your own good."

There was a burning pain right in the center of his chest. "You don't get it, do you? You can't pick and choose the things you trust me about, Vic. It doesn't work like that."

"Seth, what I did, what happened to me… There are mistakes in life that you cannot undo, mistakes that you have to pay for forever. This is mine. And I've accepted it now. I'm fine, and I'm moving on. I am so grateful for everything I have, for the amazing experience, and especially for the time I've had with you."

Seth winced a little at the finality there. The absolute conviction that this was over between them.

"What if I said I was going to withdraw, too?"

"No. I won't let you do that." Tears shone in her eyes and her voice was raspy with emotion when she said, "Scarlett is going to be okay, and my life will go back to where it was before. It's a good life. It's what I want. But your life is only beginning. No matter what. Even if you don't get the Romeo Reels job, you'll get something even better. Being with me would only hold you back."

"This is what you want?" he repeated doubtfully, frustration mixing with his sadness.

"Yes."

Seth knew he was going to hurt her. What he wanted was to take her in his arms and hold her and tell her he'd be there for her always. No matter what she'd done or what she chose to do about it. Even though he'd be willing to do just that, he wouldn't. Not when she wouldn't accept the truth. He would not enable her belief in this falsehood. By not telling him, she was hurting them both.

"That's not the truth, Victoria. That's the relief talking, and I understand that to a degree. But you're hiding behind Scarlett's injury, so you don't have to face this, whatever it is. Whatever this *thing* is that you don't trust me enough to share. As much as it hurts me, I have to accept that it's your choice to not tell me.

"But don't forget that I know who you are. The person I met the first day I came here. The determined woman who told me she wanted to win would not accept this.

"You told me you would do whatever it took to succeed. And then you set about proving that in all the best ways. As I got to know you, I realized it wasn't just the job you wanted. You want *more* for your life, for Scarlett's life, and you should get that. Not settle for less than you deserve."

"Seth, please… You don't understand."

"Maybe not. But if you give up without a fight, you will regret it. You can keep reassuring yourself that you're content with your decision, but I don't see how you're going to be able to live with the disappointment once the truth sinks in.

She looked stricken like he'd known she would. Worse, even. Tormented. Tears shimmered in her gorgeous green eyes as she stared at him, swallowing and blinking like she couldn't quite believe what she'd just heard. It nearly killed him. He wanted to take it all back.

"Seth, please, I don't—"

The pain now roared in his chest. "Once the worry about Scarlett wears off, and you see what you've lost, you will be right back where you were and… And because I love you, I have to go."

He stood. "I want to say goodbye to your family and Quinn. Of course, I'll be in touch with Scarlett. Goodbye, Victoria."

VICTORIA WATCHED SETH walk away with her heart and wondered how much agony she could endure. Curling her hands, she pressed them to her waist and rocked forward in her chair. Surely, she'd reached her quota of suffering by now.

She'd known this topic was going to come up, had even thought about broaching the subject herself just to get it over with. She'd known they were on borrowed time. But selfishly, she'd wanted it to last. Thought maybe they could get by until Romeo Reels made their decision and he had to move on. She loved him. She didn't want him leaving this way. But she couldn't ask him to stay, couldn't let his future be ruined by her past.

Sitting up again, she watched him cross the grassy expanse, each step taking him farther and farther from her. It took every last bit of her willpower not to get up and run after him. Panic built inside of her. She stood, her heart skittering, her gaze bouncing everywhere but on the house. Moving toward the dock, she climbed aboard her boat and fished the key from her pocket. Then she turned over the engine, flipped on the running lights and motored out onto the lake.

SETH DROVE NORTH toward Lafayette with no idea where he was going to go. A hotel room in New Orleans, he supposed, where he would wait to hear from Romeo Reels. Beyond the airport, he hadn't seen the city. Not that he was in the mood for sightseeing. Then again, the only thing he was truly in the mood for was some serious self-pity. He pulled off the road to get a cup of coffee. A check of his phone revealed a voicemail from Marissa, a text from Hazel asking him to call ASAP and another missed call from Henry.

He called Henry first. He didn't have the energy for the interrogation he knew would come from his sister.

"Hey," Henry said, picking up on the second ring. "Are you still with Victoria?"

"Nope. We… I… No."

"Ah. I see. I am truly sorry to hear that."

Seth exhaled a ragged sigh. "Me too."

"Where are you?"

"I'm not sure, exactly. Just left her place about an hour ago. I'm driving to…not sure yet. New Orleans, I guess."

"How about a road trip?"

"What?"

"I'm in Houston with Hazel. We're probably only a few hours from you. Four, at the most."

"You're with my sister?"

"Yes, he is," Hazel's voice came through the line, loudly, and he imagined her leaning in and shouting at Henry's phone. "And don't think I didn't notice that you called Henry first. Before me. I will forgive you if you head west immediately and drive here to apologize in person."

Seth laughed and ignored her complaint. "Henry, what is going on? What are you guys doing in Houston?"

"We're here for Victoria. We think we've

found the truth. And even better, a way to prove it. We'll tell you when you get here. Did you get a call from Marissa yet?"

"Yes, a voicemail that I haven't listened to yet. What's going on?"

"They've made a decision and want to meet with us."

"When? Where?"

"Monday morning. The where is yet to be determined."

"HOW DID IT GO?" Victoria asked Scarlett the next afternoon when she came through the door, back from her outing with Austin. At least Austin had been reasonable about Scarlett's visitation while she was recovering. He'd been over to visit, but this was the first time she'd left the house with him.

"Fine," Scarlett returned flatly, and Victoria could see it was anything but. Her gaze flitted around, at the stairs that led up to her room, toward the kitchen where Corinne was rattling pans, then at the sofa where Victoria was sitting. Up and down, back and forth, trying to decide.

"What did you guys do?" Vic asked in an attempt to keep her in the room and talking.

"We went out to lunch, and then Daddy took me out for ice cream so we could *talk*." The

emphasis on "talk" indicating she'd been sub-
jected to one of Austin's lectures rather than
engaging in any kind of meaningful dialogue.

"What did you talk about?"

"I'm not supposed to say."

Victoria tensed, thinking fast. "What do you
mean—you're not supposed to say? Your dad
is asking you to keep something from me?"

Staring down at her shoes now, Scarlett worried the toe of one against the hardwood floor
like she did when she was anxious. When she
lifted her head, tears were glistening on her
cheeks, and her voice broke on a sob that nearly
split Victoria's already-fragile heart in two.
"Mama, I don't want to…"

"Scarlett, honey, what is it?" Victoria said, on
her feet and moving, and then she was pulling
Scarlett into her arms. She knew she needed to
stay calm, but what in the world had he said to
her? Scarlett's body shook from the sobs, and
the sound of her anguish had Victoria bracing
for the worst.

When she'd quieted enough, Victoria asked,
"You don't want to what, Scarlett?"

"I don't want to see him anymore. Do I have
to?"

Leading her over to the sofa, they sat together,
and Victoria answered carefully, "Maybe not. It
would mean going to court, but we could try. I

am willing to do that, Scarlett. What did he say that upset you? You can tell me. Even if he told you not to. You can always tell me. I'm your mother. Your father should not be telling you to keep secrets from me."

"That's what Quinn said, too."

"Quinn is a very smart boy and an excellent human. One of my favorites."

That produced a smile, which made Victoria feel a tiny bit better. She plucked some tissues from the box on the end table and handed a couple to Scarlett.

"So, you know Maya Courtright?"

"Yep." A girl on Scarlett's swim team.

"So, we were at Ollie's having dinner, and Maya and her family stopped by our table. Maya asked me if it was true that you were a criminal."

An invisible punch hit her right in the solar plexus. She forced herself to breathe. Why hadn't she anticipated this? How could she explain without explaining? Apparently, she soon learned, she didn't need to worry about that. Once again, Austin had it all figured out.

"Maya's mama said, 'Maya, honey, don't be rude.' And they left. Then dinner was all polite and awkward. Amber gave Daddy a bunch of dirty looks while he tried way too hard to act normal. Then Daddy dropped off Amber and

Avery and took me for ice cream. He was way too nice and used that voice—you know the one where he calls me *sugar* and acts like I'm still three years old?"

"I know the one," Vic said. It was all she could do not to smack him when he used that condescending tone on her and called her "cookie."

"He told me that other people besides Maya would probably say things about you, and maybe him, too. Because of what you did. He said he doesn't hold it against you, even though it's upsetting Amber and causing him problems with his campaign. He told me that back when you were a teenager, you committed a crime, but you aren't a bad person, you just made a bad mistake. If you had been older, you probably would have gone to jail. But he and Grandpa helped you. And you made it right by confessing. You were sorry about it and would never do anything like it again."

"He and Grandpa *helped* me?" she repeated.

"Yes. That's what he said. They helped you to see the right way and do the right thing."

That was it. The tipping point. Like the proverbial final straw, something snapped and broke inside of her.

"Mama, is it true? Are you a criminal?"

CHAPTER TWENTY-ONE

VICTORIA STAYED BY Scarlett's bedside until she fell asleep. She'd told her daughter everything, the whole story. It was a lot of information, and she could only hope Scarlett was mature enough to understand. She hadn't seemed surprised. Only relieved. They would go to court, and Victoria would fight for the right to tell her daughter the truth. Always.

But that wasn't the only fight ahead of her.

Flipping on the monitor they'd used when Scarlet was a baby, she went downstairs and found her mom still in the kitchen. And Mémé, too.

"Good, you're both here. I need to tell you guys some…things. It might take a while? Do you have time?"

The women shared long drawn-out looks. Mama muttered something unintelligible, but she recognized the relief on her face. Then they looked at Victoria, and Mémé said, "We've been waiting twelve years for this day, Victoria. Take all the time you need."

SHE'D BEEN AVOIDING the sitting area where she'd last seen Seth, where her soul had suffered what she'd believed was the final blow. Now she headed straight there, took a seat, inhaled a deep breath, and faced the anger head-on. She should have known better than to believe there would ever be an end to this where Austin was concerned. The hits would keep coming as long as she allowed herself to be his punching bag.

She'd never thought of herself as a coward. But Seth had been right about everything. Scarlett's injury had been an excuse not to face this. Deep down, her fear had been guiding her all along. She'd maneuvered around it and compensated for it the best she could. But she would never be able to move on until she faced this. Ended it.

Scarlett's life *was* more important. Life with Scarlett was the most important thing in the world. But her life was important, too. And what kind of life would they have together anyway if she no longer had her daughter's respect?

By lying to their daughter, the way he'd always lied to her, Austin had crossed a line. Lying about her to their daughter to save himself was unacceptable. Once again, he'd backed her into a corner. But this time, she would not stay there and cower. Austin's miscalculation, his mistake, the concept that he'd failed to grasp was that he'd finally taken too much. She no longer had anything left to lose.

Pulling her phone from her pocket, she hesitated only long enough to consider who she should call first. Seth deserved an apology and an explanation. She would beg him for another chance if that's what it took. But first, she needed to prove to him that she understood what he'd been trying to make her see. She wasn't afraid. Not anymore.

She slipped the card from her pocket, memorized the number, and then keyed it in.

Three rings and then, "Hello?"

"Olivia?"

"Yes, this is she."

"Hey, this is Victoria Thibodeaux."

"Victoria, hello. How are you? What can I do for you?"

"Olivia, it's time to tell my side of the story. The truth. This isn't just about me anymore. Plus, I'm hoping you would still like for us to give karma that little nudge."

"WE WERE BUSTED," Gordon Watts said, shaking his head. Then he dunked the chip he held into a cup of salsa and ate it in one bite. Wiping his mouth with a napkin, he decreed, "Aye! That's hot. Best salsa in Texas right here."

Chasing it with a sip of beer, he continued,

"Austin dumped out the cooler that held the turtles while I drove the boat. Good thing, too, there were at least two endangered species in there. But there was nothing we could do about the fish in the live well, or at least we weren't fast enough to figure it out. Or maybe it was because Austin had already set his mind on a different plan, but…"

Seth listened as the man sitting across from him and next to Hazel at an upscale Mexican restaurant in downtown Houston relayed the story that Victoria hadn't wanted to tell.

"When we got back to the dock, Austin sprinted on up to the house and fetched Victoria. I had no idea why at the time. I just thought he wanted her with him, I guess. Game wardens were hot on our tail. They'd already called the cops, who showed up soon after. We were both in law school and knew not to say a word. My father was a judge, too, and a friend of Linus's. I didn't know what they were planning until after it was done."

"It never occurred to you to speak up?" Henry asked. "Do the right thing?"

"Honestly, no. I was happy to get out of it. I was terrified of losing my law career before it ever got started, and even more afraid of what my dad would do. And secretly, I thought it was pretty cool. You know, Victoria taking the rap for her man."

Hazel turned toward him with the full force of her glare. "You have got to be kidding—"

"Whoa," Gordy said, and chuckled. "I know what you're thinking. But trust me, it can't be worse than what I think about myself. I am not proud. But I am honest. Now, anyway. Back then, I was a spoiled, entitled, rich boy scared of his daddy. But I can assure you that I am a changed man. *That*, I am proud of. It wasn't easy, but I broke free of that good ol' boy network years ago. My father disowned me. Austin and I haven't spoken in ages. But the cool thing is, once everything is taken from you, you don't have anything left to lose, right? I live here in Houston now and work civil rights cases. A true embarrassment to my father, and I wouldn't have it any other way." A loud chuckle followed, deep and genuine, and Seth decided he liked new Gordy very much.

"So, you're not the anonymous source?" Henry asked.

"No, I am not. But it could be a number of people. I can see what the guy was trying to do by getting people talking about it. There are only three of us who were there that day who know what really went down. But plenty of others *knew* or knew enough to suspect. Those game wardens never believed for one second that Victoria caught all those fish. Not that she couldn't have, mind you, that woman could out-fish a gill net. But she was so sick she could barely hold down a glass of water. I kid you not, she almost puked on the game warden's boots."

"You think it was one of the game wardens?" Hazel asked. "Do you know their names?"

"Sure. It could have been one of them. Could also be one of the policemen. There was this rookie cop who tried to talk Victoria out of confessing."

Hazel shifted in her seat. "Gordy, would you be willing to tell this story? Back Victoria now if she came forward?"

"Heck yeah, I would! Happy to. I would have done that a long time ago if I'd known it's what Victoria wanted."

Henry sighed and leaned back in his chair. "Now all we have to do is convince Victoria."

VICTORIA STOWED THE broom she'd been using to sweep the sidewalk and dug her phone from her pocket. Still no response from Seth. Olivia had shown up yesterday, the morning after their phone conversation, to hear her story. Victoria had told it with her mama, Mémé and Scarlett all listening in. The reporter had stayed for hours, asked a ton of questions, and was extremely thorough. Mémé insisted she stay for lunch. Scarlett and Quinn charmed her socks off. Vic had no doubt when the story hit the news this time that it would finally be the truth.

Immediately after Olivia had departed, Victoria called Seth. She wanted to be the one to tell him her story before he read it online. And apologize and reiterate how much she loved him, and could they try again? No answer, and she'd ended the call without leaving a voicemail. Only his voice would do.

Maybe he wasn't ready to hear from her yet. And maybe that was what she deserved. If he hadn't given up on her, she would find a way to make this up to him.

What she needed was something to pass the time. Inside the office, she studied the schedule. Most of the campers checking out had already done so. No cabins to clean. Except for folks enjoying long weekends, it was a quiet Monday morning. Deciding she had time to spend an hour or two on the lake with her fishing pole before new reservations or drop-ins started arriving, she headed outside to find Scarlett and see if she wanted to join.

Two vehicles were driving up the lane. The first was an SUV. Fishermen, maybe? No boat, she realized when they got closer. Campers without a reservation probably. They had space available, so she waited while they parked.

A woman climbed out of the SUV, one who looked a lot like… Hazel? Yes, she realized as Henry emerged to join her. A flash of dark brown hair and there he was. Seth. Her pulse took off racing, and she tried to temper it because the second car contained Marissa and Gerard, and why would they all be here? A Romeo Reels matter seemed most likely, but what could it be that wouldn't warrant a simple phone call?

"Victoria!" Marissa took the lead, hurrying forward when she noticed her and pulled her in for a hug. "Sorry, we didn't call first. It seemed better to just show up." Stepping back, she asked, "How are you?"

"I'm good. Surprised, but a nice surprise. I'm happy to see you."

The rest of the group approached, and Victoria began doling out greetings. When she got to Seth, she wasn't sure how to acknowledge him, but he made it easy by sweeping her into one of his hugs. One of his amazingly perfect, soul-warming hugs. She wanted to hang on for dear life—and might have—if he hadn't cut it short. Was it her imagination, or did he squeeze her a little tighter than necessary?

Marissa began, "I'm sure you're wondering

what we're doing here. Do you have a few minutes to chat?"

"Of course, yes. Let's go to the house. We can sit on the porch."

"Holy cow, this place is spectacular!" This from Hazel, who fell into step beside her. Gaze bouncing everywhere, she said, "Later, maybe we can talk about your little paradise being featured on my blog?"

"We'd be honored," Victoria said.

Marissa, Gerard and Henry gathered around the picnic table. Hazel took the rocker. Victoria offered coffee and drinks, but everyone declined. She and Seth sat in two of the remaining chairs.

Marissa said, "We'll get right to the point. Romeo Reels has made a decision regarding the spokesperson position." When Victoria started to gently interrupt, she held up a hand. "We know. You withdrew. Miles Romeo didn't accept it."

"Can he do that?" Victoria asked.

"No," Gerard assured her. "And he had quite a fight with legal about it, which he lost. Technically, your withdrawal stands."

If that was the case, it seemed unnecessary to include her in this conversation. She opted not to mention that, because regardless, they had something to impart, and she was delighted to see them all. And she couldn't wait to talk to Seth.

Marissa continued, "Which brings us to the news we have to share." Her gaze swept over Victoria, Seth and then Henry. "We want to thank you guys for your stellar performances, and let you know it was an extremely close vote. We all had our favorites, but the decision truly was made by the selection committee." She smiled at Victoria. "Before this mess blew up, and you quit, Victoria, the committee had decided to hire you."

Seth and Henry exchanged knowing glances. A spike of happiness erupted inside of her. Even if it felt almost cruel to tell her now when it was too late, the fact that she'd been good enough to win was a true thrill.

"Neither of you seems surprised," Gerard said, looking pointedly from Seth to Henry.

Henry shook his head. "We're not. She's the best choice."

"Absolutely," Seth concurred. "We both called it."

"You guys!" Victoria admonished. "Either of you would be every bit as good as me. Better, even. You've both landed fish I've only seen in books and online. Compared to either of you, I'm barely adequate with a fly rod."

"None of you are doing a very good job of

selling yourself," Gerard joked. "Not that you need to, Henry."

"Why doesn't Henry need to?" Seth asked, even as Victoria was forming the same question.

Marissa looked surprised. "Henry, you haven't told him?"

"Not yet." Henry grinned at Seth. "We've been busy with other matters. I've taken another job."

"Henry is getting a better job," Gerard clarified. "He's been offered his own fishing show."

"Henry!" Victoria was ecstatic. "That's fantastic! You're going to be incredible."

"Congratulations, man!" Seth reached out one hand to shake and clapped him on the shoulder with the other. "Vic is right. You're going to kill it."

When they'd finished briefly discussing the details, Marissa picked up the thread again, "So, Victoria, in light of our own investigation and everything Henry and Hazel have uncovered about your case, we're not ready to give up on you. In fact, the opposite is now true. We'd like for you to tell your story on the national stage. You were a young woman, a girl, who was lied to and taken advantage of by a powerful man and his son. It's a story that needs to be told. You could be an inspiration to women everywhere if you will do this. You'll have the full support of the Romeo Reels legal team and—"

"Wait a minute," she interrupted. "What do you know about my story?" Had Henry told them? The idea of him betraying her confidence was shocking, but how else could they have found out? Not that it mattered now.

As if hearing her thoughts, Henry said, "I didn't tell them, Victoria. Gordon Watts did."

"Gordy? But he's Austin's friend."

"They haven't been friends in a very long time," Hazel spoke up. "It was Henry's idea to find him, which he did with my help. We asked him to tell us what happened, and he did. Everything. And he's willing to share the truth with anyone who will listen. He's supporting you one hundred percent."

"Why?" Victoria asked, growing even more empowered by the information.

The genius of Henry's strategy continued to sink in as Hazel explained, "Because of the details Gordy revealed, we've also contacted a game warden who was involved. He lives in Maine now, and he's claiming you were so ill you could barely stand up, much less fill that well with fish. He says he never believed Austin's story but was overridden by his superiors."

Henry couldn't in good conscience repeat

what she'd told him, so he'd found the only other person who could. The fact that he'd go to this much trouble for her meant the world to her. Emotion clogged her throat when she tried to speak, "Henry, I…"

"I hope you can forgive me, Victoria. I couldn't let this injustice stand. Hazel suspected something was off, too, and she was a willing coconspirator. And, of course, Seth knew there had to be a very good reason why you felt like you couldn't be honest with him."

"I know telling your story is going to be difficult for you, Victoria," Seth said, and for the first time since he'd arrived, he made full-on eye contact. Hope erupted like a geyser inside of her because those eyes of his; he still loved her. She could see it.

Between Seth's belief in her, her mama and Mémé's support, the lengths Henry and Hazel had gone to, and now this, she could barely contain her joy. She felt all sparkly and buoyant inside like she'd been lit from within.

Beaming, she looked around and told them, "I already have."

SETH EXHALED THE breath he'd been holding. The relief washing over him was almost dizzying. He'd been afraid of coming here, afraid they'd meet nothing but that same stubborn wall of resistance, and with it, any chance Victoria had of getting over this, of reclaiming herself.

"That's why I called you last night, Seth. I wanted to tell you that you were right."

"You called me?" Thinking quickly, all he remembered was seeing an unfamiliar number. He'd received several of those from reporters and bloggers. "I didn't see any missed calls from you."

"Oh… That's right. Yeah, I had to change my number. I should have left you a message, but I had so much to say. There was too much to…" she trailed off as if remembering they had an audience.

He grinned. She returned it, and he knew. Everything was going to be okay.

"Victoria," Hazel said, looking up from her phone. "Who did you talk to? I don't see the story anywhere online."

"I talked to Olivia Wallace yesterday."

"Olivia Wallace!" Seth, Hazel and Henry all protested.

"I know… It seems like an odd choice, but she apologized." Eyes on Seth, she said, "I trust her. She's going to let me know when it goes live. I wonder if I should call her and tell her about Gordy?"

The conversation steered back to the topic again. They agreed that Victoria should make the call to Olivia, who should also speak with Hazel and Henry. Or possibly even group chat with everyone about all the relevant details and the plan of attack going forward.

"Victoria," Marissa said after they'd decided how to proceed. "Before you do that, there's one more thing we need to tell you."

"Okay?"

"It's about the spokesperson job. Gerard was right when he said that Romeo Reels accepted your withdrawal. But what you don't know is what we've decided to offer you." She paused to look from Victoria to him. "And you, Seth. We'd like to offer you both jobs. It will look a little different than the original contract terms. We would split some of the responsibilities and then others you would do together. The selection committee loved your chemistry, and we'd like to build on that, too. We don't have an offer in writing yet. We wanted to make sure that it's something you two would be interested in first?"

"I'm interested!" Victoria fired off the words before Seth could form his response. "But only if there's no clause about being romantically involved. I'm in love with Seth, and if I can't have him *and* the job, I choose him."

CHAPTER TWENTY-TWO

VICTORIA'S STORY TURNED out to be much bigger than she imagined, bigger than anyone could have anticipated. It went live two days later, and Olivia, after interviewing Gordy and speaking with Henry and Hazel, worked virtually non-stop, and vastly expanded the piece. Gordy was quoted extensively, and the game warden, too. Austin and Linus Galbraith declined to comment.

The Romeo Reels promotion team was all over it and within hours it was trending on social media. *Morning Wire* invited Victoria and Olivia on their show. Victoria and Seth flew to Florida the next day for the appearance, and the story made national news.

In light of her age at the time of the incident, and with the support of several women's rights organizations, Victoria was largely understood for not coming forward sooner and praised for her courage in doing so now. Especially when faced with the wealth and privilege of the Galbraith family.

"Listen to this," Seth said, lowering himself to sit beside her on the stern of the airboat where they were currently floating on Lake Belle Rose. "A text from Hazel with a link to Romeo's press release: 'From all of us here at Romeo Reels, we are thrilled to announce that Victoria Thibodeaux has officially joined our family. Victoria is everything we could wish for in a professional angler and spokesperson. Not only does she have the skills to showcase our products, she has the ethics and integrity to be a role model for young anglers everywhere.'"

"I am going to do my best to make that true," she said, tipping her head to rest on his shoulder.

"It's already true." Seth wrapped his arms around her. She still couldn't quite believe how much feeling he could convey with an embrace, and that she could have it anytime she wanted. Victoria inhaled the comforting scent of him mixed with the bayou around them and reveled in the sweetness that was now her life.

Turned out, Victoria didn't have to choose. Romeo Reels was happy to have them sign on as a couple. Two days ago, they'd flown to Boston, to Romeo Reels' headquarters where they'd signed their contracts and discussed the details of what their new positions entailed. They'd returned to Bayou Doré early this afternoon.

Victoria was ecstatic to discover that Scarlett had continued to improve in the two days she'd been gone. Every minute she regained a little more mobility in her arm. Time would tell how much returned, but the doctors were hopeful.

They'd hung out with Scarlett, Mémé and Mama until the Duquettes had arrived to pick up Scarlett for dinner and a movie. With Mémé's guidance, Seth brewed two gallons of sweet tea for a dinner they were having that night with some "special guests." They'd been cagey about the details. Then Mémé had requested they take the airboat for a ride on the lake and not come back before supper.

"Something goofy with the motor," she'd said. "I'd like you to check it out."

But it had purred like a kitten from the moment Victoria started it up and then performed with perfection all around the lake. Upon spotting a pair of egrets, Victoria had shut the engine off to drift a bit and enjoy the scenery. Peace and quiet at last.

Everything was perfect. Almost. Thoughts of Austin kept creeping in to dampen her enthusiasm. With his campaign all but over and his political career derailed, Victoria had been expecting retaliation. So far, nothing but silence. In a particularly ominous move, he'd missed his visitation with Scarlett.

She knew he was doing it on purpose, plotting his revenge and waiting for the right moment to strike. Not a fair analogy, she decided. Austin was a million times worse than a cottonmouth. A snake acted only out of self-defense. Things were only going to get worse when he heard from her attorney. Miraculously, Mémé had managed to find one who didn't have a conflict of interest with the Galbraiths, and they were proceeding with the petition for a new parenting plan.

"What's the deal with this special dinner?" Seth asked.

"I honestly have no idea. Celebrating, I guess? They probably invited a few friends for you to meet. They both adore you and have been wanting to show you off."

"But isn't it odd that Scarlett and Quinn wouldn't be included?"

"Umm." Now that she thought about it, why would they send Scarlett off with the Duquettes? Why not just invite them? "Maybe?"

"And there is absolutely nothing wrong with this boat. If there was, your grandmother would know."

Both Mémé and her mother were meticulous with boat maintenance. It wouldn't be unheard of for them to give Victoria a specific task to perform, but this did seem odd. "That is very true. They were trying to get rid of us."

"Clearly." Seth chuckled. "What do you think is going on?"

"I do not know, but it's time to go find out."

IT MOST CERTAINLY was not a celebration, Victoria discovered a short time later when she and Seth returned to the house. The last people she ever expected to find were seated at the dining room table.

Linus Galbraith stood. "Hello, Victoria. Nice to see you. Congratulations on your new job. Sounds like you're doing well for yourself these days."

No thanks to you. Hiding her shock, she greeted him with a pleasant, "Hello, Linus. Thank you."

"Good evening, Victoria," Austin said, surreptitiously looking Seth up and down. Seth had several inches and about forty pounds of muscle on him that Austin didn't, Victoria couldn't help but notice.

"Austin," she said, and hated how her pulse resounded like thunder inside her head.

Seth took her hand, threading his fingers through hers and instantly her heart was coaxed into a more manageable beat.

Mama graciously handled the introductions. Polite chitchat made the rounds.

"Now, Ms. Effie," Linus said, "would you like to tell us what this is all about?"

"I would, Linus," she said. "And I will. But first, let's sit and enjoy this delicious meal that Corinne has prepared, shall we? Here in the bayou we believe news is best served with a good hearty meal."

What news? What in the name of all that was good on the earth was going on here? Holding tight to her composure, Victoria took a seat. Seth followed her lead.

As if on cue, Corinne emerged from the kitchen with the potatoes galette, a cast iron masterpiece and one of her specialties. And indeed, tonight's attempt was a work of art, every paper-thin potato slice arranged just so and the buttery crust a perfect shade of golden brown. When Victoria and Austin had been together, the dish had been one of his favorites. Corinne placed it between the two platters of fragrant herb-roasted chicken. Steaming bowls of garlicky asparagus, roasted radishes and a batch of fluffy buttermilk biscuits followed. Whipped butter and ramekins of boysenberry jam, strawberry preserves and rich amber-tinted honey from Mémé's bees completed the meal.

"Now, Linus," Mémé said in her most gracious tone. "I believe my friend Lettie Mayse told me that your company has given the parish a good deal on the land for the new grade school, is that right?" She followed up his confirmation with, "You are a true philanthropist. Although, I imagine there is some reward there, too, considering you'll be so generously compensated from the contract you've acquired to build it?"

Playing along now, Linus speared a piece of chicken, and accepted the backhanded compliment.

When they'd exhausted that tedious topic, Mémé moved on, "Austin, any progress on the investigation as to who sprayed all that graffiti on the post office? I don't know how they're going to get the paint off of those old bricks. That building is a treasure. Such a shame. Margaret Batton said it was some gang boys from Lafayette…"

Conversation continued this way, touching on every polite and pointless topic currently buzzing around the town of Perche. Too bad about incoming senior and the Perche Tigers' high school starting quarterback Carl Westcott breaking his leg. Would he be able to play this fall?

With each new subject change Victoria felt the tension ratchet up around the table as Linus and Austin wondered what Effie was really up to. Victoria thought she might be forming a picture now and she was reveling in her grandmother's genius.

Seth, also sensing that Effie had the upper hand, played along, strategically inquiring and commenting to draw out the suspense. Like he'd received a copy of the script beforehand.

When dinner was complete, Mémé said, "I am so happy you gentlemen were able to join us for dinner this evening. Dessert is going to be a treat. Corinne whipped up something extra special just for you Galbraith boys."

Mama, who'd already risen from the table and headed to the kitchen, taking a stack of plates and dishes with her, now returned. She placed a covered platter on the table right between Austin and Linus. With subtle dramatic fanfare, she slowly reached down and removed the cover.

Victoria nearly gasped, because on the plate was one of the most stunning, lifelike creations she'd ever seen. Her mother had outdone herself. It was even better than the bass cake. The meaning behind the object hit her next.

"What is that?" Austin asked, staring down at the table. "Is that a bird?"

"I believe that is a crow," Linus supplied. "That we're expected to eat."

"I get it," Austin scoffed. "That's very funny, Effie. But us Galbraiths will not be eating any crow for you. Not tonight. Not ever. Victoria got her revenge. My campaign is over, and she got her little job. And now we're leaving." He threw his napkin on the table and started to stand.

"Sit down, Austin," Linus said, eyeing Effie warily.

"You're going to stay here and listen to this?" Austin retorted, even as he lowered himself back down into his chair.

Effie reached over to the sideboard and picked up a file. Victoria hadn't even noticed it was there.

"Now, Austin, contrary to what you just claimed, Victoria has not gotten revenge. Not by a long shot. She got exactly what she earned through determination, study and hard work. My granddaughter is not a vengeful person. If she were, she would have come to me with the truth years ago and I would have taken care of this. But she didn't."

Shifting her gaze to Linus, she said, "Of course, the lying, bullying and intimidation made sure she wouldn't do that, didn't it? In my heart, I knew she hadn't done this foolish thing that was blamed on her. I've been waiting for this moment for a long, long time.

"Victoria, unlike some people, is a good person. And a kind and loving mother. In fact, I don't know that I've ever seen a more selfless parent. Every decision she makes, every action she takes, she puts Scarlett first. A phenomenal, admirable trait in a single teenaged mother, don't you think?"

Several seconds stretched by while she stared at Austin until he stuttered, "I, uh, I've always said she was a good mother."

"While you, on the other hand, are the complete opposite. I have never in all my life seen a more selfish, self-centered, useless parent than you. Thank the stars above that *her* child has taken after her."

Victoria felt tears gather but willed them away. No way would she cry in front of these men. Never again. Under the table, Seth took her hand.

"Now, I recall you telling me something years ago when you were caught cheating on Victoria. Which, knowing your character, was no surprise and didn't bother me nearly as much as the manner in which you discarded her, without apology or support.

"At the time, I said that I would never forget what you'd done. You laughed and replied 'Of course, you won't forget—you're a poor, old woman who's got nothin' but a lot of sad, sorry memories. You're the same as your grandmother, and her grandmother, too. Everyone knows that about the Thibodeauxs in this town.' Do you remember saying that to me, Austin?"

Linus gave his head a little shake as if he couldn't quite believe what he was hearing. Austin shifted in his seat, fidgety and reluctant to answer.

Effie repeated the question, "Do you remember your words to me, Austin?"

Wisely, Linus said, "Just answer, Austin."

"Yes, ma'am, I do believe I said that in anger."

"Oh, in anger?" Effie repeated with a bitter chuckle like it was anything but a funny joke. "No matter if it was anger or mirth, I remember. And I am here to assure you that you were right."

The table went silent.

"Yes indeed, I'm about to show you just how good a memory like mine truly is." With that she opened the file and removed a thick sheaf of papers. "I'll start here. This is a copy of what I like to call the *Where's Daddy Papers*, beginning at day one."

Victoria recognized the pages where she kept track of Austin's time spent with Scarlett, and the long list of excuses when he couldn't.

"I'm sorry, it's what?" Linus interjected.

"A journal, Linus," Effie stated, "Of Austin's time spent with Scarlett since the divorce. Now, I didn't go on to college like you all, but I have managed to run this business for nearly all of my adult life, which requires a fair amount of math. As such, it wasn't difficult for me to calculate that Austin has exercised his parental visitation twenty-two percent of the time. That means that seventy-eight out of the hundred times he should have spent time with his daughter he chose not to. That is well over four hundred missed opportunities not including numerous birthdays, holidays and so on. Every single excuse documented."

She pulled another sheet of paper from the file. "And this shows the amount of child support Victoria receives. As you are well aware, this figure is based on the salary you were receiving at the time of Scarlett's birth. Your income has increased exponentially in that time and yet your child support payments have remained the same."

"Victoria never requested more!" Austin blurted.

"Or perhaps your visitation commitment is in direct correlation to your financial commitment?" Effie graced him with a pleasant smile that Victoria knew was anything but. "Either way, you can tell my friend Lettie Mayse all about that when you appear before her in family court. Or wait, I guess you would know her as Judge Leticia Fletcher, wouldn't you? She uses her married name on the bench. I believe you've had some courtroom run-ins with her in the past."

Austin swallowed uncomfortably. Victoria didn't know what that was about but could assume that Austin had ticked off the wrong judge.

"But I am sure that what you are *not* paying in child support is being put to good use decorating that grand old mansion your daddy built for you. Speaking of, this sheaf of papers here…" A quick shuffle and she produced a stapled stack, the top sheet printed in bold black letters with Austin's address. With a flat palm, she gave the pile an affectionate pat. "This is like a storybook. We'll call it *Construction Adventures* by Linus and Austin Galbraith.

"My favorite chapter is the one where some, uh, rather firm restrictions were bypassed to import that Italian marble you're so proud of. But I also like the part where building supplies were purchased at extravagantly inflated prices. Workers were hired for cash and paid less than minimum wage. Now, my friend Walt Westcott, that would be young Carl's dad, he works for a nonprofit that advocates for workers' rights and assures me that could be construed as unethical. Now, I'm sure there's a perfectly reasonable explanation for—"

"This is ridiculous!" Austin interrupted. But Victoria could see the concern in his eyes, which were shifting between Mémé, the papers and Linus. Sweat was forming on his upper lip.

Effie's enigmatic smile was still in place. "Young man, if you interrupt me again, this day will certainly go from bad to worse for you."

No doubt from his extensive years of unethical corner-cutting and corruption, Linus was much more composed. Folding his hands on the table in front of him, he smiled benignly and said, "I apologize for my son's breach of etiquette and lack of manners. But, Ms. Effie, if you are accusing us of illegal activity, or even implying such, you need more than your little journal there and the word of some blue-collar laborers."

"Do I, though?" Effie shuffled through the papers and a photo slid out. "Oops, how did that get in there?"

She placed the photo above the file. Tapping a finger, she said, "This is a good one though, don't you think? Me and Denny go way back. See this canoe we're standing by? I made it for him. I think it's my best one to date."

Linus paled. Austin was clueless.

"Tadpoles from the very same swamp, can you believe that? My best friend from childhood, Dennis Eugene Landry, is the biggest construction contractor in the state of Louisiana. Out of Baton Rouge now. Where you're from. Says he knows you? I mean, we were just little tykes together tromping around the swamp catching bullfrogs, fishing for whatever we could catch.

"This one time, when we were older, I saved his dog, Luna, from a gator. I used a canoe paddle that I'd made, and I pulled Luna right out of that gator's mouth…" Trailing off, she waved a breezy hand through the air. "But that's a story for another day. I don't think I need to go on about what an experience like that will do for a friendship."

Looking at Victoria, she commented, "Kind of like our Scarlett and Quinn."

"I agree," Victoria said with a smile. "I've often thought their friendship was very much like yours and Mr. Landry's."

She focused again on Linus. "Anyway, you might not know that his son, Jason, has gone and got himself elected state attorney general. Isn't that something? So proud of him. He's a good boy. Smart as a whip just like his daddy."

"Now—" Effie paused and folded her hands

atop the file "—I'm not accusing anyone of anything criminal, Linus. I am certainly not qualified to draw those types of conclusions. Fortunately, I have friends who are."

"You've made your point, Effie," Linus said. "What is it you want?"

"It's not a matter of what I want, Linus. We're going to negotiate the same way you negotiated with Victoria twelve years ago. Meaning, I'm going to tell you what you're going to do. First, you are going to set my granddaughter free. Victoria will no longer live in fear of retaliation or slander or even so much as an uncharitable frown from any member of the Galbraith family, or your accomplices—pardon me, I mean your friends. The only words out of your mouths regarding Victoria will be ones of apology, pleas for forgiveness or compliments.

"Second, you will release my great-granddaughter of any further obligation to visit her father. Scarlett will see Austin on her terms only.

"And you." She pointed a finger at Austin. "You will never again lie to Scarlett and attempt to turn her against her mother. Do you understand me, Austin, you arrogant, deceitful, condescending, good-for-nothing, two-bit piece of entitled trash? No. More. Lies. Not about Victoria or any member of this family."

Linus elbowed Austin who managed a weak, "Yes, ma'am."

"Now," Corinne said sweetly, producing a knife that was way too large for the job, and chopping the crow's head from its body with one fell swoop, "Time for cake."

EPILOGUE

THE ROD TIP arched with a sudden, almost violent force when the fish hit the lure and kept right on going. "Fish on!" Seth cried, as the reel emitted a zinging sound, taking yards of line along for the ride.

"Holy cow," Scarlett uttered, giving the pole a sharp tug to set the hook.

"Keep your tip up. Good, yes, just like that," he encouraged.

"Is it a steelhead?" she yelled as a silver flash broke through the surface of the Opal River.

"Yes, it is." Seth answered. "That is a *nice* fish, Scarlett."

Seated in Seth's jetboat, Victoria couldn't help the joyous laugh that escaped her while she filmed her daughter's dream coming true. After a moment, she panned the camera over to capture Quinn who looked to be about equal parts nervous and excited. Scarlett still hadn't regained all the strength in her hand, and she could see how Quinn was both trying not to hover and yet be there at the same time in case she lost her grip.

Sort of like she and Seth had done for each other the last few months.

Romeo Reels had kept them very busy lately with photo and video shoots, guest appearances, interviews and various other promotional activities. Besides fishing, Victoria's favorite parts of the job were the fishing workshops she presented and the guest appearances where she got to talk about fishing. There was something so satisfying about teaching people technique and sharing in their success. But she'd discovered that the television spots were kind of fun, too. Next month, when they got back from vacation, they were scheduled to appear as guests on Henry's new fishing show, which she knew would be an absolute blast.

Seth, in a stroke of pure genius, had arranged for this two-week break when they'd negotiated their contracts. So here they were, right in the middle of July, their first day of fishing and sightseeing in Alaska. And already having the time of their lives. The Opal River was one of the few southeastern Alaska waterways with a notable summer steelhead run.

"I'm so excited I'm shaking!" Scarlett said, easing up on the retrieval while hefting the rod, and shifting her body with the fish's movement. "It's running again."

"That's okay," Seth said calmly. "You're doing great. Keep it up. It'll get tired."

They'd given Scarlett a lighter, more flexible rod so she could experience the full fight of the fish. Seth and Victoria had discussed the fact that it meant she could more easily lose a fish once hooked, but they'd opted for it knowing that it greatly enhanced the excitement factor. Watching her now, Victoria was pleased with their decision. Scarlett had the skills and patience of an experienced angler.

"Mama, are you filming this for Gram and Mémé?"

"Yes, Scarlett, I sure am." Effie and Corinne had opted out of the trip to mind the resort with a promise to visit during the off-season.

Nineteen minutes later, an exuberant Scarlett was posing with her catch, grinning from ear to ear, and jabbering ninety miles an hour.

Seth told her, "Bering is going to be very happy, young lady. He wanted us to keep one for the barbecue tonight."

Victoria felt a twist of nerves at the reminder of the gathering. The barbecue where they would be meeting the rest of Seth's family. She was particularly grateful for the friendship that had grown between her and Hazel. And since she'd already met Tag and Bering, and their friend Cricket, at least she wouldn't be among a crowd of all strangers.

Seth beached the boat in a shallow inlet just above a stretch of river that contained a series of rapids with deep pools, his favorite steelhead spot. It was easily fished from the bank and he had motored through the stretch twice, explaining and giving the kids advice on how to best proceed from that vantage point.

"What about bears?" Quinn asked, scanning the woods along the bank as they got out of the boat.

"Oh, so maybe the Alaskan woods aren't quite as boring as you anticipated?" Seth teased.

Quinn laughed. "Slightly less boring," he agreed. "But imagine how cool bears and snakes would be together."

Seth shook his head, hooked bear spray to both of their belts, and sent them on their way toward the good spot along the bank.

When Victoria began to ready her own pole. Seth said, "Hand that to me for a sec, I have a new lure for you to try."

"Okay, cool."

Several feet away, he crouched in front of his tackle box and went to work attaching the lure.

Adjusting her baseball cap, Victoria studied the river, trying to read the water. "You know that I am thrilled that Scarlett caught one first, right? But I can't help it, Seth, I want to catch one, too."

He chuckled. "I know. You will."

Pointing upstream, she told him, "I like the look of that spot right there." There was a giant submerged rock with a nice roiling pool behind it. She could imagine the fish lying in the lee on the downstream side.

He was watching her in this odd way. She couldn't quite put her finger on what it meant but it sent a nice mix of nerves and heat flooding through her.

"What is the matter with you, Alaska?"

Sheepishly, he offered a one-shouldered shrug. "Just happy you guys are here. Excited to show you all my favorite places and introduce you to my favorite people."

Victoria felt that now-familiar outpouring of love for him. "Oh, Seth, I'm excited for all of that, too. You've seen plenty of Louisiana by now." Seth had spent most of his off time with her and her family, and Victoria had enjoyed showing him around.

"Okay, so you should cast right up there and bring it fast behind that rock," he explained, swinging the pole around and casting in the exact spot she was thinking. The reel clicked as he handed over the pole.

Gripping the rod, she began to reel but knew instantly something wasn't right "Feels funny. Blade isn't spinning right."

"Pull up. Give it a little jerk."

"Did that." she said, tossing him a knowing look. "It's juking and diving like the hook snagged in the swivel when you casted."

"That's probably it. It's a homemade lure."

Reeling in the rest of the way, she lowered the butt of the rod and placed it on the ground and then swung the line forward for closer inspection.

"What is this?" The shape wasn't like anything she'd ever seen in a lure before, and it took her a few seconds to register what was happening. Her breath caught. *Was that...a ring?* Her pulse went fluttery. Reaching out, she grasped the lure and found a silver band attached to the body of the spinner. Definitely a ring, decorated with the same Celtic knot as her necklace. Her heart seemed to expand inside her chest, going full and light like it might whisk her off her feet.

"It's a ring," he confirmed, stepping close. "Kella made it."

"I see that," she whispered reverently before meeting his gaze. "Seth..." His name was just a breath because the love she saw there stole her words.

Seth came forward and unhooked the ring from the lure and slipped it on her finger. "I love you, Victoria. Will you marry me?"

"Of course." She threw her arms around him. "Of course, I will. I really want to be married to you. Thank you. It's gorgeous and perfect and I love it. And I love you."

"Wow," he said, and then exhaled a sigh of relief. "That is the best possible news. I couldn't decide if I should wait until the end of the trip to ask so if you said no I wouldn't be miserable for two weeks, or at the beginning so I could feel like this."

"That second option is working for me, too, because I can't imagine being any happier than this." She pulled back enough to kiss him, to show him how much she meant the words.

"Plus, I really wanted to introduce you to everyone as my fiancée."

That made her laugh. "I'd love to meet everyone that way. We need to tell Scarlett."

"She already knows."

"Seriously? She didn't say a word."

"Hey, I had to run it by her first. And Quinn. Make sure the lure proposal wasn't too over-the-top."

"Yeah," she said dryly, "definitely you should rely on two middle school kids for romantic advice."

"I see your point," he said, and chuckled. "But in this case—"

"Psst, Seth!" Scarlett interrupted with a loud stage whisper from somewhere in the brush behind them. "What did she say?"

Victoria paused to laugh before shouting, "She said yes! Come on out, you two."

Giggling and chattering, Scarlett and Quinn hurried to join them.

"Congratulations, Mama!" Scarlett hugged her. "I'm so happy. Seth said he was going to live in Louisiana with us but that we'll visit here whenever we can."

"Thank you, Scarlett. Me too. That sounds like a perfect plan."

Standing next to Seth, Quinn congratulated them both. "Well done," he added, clapping Seth on the shoulder.

"Thank you, Quinn. Luckily, it went pretty smoothly."

Louder, to Victoria, Quinn announced, "And just think, Ms. T, how many people can say they went fishing in Alaska and caught themselves a Mr. Right?"

They all laughed.

* * * * *

Get 4 FREE REWARDS!

We'll send you 2 FREE Books plus 2 FREE Mystery Gifts.

Love Inspired books feature uplifting stories where faith helps guide you through life's challenges and discover the promise of a new beginning.

FREE Value Over $20

YES! Please send me 2 FREE Love Inspired Romance novels and my 2 FREE mystery gifts (gifts are worth about $10 retail). After receiving them, if I don't wish to receive any more books, I can return the shipping statement marked "cancel." If I don't cancel, I will receive 6 brand-new novels every month and be billed just $5.24 each for the regular-print edition or $5.99 each for the larger-print edition in the U.S., or $5.74 each for the regular-print edition or $6.24 each for the larger-print edition in Canada. That's a savings of at least 13% off the cover price. It's quite a bargain! Shipping and handling is just 50¢ per book in the U.S. and $1.25 per book in Canada.* I understand that accepting the 2 free books and gifts places me under no obligation to buy anything. I can always return a shipment and cancel at any time. The free books and gifts are mine to keep no matter what I decide.

Choose one: ☐ **Love Inspired Romance**
Regular-Print
(105/306 IDN CNWC)

☐ **Love Inspired Romance**
Larger-Print
(122/322 IDN GNWC)

Name (please print)

Address _____ Apt. #

City _____ State/Province _____ Zip/Postal Code

Email: Please check this box ☐ if you would like to receive newsletters and promotional emails from Harlequin Enterprises ULC and its affiliates. You can unsubscribe anytime.

Mail to the **Reader Service:**
IN U.S.A.: P.O. Box 1341, Buffalo, NY 14240-8531
IN CANADA: P.O. Box 603, Fort Erie, Ontario L2A 5X3

Want to try 2 free books from another series! Call 1-800-873-8635 or visit www.ReaderService.com.

Get 4 FREE REWARDS!

We'll send you 2 FREE Books plus 2 FREE Mystery Gifts.

Love Inspired Suspense books showcase how courage and optimism unite in stories of faith and love in the face of danger.

FREE Value Over $20

Get 4 FREE REWARDS!

We'll send you 2 FREE Books plus 2 FREE Mystery Gifts.

Both the **Romance** and **Suspense** collections feature compelling novels
written by many of today's bestselling authors.

YES! Please send me 2 FREE novels from the Essential Romance or
Essential Suspense Collection and my 2 FREE gifts (gifts are worth about
$10 retail). After receiving them, if I don't wish to receive any more books,
I can return the shipping statement marked "cancel." If I don't cancel, I will
receive 4 brand-new novels every month and be billed just $7.24 each in the
U.S. or $7.49 each in Canada. That's a savings of up to 28% off the cover
price. It's quite a bargain! Shipping and handling is just 50¢ per book in the
U.S. and $1.25 per book in Canada.* I understand that accepting the 2 free
books and gifts places me under no obligation to buy anything. I can always
return a shipment and cancel at any time. The free books and gifts are mine
to keep no matter what I decide.

Choose one: ☐ **Essential Romance**   ☐ **Essential Suspense**
                     (194/394 MDN GQ6M)   (191/391 MDN GQ6M)

Name (please print)

Address   Apt. #

City   State/Province   Zip/Postal Code

Email: Please check this box ☐ if you would like to receive newsletters and promotional emails from Harlequin Enterprises ULC and
its affiliates. You can unsubscribe anytime.

Mail to the **Reader Service:**
IN U.S.A.: P.O. Box 1341, Buffalo, NY 14240-8531
IN CANADA: P.O. Box 603, Fort Erie, Ontario L2A 5X3

Want to try 2 free books from another series! Call 1-800-873-8635 or visit www.ReaderService.com.

---

*Terms and prices subject to change without notice. Prices do not include sales taxes, which will be charged (if applicable) based
on your state or country of residence. Canadian residents will be charged applicable taxes. Offer not valid in Quebec. This offer is
limited to one order per household. Books received may not be as shown. Not valid for current subscribers to the Essential Romance
or Essential Suspense Collection. All orders subject to approval. Credit or debit balances in a customer's account(s) may be offset by
any other outstanding balance owed by or to the customer. Please allow 4 to 6 weeks for delivery. Offer available while quantities last.

Your Privacy—Your information is being collected by Harlequin Enterprises ULC, operating as Reader Service. For a complete
summary of the information we collect, how we use this information and to whom it is disclosed, please visit our privacy notice located
at corporate.harlequin.com/privacy-notice. From time to time we may also exchange your personal information with reputable third
parties. If you wish to opt out of this sharing of your personal information, please visit readerservice.com/consumerschoice or call
1-800-873-8635. **Notice to California Residents**—Under California law, you have specific rights to control and access your data.
For more information on these rights and how to exercise them, visit corporate.harlequin.com/california-privacy.

STRS20R2

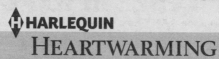